The Scientific Romances of
J.-H. Rosny Aîné

THE WORLD OF THE VARIANTS
And Other Strange Lands

The Scientific Romances of
J.-H. Rosny Aîné

THE WORLD OF THE VARIANTS
And Other Strange Lands

translated, annotated and introduced by
Brian Stableford

A Black Coat Press Book

Acknowledgements: I should like to thank John J. Pierce for providing valuable research materials and offering advice and support. Many of the copies of Rosny's works and critical articles related to his work were borrowed from the London Library. Also thanks to Paul Wessels for his generous and extensive help in the final preparation of this text.

Visit our website at www.blackcoatpress.com

Table of Contents

Introduction

This is the second volume of a six-volume collection of stories by J.-H. Rosny *Aîné* ("the Elder"), which includes all of his scientific romances, plus a number of other stories that have some relevance to his work in that genre.[1]

The contents of the six volumes are:

Volume 1. THE NAVIGATORS OF SPACE AND OTHER ALIEN ENCOUNTERS: The Xipehuz, The Skeptical Legend, Another World, The Death of the Earth, The Navigators of Space, The Astronauts.

Volume 2. THE WORLD OF THE VARIANTS AND OTHER STRANGE LANDS: Nymphaeum, The Depths of Kyamo, The Wonderful Cave Country, The Voyage, The Great Enigma, The Treasure in the Snow, The Boar Men, In the World of the Variants.

Volume 3. THE MYSTERIOUS FORCE AND OTHER ANOMALOUS PHENOMENA: The Cataclysm, The Mysterious Force, Hareton Ironcastle's Amazing Adventure.

Volume 4. VAMIREH AND OTHER PREHISTORIC FANTASIES: Vamireh, Eyrimah, Nomaï.

Volume 5. THE GIVREUSE ENIGMA AND OTHER STORIES: Mary's Garden, The Givreuse Enigma, Adventure in the Wild.

Volume 6. THE YOUNG VAMPIRE AND OTHER CAUTIONARY TALES: The Witch, The Young Vampire, The Supernatural Assassin, Companions of the Universe.

The first volume of the series includes a long general introduction to Rosny's life and works, which there is no need to

---

[1] *Le Félin géant* (*The Giant Cat* a.k.a. *Quest of the Dawn Man*) and *Helgvor du fleuve bleu* (*Helgvor of the Blue River*) will be reprinted in their original English translations in a seventh volume.

repeat here; the following introduction will therefore be limited to a brief account of the stories included in this volume, which will be supplemented by a more detailed commentary contained in an afterword.

The first six stories included here are Rosny's shorter ventures in the subgenre of "lost land" stories, which features remote enclaves on the surface of the Earth whose isolation has permitted biological evolution to follow a distinctive track. The majority of 20th century exercises in the subgenre feature survivals from prehistory, after the fashion of the subgenre's archetypal texts, Jules Verne's *Journey to the Center of the Earth* (1864; revised 1867) and Arthur Conan Doyle's *The Lost World* (1912), but Rosny's ventures—the first four of which antedated Doyle's novel—attempt extrapolations of a subtly different sort, being primarily concerned with a series of alternatives to the human "dominance" that is the most marked feature of our world, substituting variant human species, or species of a different sort.

The plausibility that evolution might have taken a different path in isolated enclaves had, of course, been ensured by 19th century accounts of the extent to which animal life in Australia differed from animal life everywhere else on the globe. Unfortunately, by the time that anyone began to build serious speculative fictions based on that analogy, the world was running short of places where such isolated enclaves might plausibly be located, and the subgenre always seemed a trifle belated, fit only for popular adventure stories that made no serious claim to rational plausibility. In the latter years of his career Rosny wrote several such adventure stories, but never entirely sacrificed the quest for serious speculative content. *L'Etonnant voyage de Hareton Ironcastle* (1922; tr. in vol. 3 as "Hareton Ironcastle's Amazing Adventure") eventually becomes closer in theme and in spirit to *Le Trésor dans la neige* (1920; tr. herein as "The Treasure in the Snow") than to "Les Hommes-Sangliers" (1929; tr. herein as "The Boar Men"), and its concluding section is more ambitious than either. *La Sauvage aventure* (1935; tr. in vol. 5 as "Adventure in the Wild"), although it is a straightforward exercise in pulp fiction, is actually a transfiguration of "Les Hommes-Sangliers," but I thought it important to include "The Boar Men" here rather than placing it in the same volume as the expanded text, along with a translation of "Dans le monde des Variants" (as "In the World of the Variants") in order to illustrate the continuity between Rosny's lost land stories and certain other elements of his work.

It is difficult to determine when the stories included in this volume were originally written, because some of them were almost certainly begun, if not actually finished, long before they were published. Although he never mentioned the title under which the story actually appeared, it seems likely that "Nymphée" (1893) was derived from one of the numerous fragmentary manuscripts that Rosny brought to Paris when he moved his family from London at the end of 1884. It certainly bears all the indications of having been completed in great haste, and very awkwardly, for its two-part publication in *Le Bambou*. The manuscripts he did mention having worked on in 1885 included a putative novel called *Cavernes*, which was presumably never completed; it seems likely that "La Contrée prodigieuse des cavernes" (1896; tr. herein as "The Wonderful Cavern Country") is derived from that manuscript, even if "Nymphée" was not. Whether "Les Profondeurs de Kyamo" (1896; tr. herein as "The Depths of Kyamo"), which features the same protagonist as the latter story, dates from the same period is unclear, although appearances suggest that it did not emerge from the same manuscript source. "Le Voyage" (1900; tr. herein as "The Voyage") is similar in theme, if not in tone, and obviously takes its inspiration from one of the prose poems included in "La Légende sceptique," another piece that Rosny reported working on in 1885, although it did not see print until 1889; appearances suggest, however, that "Le Voyage" was probably written some time after the earlier lost land stories.

A long gap in publication dates separated these early stories from "La Grande énigme" (1920; tr. herein as "The Great Enigma"), a brief quasi-poetic piece whose substance was expanded into an adventure story as *Le Trésor dans la neige*; it seems probable that the belated recruitment of the name of the protagonist of "Les Profondeurs de Kyamo" and "La Contrée prodigieuse des cavernes" to the latter story was a sudden afterthought, but it is not impossible that they too are based on earlier materials. Some bibliographical lists give the date of *Le Trésor dans la neige* as 1910, while others have 1922, but it seems unlikely that it appeared in a periodical before its appearance in the Flammarion booklet series *Une heure d'oubli*, and the copy of that booklet recently scanned by Google is dated 1920—the date universally credited to another booklet by Rosny issued in the same series—so that seems to me to be the likeliest alternative.

Although it deliberately recapitulates the basic formula of "Nymphée" and its companion-pieces, "Les Hommes-Sangliers" has a markedly different focus of concern, and a markedly different tone, which links it more significantly to such late works as "Dans le monde des Variants" than to the novel more explicitly derived from its plot. In "Les Hommes-Sangliers" the plausibility of the lost land theme is not really an issue, as the framework merely serves to support a cruel parable.

"Dans le monde des Variants" (1939) is also a new variant of a much older story—"L'Autre monde" (1895; tr. in vol. 1 as "Another World")—but, as with "Les Hommes-Sangliers," it focuses on a very different central concern. It was published in 1939, only a few months before Rosny's death, but might have been written some time before publication; the nature of its thematic adjustments suggest that it might have been written not long after *Les Navigateurs de l'infini* (1925; tr. in vol. 1 as "The Navigators of Space") and before "Les Hommes-Sangliers," but that is pure speculation. The story does, however, serve to round off this volume nicely by extending the scope of "strange lands" to illustrate the wider range of Rosny's concerns.

The version of "Nymphée" translated here is that in the book bearing that title, published by the Societé Française d'Imprimerie et de Librairie in 1909 (which also includes another novella). The versions of "Les Profondeurs de Kyamo" and "La Contrée prodigieuse des cavernes" are those in the 1896 Plon collection bearing the former title. The version of "Le Voyage" is from the Plon collection *L'Epave* (1903).

The version of "La Grande énigme" is from the 1985 Laffont omnibus of Rosny's *Romans préhistoriques*. The versions of "Le Trésor dans la neige," "Les Hommes-Sangliers" and "Dans le monde des Variants" are from the 1975 Marabout omnibus of Rosny's *Récits de science-fiction*. I have no reason to think that these versions differ substantially from any other extant versions of the stories.

Brian Stableford

NYMPHAEUM [2]

Preface

It has always been my conviction that, in spite of our armies of explorers, many secrets remain in the world, including territories and astonishing beings. This conviction was confirmed by an extraordinary adventure that I had in eastern Asia, and which I shall relate here.

Yes, there are still many mysterious regions: marshy regions, subterranean regions with marvelous rivers, mountain ranges and forests. Travelers have doubtless skirted them, but they have only covered a fraction of their vast surfaces; either putrid waters and mud have blocked their progress, or hunger, thirst and disease. Impenetrable vegetation has restricted them to the margins. As for cavernous regions, you know that there are prodigious unexplored examples even in France. I can only speak, in any case, of Europe, Asia and America, for Africa guards its mysterious heart, Australia has only made fragmentary revelations and the extreme Arctic and Antarctic latitudes remain inviolate.

What I shall relate here is the absolute truth—and since I have invented nothing I believe I can affirm without immodesty that it is one of the most gripping adventures ever told. If it

---

[2] In ancient Greece, a *nymphaeum* was a sanctuary dedicated to water-nymphs. The word was imported into French, as *nymphée*—not to be confused with *nymphéa,* which is a kind of water-lily—because it was borrowed for reference to fountains decorated with sculpted nymphs, but never made it into English, save for technical references to the Greek institution.

does not appear so, it will be because I have not done justice to it; even in that case, it will not fail to excite the mind.

In order to enhance understanding of the story, and in order not to burden it with fastidious preliminaries, it is necessary to know that I accompanied a Geographical Expedition in 1891 to the regions of Amur,[3] in the hinterlands of Russian and Chinese Asia. In spite of my youth, I was attached to that expedition, expressly commissioned by the French government, as a naturalist and physician. Its leader was the celebrated Jean-Louis Devreuse, the captain of the cruiser *Hero*, whose glorious explorations in the Antarctic regions are well-known.

The story begins in the eighth month of our voyage.

Robert Farville.

---

[3] Amur, or Sakhalin, is a province of eastern Siberia, north of Manchuria. The French spell the name Amour, so Rosny's choice of it as a location has a certain metaphorical resonance.

Part One

I. The Great Marshes

A remarkable fecundity reigned in the region through which we were traveling. Humans were scarce there. Around the vast marshes the silence was stagnant; animals, free to increase, had multiplied on land and in the waters. Birds filled the air all the way to the clouds, and the rivers were seething with copious life.

The soul expanded to its full breadth there; I had a sensation of vastness and full life for months on end. My imagination flowed like a great river, and grew like the terrible forests; I witnessed considerable migrations of wolves, cranes, horses, bears and wood-pigeons. I was foolishly besotted with the wind, the glitter of the streams, the softness of the grass and the rustling of willows and reeds.

Then the marshes impeded us. An equivocal region extended to our left, punctuated by long promontories where thoughtful herons flocked and rails ran through the reeds. We waded through weed-infested lagoons and crossed one deep marsh on a raft made from an alder-tree felled by lightning. Then the black country broadened out, replete with subterranean forces, and feverish reptilian life. Giant toads roamed the shores; serpents plunged into the mud and the withered grass; insect swarms burrowed in the soft Earth to shelter their reproduction. The insipid and mortal gases, the mysterious stirrings of the mud and mire, the flickering flames that lit up by night, and—most especially—the exceedingly low and opaque cloud-layer overlying the strips of land lost in the sinister waters and the green algal scum, filled us with a sentiment of terrible grandeur.

We continued going forward, no longer having the courage to retreat, determined to find a way through.

It was toward the end of August. We had already been wandering at hazard for three weeks. We had lost our tents in some rapids; the men had become discouraged, but our leader remained committed. Endowed with a restless exploratory spirit and an obstinate, stern, implacable and almost cruel energy, armored against anxiety and tenderness, he was one of those men who knew how to fight hard, overcoming people and things, and to die heroically if he must, but whose inner life was morose and monotonous, almost non-existent. He kept us under the yoke of his determination.

Our Asiatic guide no longer had the slightest knowledge of the region; he replied to all our questions with the impassive sadness typical of Orientals: "Not know…land of wicked men…know nothing about it."

Our men were beginning to show signs of rebellion. Personally, I was only anxious on behalf of the captain's lovely daughter, Sabine Devreuse. How she had contrived to accompany us is incomprehensible. Doubtless the captain had thought that the expedition would be brief and not at all perilous, and the young woman's pleading had done the rest. Then again, world-travelers end up becoming immeasurably optimistic, with a singular belief in their lucky stars.

Sabine Devreuse had become dearer to me with every passing day; thanks to her, a hint of grace and a superior joy accompanied the journey. Thanks to her, the evening halts were becoming an incomparable poem. In spite of her sensitive features and delicately soft lips, she was very resilient— never ill and rarely weary. Oh yes, she was the charm of our expedition, the exquisite wild rose on our rude masculine bush.

One morning, we thought we had reached a more hospitable territory. The commander was already triumphant as we crossed a kind of feverish plain, scarcely dotted with a few small pools.

"We'll come out on the eastern side," he said, "probably in grassland—as I expected."

I did not share his optimism. With my eye fixed on the horizon, I anticipated more considerable perils. Soon, in fact, the waters returned, perfidious and pernicious. Furthermore, an interminable rain began to fall. The plain was stony in parts, covered in others by spongy mosses and slimy lichens. The marshes became more numerous; we lost days going around them, while all kinds of marsh animals slithered around us, frightening our horses. Our waterproof clothing had holes, and provided poor cover; we were soaked to the skin.

The halt of August 30, on a small rocky eminence devoid of shelter and combustible material, was among the most depressing of our journey. The commander, as rigid and stern as the Assyrian overseers leading captives on the bas-reliefs of Khorsabad, said nothing. An abominable twilight died away in the deluge. The implacable moisture, the funereal grayness and the indigent and feverish ground were soul-crushing. Only Sabine Devreuse found the strength to smile. The dear girl, symbol of hearth and home, and the familiar grace of Europe, was a silvery voice amid the rain-clouds. Oh, how serene I felt in listening to her, forgetting my anguish and lassitude!

Can you imagine how we bedded down on the viscous soil, in absolute darkness—for it was the dark of the Moon— beneath a sky triply covered in clouds from dusk to dawn? I slept, though, with intermittent dreams and frightful nightmares.

About an hour before dawn, our horses became agitated, snorting in terror. They would certainly have run away but for the sturdy tethers with which we were accustomed to hobble them.

The guide touched my arm, and said: "A man-eater!"

You cannot imagine the horror of these words, in the ink-black night, beneath the indefatigable cold deluge. However, getting up with a start, I had the presence of mind to load my rifle, which was protected by a sheath of oiled leather. I peered into the darkness, but I might as well have been trying to look through a wall.

"How do you know?" I asked.

A muffled growl went up on the plain, dispelling all doubt. It was really *Him*, the largest wild beast in the world, the immense tiger of the North, which crosses frozen rivers to ravage the little towns of Amur, a successor, if not a descendant, of the formidable dominator of the Quaternary Era.

It was not the first time we had encountered one—but while we had a dozen good marksmen, well-armed, behind a blazing camp-fire, they had never alarmed us to the point of terror, whereas we were incapable of keeping track of the monster's movements in that funereal night. We could only wait; the other could see in the darkness admirably.

"Form a square!" murmured the commander.

We were standing up, our horses increasingly restless. We should have been able to shield ourselves with their bodies, but they were panicking, and it would probably have been more dangerous close to them.

"Him coming...me hear him!" said the guide.

No one doubted the Asiatic's prodigious hearing. Oh, that damp wall, that dark rain, that unspeakable mystery! Soon, I perceived the footfalls of the great beast myself, gliding, then stopping. The feeling that it could see us, that it was preparing itself, calculating its attack, and was about to pounce without warning, was enough to dishearten the bravest of men!

There was a pause. The beast must be hesitating over the choice of a victim. In this wilderness, where there is no contact with humans or horses, both are doubtless astonishing.

Eventually, the movement in the darkness resumed. We perceived that the tiger was to the left, closer to our square than the horses.

"Take a blind shot," Devreuse instructed me. I was unquestionably the best marksman in the party; I could hit a target at 100 paces.

A roar followed the shot: we heard a heavy body land three times. The tiger was now very close. Its breath was harsh and jerky.

"Alcuin, Lacal—fire!" ordered the captain.

By the light of the muzzle-flashes we glimpsed the mighty silhouette, crouched for a final leap—then, before Devreuse was able to give any further order, the beast was upon us. An agonized scream rang out in the impenetrable darkness, followed by two seconds of infinite horror. No one dared fire! Then there was another scream, and a crunch of jaws. Finally, someone fired.

The flash of light showed us two of our men down, and the tiger rearing up, ready to fell a third. By the same token, the beast's position was known. Rifle-shots rang out: four shots—and the beast uttered a frightful groan. A brief silence followed.

"Him wounded!" whispered the guide.

Scarcely had he spoken than a hoarse growl replied. I sensed the movement of a formidable mass; I was seized implacably and irresistibly, rolled over and shaken, then carried away like a sparrow by a lynx.

I'm doomed! I thought.

I was overwhelmed by an incredible resignation. I abandoned myself to death. I felt no pain; I was in a state of lucid delirium. I held on to my rifle, mechanically...

An interminable time went by; then there was an abrupt halt. I was lying on the ground. I felt strong fetid breath on my face...and suddenly, my resignation evaporated, changing into an immense terror and an immeasurable regret for the loss of life.

A taloned paw came down; I thought that I was about to be torn apart, pounded and devoured. "Adieu!" I cried, feebly—and yet, with a desperate instinct, I had raised my rifle. There was a flash, and a bang!

The beast howled and leapt into the air—and leapt again.

I was still lying down, still expecting to die. I heard a colossal groan three paces away. A faint hope crept into my heart. *What's happening? Am I going to die, or to live? Why am I free? Why is the beast groaning without seeking vengeance? A movement! It's getting up again—I'm going to*

19

die...no, it's fallen back, no longer growling. Silence! A great silence!

How long did all that take?

Terror and horror give rise to infinity. I found myself standing up without knowing how, without any mortal injury. Human footsteps were approaching, and a voice—that of the Asiatic: "Him very dead!"

In the darkness, his hand had grabbed mine. I replied with a powerful grip—but the anguish remained: doubt as to whether the beast was really dead...or whether it would get up again and pounce.

It was certainly not moving, though, not breathing. Nothing could be heard but the monotonous fall of the rain and the tentative footfalls of my companions.

The captain's voice rang out: "Robert, are you all right?"

"Yes."

I succeeded, after several attempts, in lighting a match under cover of my overcoat. In that faint gleam the apparition was gripping: the giant beast in the red mud, still beautiful in its attitude and menace, its mouth tightly closed over its immense carnivorous teeth, one paw advanced, showing its sharp talons. In truth, it was no longer moving, no longer palpitating! How had that come about? Was it possible that I was here, among the living, saved from the hideous peril? Was it me who was breathing? Oh, I had really thought that my last moment had come, and felt the icy breath of annihilation.

"Him very dead!" the Asiatic repeated.

Groping our way, we rejoined the captain and went back to the eminence. There, a soft and tremulous voice made my heart beat faster.

"Are you hurt?"

"No, Mademoiselle...not grievously, at any rate. The beast must have held me by the leather and rubber of my garments. How are the others?"

"As for me," said Alcuin, "I seem to have a nasty scratch on my chest. The tiger left me right away..."

A second voice, more muffled and more plaintive, said: "I'm wounded at the hip...but the shock was the most terrible thing..."

We were no longer paying any heed to fatigue or the rain; our escape from terrible peril filled us with an almost joyful excitement. A faint grayness was beginning to tint the eastern horizon. For some time, that light remained uncertain, scarcely allowing us to see one another. Finally, it increased, and there was daylight: a miserable daylight in a desolate region, where the rain was causing the marshes to overflow. The excitement died away in confrontation with the wretchedness of the landscape; a profound sadness penetrated our souls. Personally, I only had eyes for the brilliant Sabine, who illuminated my destiny as the pole star did for ancient mariners.

Our wounds were not serious enough to force a delay.

Another day went by in the horrid wilderness, beneath the implacable, energy-sapping rain. The men complained incessantly. They kept their distance, conferring in secret. When I approached them, they looked at me mistrustfully. It was not difficult to deduce that they were plotting—and although I, personally, was willing to follow the captain to the ends of the Earth, I understood their discontentment and felt sorry for them.

At about 4 p.m., Devreuse decided to call a halt. In addition to our excessive fatigue, and the care we had to give the wounded, the halt was determined by the unexpected discovery of shelter. In the midst of the plain there was a bizarre protrusion of rock almost 90 meters high. We climbed it by means of a large fissure that seemed to have been completed by human hands. The summit of the hill formed a plateau, in which there was a cave. The sloping floor of the cave was quite dry; the whole formed a large space, fairly well-lit.

After two days of downpour, the shelter seemed rather providential, so our men manifested the intention of spending the night there. The captain could not refuse such a reasonable request. Our little horses were brought up without difficulty, and we found ourselves lodged in unexpected comfort—unexpected in that, in addition to the cave, properly speaking, we found corridors and coverts where we could take care of a few hygienic concerns. There was no lack of water—a depression in the plateau formed a small pool, all the fresher because it was continually running.

An hour later, with our wounds well-dressed and some of our clothes hung up to dry, we finished eating the provisions remaining from our last hunt—a few slices of venison cooked in advance. It would have been nice to drink a cup of hot tea, though! Alas, we had no fire.

"It would be useful to go cut a few branches," said one of the men.

"They wouldn't have time to dry," said the captain, morosely.

"Really!" the man replied. His tone disturbed me. At that moment I was standing on the threshold of the cave with Sabine. We were contemplating the country through the melancholy curtain of rain. I was savoring the delight of the moment. How graceful she was! In her gray mantle, her damp hair negligently braided and her complexion diaphanous, Sabine retained a palpitating sensation of life and sacred youth. All nostalgia and all anxiety vanished in the curve of her mouth, her mysterious smile... The man's voice—it was Alcuin's—caused me to turn around, though.

Devreuse had also been struck by the reply. "What did you say?" he snapped, with severity.

Alcuin, anxious at first, replied with respectful firmness: "It's just that we're very tired, captain. We need a few days' rest...and Lefort's wound requires care."

His companions nodded their heads approvingly—which gave the captain pause for reflection. As usual, though, the obstinacy of his will prevailed. "We're leaving tomorrow morning!"

"We can't!" And Alcuin risked adding: "We need five days rest. The shelter's sound—we can get our strength back."

A shadow of indecision passed over the commander's hard features—but the man was too inaccessible, absolutely resolute to the point of obsession, with a superstitious belief in his own prescience. He had decided, privately, that there was a way out to the south-east, and he did not want to lose a single day.

"We're leaving tomorrow morning!"

"And what if we can't?" Alcuin asked, softly.

Devreuse's expression hardened. "Are you refusing to obey my orders?"

"No, captain, we're not refusing, but we can't go on! The expedition was only supposed to last three months."

Devreuse, who was agitated, evidently recognized that there was some justice in his subaltern's claim, or he would not have delayed his response. I still hoped that he might yield to common sense and grant the respite—but no; it was impossible for him to give in.

"That's all right," he said. "I go on alone." Then he turned to me. "Will you wait for me here for ten days?"

"No!" I cried. "If these men abandon you, I can't blame them—but for myself, I swear that I won't leave you until we reach civilization!"

The men remained impassive. Devreuse's stern lips displayed an unaccustomed emotion. "Thank you, Robert!" he said, emphatically. Addressing the others, disdainfully, he said: "I shan't hold your conduct against you, considering the length and fatigue of the journey, but I order you to wait for us here for a fortnight. Further disobedience, save in the case of *force majeure*, will be considered treason."

"Until the evening of the 15th day, at least!" Alcuin replied, humbly. "And we regret…"

Devreuse cut him off with an imperious gesture. We remained in somber silence for some time.

II. Confession

I got up at dawn. Everyone else was still sleeping soundly. I was nervous, full of anxiety for the delicate Sabine, whose father was about to expose her to new perils. I reproached myself for my resolution; perhaps, if I had sided with the others, the captain would not have been so stubborn. The idea gnawed away at me—and yet, intractable as he was, the opposite seemed more probable. Would he not have left on his own, taking Sabine? That separation would have been more bitter to me than death.

Thus I reflected, on the threshold of the plateau. A dismal day was beginning in the inexhaustible rain. The entire country was waterlogged; the water was triumphant over sky and Earth alike.

Suddenly, I heard a slight noise behind me—light and prudent footsteps. I turned round; it was her, Sabine. Wrapped in her little cloak, she approached with an air of gracious mystery. With that, all fear and sadness was dissipated. Even the rain became charming.

Immobile, hypnotized, I was about to stammer a polite greeting when she said: "I've come to talk to you."

These simple words held an infinity of mystery and anxiety. "I was very touched by your devotion," she continued. "My father, who will be eternally grateful to you, doesn't know how to express gratitude. May I thank you on his behalf?"

Oh, the morning hair, falling loosely over the dazzling nape of her neck! The humble gray mantle, more beautiful than a fairy's robe! The delightful cave-entrance, the soft rhythm of the rain, accompanying my beloved's words! I no longer felt anything but the force of adoration; my every nerve was charged with love. But I was gripped by anguish—the moment was too beautiful! It had—how can I know why?— completed my passion at a stroke. It was the flash of lightning that unleashed the storm. Everything was doubtless ready; the profound and durable tenderness had been flowering in my soul for a long time—but so often, love, even when powerful, founders in long silence, in a silence that can never be broken. One slight venture—one nice gesture, like Sabine's at that moment—may leave no further alternative but happiness or distress, triumph or mortal, unanswered, love. That morning, I knew that I was about to speak, I knew that I was about to interrogate my destiny. From what tortures the next minute might deliver me—or what a curse might love become!

"If I was able to please you in saying what I did…the recompense is too great!"

She looked at me with her lovely clear eyes, and the spell was further increased. "Too great?" She was blushing now. As for me, my breathing was so rapid that I lost my voice momentarily. How could I dare to speak to her? And if I spoke, what if it was for nothing? What if she refused? What if those hands were never to grip mine, or those red lips…? Harsh, powerful doubts—how they squeezed my heart!

Finally, I was able to speak. "Yes, too great. Your thanks would repay any peril and any devotion!"

She lowered her eyes. Her lips quivered over the pallor of her teeth. Sabine was my destiny; she embodied Life and Nirvana in her lowered eyelashes.

Tremulously, I said: "Does my devotion alarm you?"

"I would have to be very timid, if so," she said, with slight irony—but a very gentle, almost tremulous irony!

The doubt persisted: the terror of losing everything on a single throw of the dice.

At hazard, I stammered: "Don't you want me to follow you *forever?*"

"Forever?"

"Yes, for as long as I live?"

She assumed a serious expression. I felt faint. But there was no going back; I had thrown the dice.

"Would you like me to ask your father if he wants me as a son?"

Doubt passed over her face; then, with charming bravery, she said: "Yes, ask him!"

"Sabine!" I cried, with an almost painful joy. "Can I believe that you love me?"

"What else can you believe?" she said, the hint of irony returning—that tender and affectionate irony.

Silhouette of happiness, rain-swept early morning, paradise of marshland! Gently, I had taken her pretty hand and raised it to my lips.

And I felt that I was the Master of the World.

III. The Man of the Waters

The captain, Sabine and I had left the men behind two days before. We were advancing through country that was even bleaker, but possessed of a tenebrous and grandiose beauty. Whether there was a way through or not, the march was becoming more painful by the hour. Fortunately, we had only brought Sabine's little horse; our own mounts would have been more of a burden than a help.

Toward the end of the second day, the rain stopped. We were surrounded by pools on all sides. We were making slow progress along a ridge.

"It's getting dark! One more effort!" said the captain.

Night was, indeed, falling. The light was fading as the Sun set. We were heading for what seemed to be a hillock. I don't know what happened to Sabine's horse, but it suddenly bolted, passing to the left of the hillock like lightning. Sabine uttered a loud scream. Her mount had just plunged into the marsh. I had no time to think; I was beside her within a second; the soft Earth dragged me down in my turn.

For a few minutes, we tried to break free.

"Moving only makes us sink deeper!" Sabine remarked.

That was incontestable. Trapped in a tangle of plants, we could neither go forward, nor retreat, nor climb back up. It was one of those traps in which inert nature seems to swallow living beings with a slow but sure ferocity.

The captain had not lost his presence of mind, however. He advanced indirectly, along a small promontory whose tip slanted toward us. He had uncoiled several meters of the rope that he always carried on his person, and was getting ready to throw us one end. He was our only hope, and we watched him anxiously.

Suddenly, he slipped, stumbled, and tried to step back. The soil of the promontory at the place where he was standing, doubtless composed of a thin vegetable crust, had collapsed into the green water. Devreuse reached out his arms, clutching at random, but his hand only encountered an illusory support; his situation had become identical to ours!

And night was falling! Only vague shapes were now distinguishable. Animals were sighing or wailing in the half-light of the vast wilderness. Will-o'-the-wisps were flickering over the marsh. We were prisoners of the mud! Every movement caused us to sink deeper; every minute marked a stage in our frightful death-throes. A faint and murky crescent moon appeared between the misty clouds, seemingly immense as it posed atop a distant curtain of poplars, already on the wane. Sabine's horse was rump-deep; she looked at me, beginning to despair.

"We're doomed, Robert!"

I tried to find something nearby to hold on to, but everything gave way, and every attempt hastened the moment when...

"Well," said the captain, "if no help arrives—and I don't see where any can come from—we are indeed doomed, my poor children."

His harsh voice had taken on an inflection of tenderness; that made me feel even worse. Sabine's eyes dilated in horror. She looked at us in turn, and all three of us abandoned ourselves to that hideous state in which struggle is futile, in which the elements are devouring you, draining more of your strength with every passing minute.

"My God!" Sabine sighed.

The Moon, chasing away the mist, shone brightly over the lagoon. A few solitary stars appeared in the south, like a little archipelago in the bosom of an ocean. The wind skimmed the marsh slowly, with a heavy and toxic gentleness.

The mud reached my shoulders; another half-hour and I would disappear. Sabine put out a hand to help me.

"We'll die together, my dear Robert!"

Lovely girl, be blessed in death!

Suddenly, a confused melody rippled over the algae: a strange, unknown music from another time and another place, indistinguishable to our gross senses at intervals, and yet perceptible.

I looked around. The Moon was in a clear patch of sky; its light fell brightly. I saw a slender human silhouette standing on a tongue of land, a sort of long, low-lying islet. His fingers were holding a slim object whose form I could not quite make out.

And we saw an extraordinary scene unfold.

Giant salamanders were climbing on to the islet and gathering around the man, along with newts, olms and water-snakes. Bats were flying around his head, grebes were dancing to the rhythm, and yet more vague forms accumulated, including rats, water-fowl and owls. The man continued to play his bizarre music, and a great calm descended upon the scene: a sentiment of pantheistic brotherhood that I felt strongly, in spite of the horror of our situation.

We uttered cries of distress. The man stopped playing and turned toward us. When he saw our situation, he leapt from his islet and disappeared into the algae. Anguish and hope, interlaced like lianas, held us motionless.

Suddenly, the man reappeared nearby—and, without a word, he raced toward us. We could not take full account of his movements, but I felt myself grabbed and dragged away, along with Sabine. A few moments later we were able to wade through mud that was less treacherous, and finally to come ashore.

Devreuse rejoined us after a few minutes, and the man stood looking at us with a tranquil expression He had thin hair, like stringy lichen. There was no hair on his body or his face. His skin—in spite of the mud into which he had plunged—was clean, and slightly oily. He was almost naked, having only a short fibrous garment around his loins.

Devreuse thanked him in various languages. The man listened patiently and shook his head. Evidently, he did not understand. In the joy of our salvation, we took hold of his hands enthusiastically. He smiled, and spoke incomprehensibly. It was not a human voice, but some guttural amphibian pronunciation.

He saw us shivering, though, and made a gesture bidding us to follow him. We went along a slender natural causeway, firm and solid. It broadened out and became more elevated, allowing us to attain a sort of plateau in the middle of the waters. The man signaled to us to stop there, and disappeared again.

"Is he abandoning us?" Sabine asked me, anxiously.

"It doesn't matter—we're safe."

"And so strangely!"

The Moon was high, almost white, and bright. The marshes extended as far as the eye could see, a realm of Dismal Waters. Various things were drifting through my mind, in a sort of hallucination, when I saw the silhouette of the man again, coming back with Sabine's horse.

"Poor Geo!" she exclaimed, with affectionate tears.

The man was also carrying plants, wood and eggs. He offered us the eggs and a few handfuls of edible nuts. At the same time, he heaped up armfuls of wood and dry stems, and we lit a fire.

When that was done, he smiled slowly—then, leaping down from the top of the plateau, he disappeared again beneath the water, which was deep in that vicinity. We stood there watching the place where he had dived; we could not see anything.

Not knowing what to think, we looked at one another in amazement.

"What is he doing?" I exclaimed.

"This is certainly the most incredible thing I've encountered in 15 years of traveling," Devreuse replied, pensively. "But whatever is going to happen will happen—let's eat!"

We ate heartily, drying our clothes in the firelight. The evening was warm, which helped us go to sleep.

In the middle of the night, however, I woke up. Our savior was playing his bizarre music again in the distance, over the silent marsh. The musician was invisible. It seemed to me then that I had entered a new life, a reality more enchanted than the most magical of fairy tales.

We awoke at dawn, having slept well.

"Captain!" I exclaimed. I pointed to our clothes, which had been cleaned and were perfectly dry.

"It's our water-man!" Sabine replied. "I'm beginning to think that he's some benevolent faun."

We still had some eggs and nuts, which provided us with a good breakfast. The Sun came out softly, refreshed by light clouds. The gloomy marvel of the marsh made us thoughtful. Some herons flew by, then a group of teal. Although fortified and feeling quite well, we could not help feeling some anxiety.

Suddenly, Sabine uttered a faint exclamation: "Look!"

A floating object was advancing rapidly toward our haven; we soon recognized it as some kind of raft. It seemed to be moving through the algae of its own accord, and that life-like movement of an inert object seemed disturbing—but a head appeared, and then a body, springing from the green water; we recognized our bizarre providence. To our gestures of welcome the Water-Man replied with unequivocal cordiality.

His appearance astonished us even more than it had in the moonlight; he had skin as green as new grass-shoots, violet lips, strangely rounded eyes almost devoid of sclerotic, with irises the color of carbuncles and very large, deep pupils. He also had a peculiar gracefulness, and a great apparent youthfulness. I examined him for a long time, especially his singular eyes; I had never seen anything analogous in any other human being.

He beckoned us on to the raft, after having hitched Geo to its rear end. We obeyed, not without a slight suspicion, which increased when we saw him disappear underwater again, and the raft resumed its progress in the same strange way that it had arrived.

We were able to catch occasional glimpses of our conductor under the glutinous muddy water encumbered with vegetation. We drifted for 20 minutes without him emerging once. We were making good headway; the place where we had spent the night was already distant. The locale began to change; the water was fresher and we skirted some delightful little islands.

The Water-Man's head reappeared; he pointed to the south and dived again. The breeze brought purer air. Soon, the marsh became narrower, and we went along a sort of shallow channel. Then we found ourselves in new waters—lake waters, clear and fresh, where the atmosphere was invigorating.

IV. Lake Nymphaeum

The lake, which extended for several leagues, was strewn with islands, whose shores were decorated with huge pale-flowered water-lilies, planted with an infinite vegetation of grasses, flowers, bushes and tall trees. Our suspicion had vanished along with the heavy, somnolent and morbid air of the marsh. Our lungs were breathing in the good health, and our hearts were full of hope and lacustrian poetry.

The raft came to a stop at the point of a promontory. The Water-Man emerged and signaled to us to follow him.

We found ourselves confronted by the most extraordinary spectacle. Thirty human beings were gathered on the shore of the isle: old and young, men and women, girls and little children; they were all green in color, with smooth skin, eyes like carbuncles with large flat pupils, hair like stringy lichen and violet lips.

At the sight of us, the children ran forward, along with adolescents of both sexes and an old man. They crowded around us with batrachian exclamations, exhibiting a great and hilarious excitement.

While we were standing there, other Water-Men emerged from the lake and came on shore. We soon found ourselves surrounded by an entire aquatic population, not merely very human but closer, in their general features, to the white race than other terrestrial races. Their green color and the oily sheen on their skin were not disagreeable to look at. The younger ones were a pretty pale green, as light as that of new spring vegetation; the older ones often had the velvet green of moss or lotus-flowers. A few of the young women presented a slimness of figure, slender fingers and a delicacy of feature that rendered them veritably seductive.

It would be vain for me to attempt to describe our amazement. What we felt can only be represented by those dreams in which the soul glimpses the youth of the world, the divine time of geneses. For the captain and myself, that was combined with a scientific pride—what discovery could compare to this one? Was it not a realization, without ancestral mythical apparatus, or the monstrosities of beast-men or fish-men, of one of the most attractive traditions of all peoples? Were we not verifying, once again, that legends are usually founded in truth? In the same way that the gorilla, the orangutan and the chimpanzee have justified the fiction of fauns and satyrs, Ctesias' account of the Cynocephali,[4] and the passage

---

[4] Ctesias was a Greek historian and physician of the 5th century B.C., contemporary with Herodotus, who produced an account of India, some fragments of which survive, most fa-

in Hanno's *Periplus* regarding the hairy men of the Gulf of the Southern Cape,[5] were we not seeing a realization of the immense legendary cycle of merfolk? What made our discovery all the more exciting was that the people we had before our eyes were true men, not anthropoid apes.

When our initial astonishment had passed, all that remained in me was a kind of mystical intoxication, which I could see that Sabine and Devreuse shared.

Our savior led us toward a grove of ash-trees. There we found a group of huts. Aquatic birds were wandering around: ducks, swans and other water-fowl, evidently domesticated. We were brought fresh eggs and a grilled perch. After the meal, we returned to the shore.

The weather was mild. All afternoon we watched the comings and goings of the Water-People. They swam like huge batrachians, diving and disappearing—then a head would emerge, and a body would leap out on to the island.

Fascinated by the pleasure of their double life, I continued to examine them with avid curiosity, trying to discover what adaptation permitted them to remain under water for such a long time. Save for a large thoracic capacity, however, I could not find any clue to enlighten me in this matter.

That afternoon, we were never left alone. We were constantly surrounded by a crowd, whose members tried to talk to us, showing an innocent benevolence toward us. In spite of the seductiveness and marvelous quality of these strange beings, we made plans to leave the following morning, intending to come back as quickly as possible, having communicated with our men. In view of the superior importance of the discovery, the captain renounced his famous south-west passage.

---

mously a passage dealing with the Cynocephali—a race of "dog-headed" people.

[5] Hanno was a Carthaginian navigator of the 5th century B.C. who allegedly led an expedition southwards along the west coast of Africa; a Greek account of the voyage is preserved in the *Periplus.*

Fate, however, modified our plans. I was woken up in the night by Devreuse.

"Sabine is ill!"

I got up with a start. By the pale light of an ash-wood torch, I saw my beloved writhing in a fever. Gripped by alarm, I examined her and listened to her chest. I was slightly reassured.

"Is it serious?" her father asked.

"A few days of absolute rest should set her right."

"*How many days?*"

"Ten."

"At least?"

"At least!"

He scowled, expressing his helplessness. He looked at me in the dim light. "Robert, I can entrust your fiancée to you. There's no doubt that I'll be able to reach an understanding with the men, so that they'll extend their stay for a couple of months. I'll be back here at the end of the week." He spoke agitatedly, marching back and forth. "Besides," he continued, "if the weeks that I expect to spend among these extraordinary beings are insufficient, we'll certainly be able to organize a further expedition. We have time. I'll resign, if I must, in order to have years at my disposal. All the more reason for me not to abandon my men!"

"But it's my job to go and warn them," I protested.

"No! Your care is indispensable to Sabine. I'd be no more help than a block of wood." He put his hands on my shoulders. "Isn't that so, Robert?"

"I'll do as you say," I said.

Although she was slightly delirious, Sabine had understood us fully. She propped herself up on her elbow. "I'm strong enough to go with you, Father!"

"Obey the doctor's orders, little girl," Devreuse replied, authoritatively. "Within six days I'll be back, having accomplished my duty. Do you want to hold me back?"

Sabine gave in, making no reply. We remained taciturn for some time. The fever began to make the young woman agitated again; then she fell into a semi-sleep. I watched her by the poor light of the torch. I felt an indefinable presentiment.

The captain's voice pulled me out of my reverie. "Are you sure that it's not dangerous?"

"In medicine, one is never certain."

"But as sure as you can be?"

"So far as I can judge, Mademoiselle Sabine will be fully recovered in a fortnight."

"I'll go, then."

The illness was even less serious than I thought. After three days, Sabine was convalescent, and was able to get up for a few hours. The weather remained fine. A fluid beauty spread over the island and the lake. Our lake-dwelling hosts were full of goodwill, politeness and sympathy.

A week went by. The young woman was almost entirely well again, but a great anxiety was born: the captain had not come back.

One afternoon, seated on the shore, I was doing my best to console Sabine, without succeeding in calming her anxiety.

"I'm afraid!" she repeated.

I no longer knew what to say. A shadow extended nearby. On turning round, I saw that it was the Water-Man who had rescued us, with whom we had established a particularly amicable relationship. He smiled, and showed us a large gray swallow peculiar to the region, and very friendly. When he came closer, he handed the bird to me.

"What is it?" asked Sabine.

I immediately spotted the shaft of a quill attached to its pale underside, which I detached. It contained a thin sheet of tissue-paper.

"A letter from your father!"

There were only the following words:

Reached port. Ankle sprained in fall. Nothing serious, but am delayed. Don't worry, but above all, wait for me. Don't leave the island.

Sabine burst into tears. Personally, I was astonished that the captain had thought of making use of the little messenger. The Water-Man's smile suggested to me that the idea had not originated with Devreuse. My companion continued to show distress.

"Sabine!" I whispered, gently. "It's not dangerous...a sprained ankle. The effect will only last a couple of weeks..."

"Are you sure?"

"Absolutely."

The Water-Man had disappeared. Sabine was no longer crying, but she was mournful. I put my arms around her slender neck. Her blonde head rested on my shoulder, and my eyes were reflected in hers. I had never been so happy, in spite of our tribulations.

She was weak and tired. She only wanted reassurance. The clear sky and the tremulous shadows enveloped her with divinity. Oh, the mysterious power that has created Love, the vanquisher of Death!

V. The Inhabitants of the Lake

The days went by.

We were becoming increasingly fond of the marvelous lake, going to visit its islands with our aquatic friends. Groups of young men and women pushed our raft playfully, swimming around us in the near-transparent water. We took breaks on cool shores, beneath slender willows or tall poplars.

The best thing about that delightful life, however, was the superior charm of our hosts themselves, whom we were beginning to understand, and with whom we could exchange a few words. It was, however, them who were learning our language. Our ears remained impotent to analyze the sounds they exchanged with one another.

Their mores were simple and facile. The notion of family was entirely foreign to them. I think the entire population of the lake amounted to about 1200 individuals. Men and women raised the children without distinction, we never saw any of them neglected.

Their dwellings were made of wood covered with moss and twigs, with gaps for windows. They made little use of them during the fine season, and must have been used mostly as shelters for hibernation. Their cooking was done in the open air, and their diet consisted entirely of fish, eggs, mushrooms and a few wild vegetables. They did not eat their domestic birds or any other warm-blooded animals. We understood that they would be disgusted by seeing us eat them, so we contented ourselves with their dietary regime. Our health thrived on it.

They had a few weapons, including a kind of helical harpoon, which they could not only throw over the water in a straight line, but also in a series of curves, making it come back to them like an Australian boomerang. They used it to catch big fish. It must be said that the fish in the lake were the cleverest I have seen, doubtless because of the presence of the aquatic men—who, over the generations, had accustomed them to more subtle defenses than are customary. Our hosts had succeeded in domesticating many; they did not kill those, only consuming their eggs. On the other hand, they were keen hunters of pike and perch.

Their industry was uncomplicated, although they were familiar with the art of pottery and the elements of carpentry and joinery. They did not use metals at all, but fashioned their harpoons, saws, axes and knives from a kind of strong, hard jade.

All in all, the simplicity of their material needs scarcely inclined them to industry. Their way of life was more poetic than practical. I never saw creatures freer from all concern with the encumbrances of property. They seemed to have retained only the elements of happiness, ridding themselves of all vain suffering. Not that they were lazy, though; they loved exercise, undertaking aquatic journeys to the point of exhaustion. They were incessantly in motion, like cetaceans. Unlike savages, who follow determined hunts with long days of idleness, they remained untiringly active.

This prodigious activity had no productive aim, however; it was *their dream*. They swam, sailed and bounded as other people rest. Apart from underwater hunts—only undertaken against carnivorous fish—theirs was *movement for movement's sake*.

I saw them solve extraordinary problems of movement, exhibiting a variety of attitudes and trajectories compared with which the suppleness of a swallow or a salmon is clumsy. Their games were merely a continuous deployment of the art of dance-swimming, complex and suggestive ballets. On seeing them darting and turning, describing spirals around one another, precipitating themselves into whirlpools 20 or 30 at a time, one sensed that they had a kind of dynamic, or muscular *consciousness* unknown to other humans.

They are particularly admirable in the moonlight. I witnessed underwater festivals so beautiful, so graceful and so dreamlike, composed of evolutions so various, that nothing in this world can compare with them. When large numbers participated in them, these festivals were accompanied by a strange phenomenon. The water, moving rhythmically by virtue of their ballet, gradually acquired a euphonic voice. That voice, party to an indescribable melody, a secret murmur, a harmonious whisper, increased slowly and ineffably. The Element trembled and sang, sending forth a great moist hymn—O untranslatable softness, O prodigiously penetrating voice!—which caused us to weep tears of exaltation.

Then, I remembered the Legend, of the victorious voice of Sirens, which the navigators of old thought they heard over the waves. Was that not what we heard in the silvery night, but so benevolent and fraternal! And how superior it was to the myth, for it was the Water itself, the Lake, that was singing—it was the great rumor of the waves, submissive to the rhythm of the Water-Men, as Forests here may sometimes be submissive to the rumor of the Winds.

The thoughts expressed by the movements of our hosts were not only general and poetic. They often became specific; I understood that they served to express *precise* notions. For example, I was able to observe veritable dialogues in a few instances, of which I ended up grasping some vague traces, doubtless insufficient for me to follow the thoughts of the swimmers, but sufficient for me to understand that what I was seeing was a conversation. During aquatic lessons given to children, which I took pleasure in watching, my conviction was confirmed; the individuals informing the children expressed their approval or disapproval by means of swimming gestures, at least two of which I came to understand—one that brought the lesson to an end, another that changed the subject.

Love found its natural expression there. The Water-Men were able to deploy an artistry of tenderness, supplication and pride, which varied between individuals—an artistry more unexpected than their collective art, exceedingly subtle and delicate, and perhaps superior to our conversational idylls.

They did not seem to have any metaphysical consciousness, being little inclined to abstraction. I saw no trace of religion or supernatural belief, merely an intense love of nature. I have mentioned their gentleness toward birds and mammals, and also toward domesticated fish. That gentleness put them in intimate communication with the creatures in question. They were able to make themselves understood to an admirable degree. I have seen them giving instructions to salamanders, to bats, to birds and to carp—instructions the mere idea of which would seem chimerical to us: to go to a designated place for instance, an island or a particular part of the lake. Swans might make journeys of several leagues in response to such orders; bats might suspend their hunting for several days; carp might cease temporarily to shelter in their favorite spots.

The scene that had transpired during our first encounter with the Water-Men was often repeated before my eyes. With the aid of a reed, in which grooves of different lengths and depths were engraved, and by means of the friction of a stone hook, a musician could produce those finely cadenced notes.

The sounds caused animals to gather and held them spell-bound: reptiles, birds and fish came to listen to them, and beasts of prey granted their victims a truce.

How often those scenes enchanted us! How many hours we spent watching some male or female musician renewing the ancient fables—and with such a rudimentary instrument! What an extraordinary felicity there was in all the play, and in all the life, of those amphibious people!

I have said that their mores were free—but with one reservation; their unions lasted a lunar month. Generally, the new moon coincided with the period of selection. Young men and women paired up then, until the phases were complete. All the same, it was a sort of marriage, a marriage both physiological and astronomical, inasmuch as the young women were perfectly in tune with the star.[6]

These mores did not give rise to any disorder. They were accompanied by a great fidelity. We saw no shadow of dispute, much less of combat, between our male hosts. Once a choice was made, everyone observed it until the end of the lunar cycle; everyone remade it until the end of the following cycle. It was not prohibited to continue a marriage for a further term, but it rarely happened. They were more frequently resumed a few months later. As for the children, they stayed with their mothers for a few months, but the entire community watched over their wellbeing.

With respect to an adaptation that might explain how they can remain so long underwater, I never found any trace of one.[7] The time that a Water-Man can dive without coming up to the surface is sometimes more than half an hour. If you add to that a swimming speed that reaches 30 to 45 kilometers per hour, you will see that they can rival cetaceans. They have one

---

[6] Rosny's narrator inserts a footnote here: "All this, of course, I only learned later."

[7] Rosny's narrator inserts another footnote: "As I never had the corpse of a Water-Man in my possession, my experimentation was necessarily limited."

veritable superiority over the latter, in their eyes, which are admirably adapted for aquatic vision. A simple inspection of that organ already makes that apparent: their immense flat pupils are as favorable to underwater vision as a falcon's eyes are to aerial vision. The superiority of the organ is abundantly demonstrated *a posteriori* by the subtlety of their movements; they accomplish marvels of precision in co-ordination, calculating, almost simultaneously, darts that, if they were incompetently executed, would result in terrible collisions. In their fish-hunts, they can perceive the smallest fish from hundreds of meters away. On land, they suffer from a kind of presbyopia; within a radius of ten meters their sight is blurred, but they can see distant objects quite well.

Their hearing is also noticeably different from ours. I have mentioned their music, which is punctuated with veritable commas, and their bizarre articulation of speech. This is, I believe, because their ears—like their eyes—are adapted for aquatic life rather than life in the air. It is well-known that the speed of sound in water is more than quadruple that in air, which necessarily creates significant divergences between an ear developed in an aquatic milieu and one developed in the medium of air.

It might be objected that the inhabitants of water are very often mute, and that ears developed with the rarefaction of air, but I shall not debate the problem here—experience is on my side, in regard to the Water-People, and takes priority over theory. I shall limit myself to saying that, once originated, hearing has been able to receive modifications due to the very media that retarded its birth. Thus, even if a very dense atmosphere might have opposed the production of an auditory sense, there is no proof that a relevant organ, *already produced*, would not have been capable of adapting, if the animal were subsequently led to live in a dense atmosphere. Furthermore, the fact that hearing has developed on Earth in the aforementioned conditions does not demonstrate peremptorily that it could not have developed otherwise, although it would doubtless have required a few million years more. Finally, and most importantly, the present affirmations of science on this subject might be no more definitive than the assertions of our immediate predecessors—such as, for example, that which attributed the vast development of the reptiles of the Secondary Age to the presence of large quantities of carbon dioxide, whereas today it is attributed, on the contrary, to an excess of oxygen.

VI. The Attack

One morning, Sabine and I were drifting idly on the lake. At first, our friend had followed us on our lazy excursion. He darted away, returning in unexpected leaps, and sometimes drew our raft along. We paused in the shade of a clump of ash-trees on an islet.

Snowy water-lilies were dreaming on their dark leaves; humble water-crowfoots raised themselves up above thin archipelagoes of algae; arrowheads deployed their pale petals, their gleam softened like clouds in the dawn light; and sharp-snouted fish, emerging in schools, darted forth joyfully. Plants and animals alike were glorying in the sunlight; the hour was sounded by carillons of shadow, the rippling of the water and the swaying of the reeds. Warm caresses sought one another in the imponderable clouds of pollen and flowers emerging tenderly from the depths toward other flowers. The world of the Waters, father of life and fecund ancestor, multiplied its indefatigable magic.

Sabine's gaze was impregnated with the freshness of the lake and the palpitation of the daylight. I trembled with emotion as I looked at her. The Eternal Eden of Nature around amorous youth!

I remember the passage over her face of a sunbeam filtered through a gap in the foliage. She was standing up, her eyelashes lowered toward me. The sunbeam began to tremble in her hair as the leaves stirred. A bough dipped; a shiny insect

42

wandered over her neck—and happiness seemed to be posed upon the bluish water, on the nacreous edges of petals. I clasped her to my heart; a perilous softness commanded us.

"Forever!" I murmured.

Then, I felt afraid; I drew away from her. We dared not say any more; an overly charming threat was prowling around us; the susurrus of the leaves, the flutter of a sparrow and the hum of insects seemed like the sighs of the beyond...

A rumor drew us out of that ecstasy.

It was coming from our left, from an isle of poplars.[8] Some 30 human beings were moving about there. Others soon joined them, emerging from the lake.

"Water-People," I said.

"But look...they're different from the ones we know!"

Indeed, these were darker in color, a kind of blue-black. Sabine huddled closer to me, impelled by dread. "Let's go back to our friends!"

"I think we should," I said.

I was about to cast off when a violent commotion lifted up our raft. Half a dozen men emerged near the islet. Like our hosts they had bizarrely round eyes almost devoid of sclerotic, with slightly indented pupils, but their color and their hair were quite different, as was their attitude.

They watched us from a distance. One of them—an athletic young man—never ceased staring at Sabine. Armed with harpoons, they seemed redoubtable. I shivered as I saw them drawing closer. Sabine was very pale.

Suddenly, the one who was staring at Sabine spoke, in the moist, rippling voice of his race. I made a gesture of incomprehension; they uttered menacing cries and brandished

---

[8] The phrase "île des peupliers" [isle of poplars] has a particular significance in France because it is the name of the burial-place of Jean-Jacques Rousseau, the popularizer of the notion that people uncorrupted by civilization are—or were—happy and peaceful, which became a key element of French Romanticism.

their harpoons. The situation was becoming critical. I still had my rifle, which I kept in readiness—but once the two barrels had been discharged, how could we defend ourselves against these beings, familiar with an element in which they could hide? Besides, even supposing that I could stand up to them, was there not a multitude within 100 meters, ready to come to their aid?

While I reflected on the peril, the young athlete began to speak again; his gestures indicated that he seemed to be demanding a reply. Then I raised my voice. They were struck with amazement. Having paused momentarily to confer with one another, their harpoons were raised again, and they resumed shouting, more menacingly. It became evident that they were preparing to attack me.

I raised my rifle. There was a moment of horrible silence. I thought we were doomed, and prepared myself to die courageously.

A shout went up from the open water. My antagonists turned round. I could not retain a joyful exclamation. A troop of our hosts was swimming toward the islet. Our friend, at their head, made signs to the aggressors. In response to these signs, the harpoons were lowered. Soon, Sabine and I found ourselves in the midst of our friends again.

Then, we witnessed a kind of ceremony in which our Water-People welcomed the others. The entire dark horde came from the isle of poplars. Presents were exchanged, along with strange embraces. It seemed to me that I discerned a certain falsity in the demonstrations of the two races, especially on the Dark side.

The young athlete continued to stare at Sabine from a distance, in a manner that I found extremely annoying.

When our hosts had taken us back to their own island we were greatly relieved to find ourselves under their protection again. Nevertheless, a subtle anxiety continued to haunt us. I thought it was shared—our rescuer, in particular, seemed troubled. He no longer left our side. He had shown us an admirable devotion and, affection generating affection, I had come to love him like a brother.

The afternoon passed without incident.

An hour before dusk, a deputation of dark Water-Men arrived on the island; among them I recognized the young athlete. He seemed to be acting as their leader. Our hosts received the deputation honorably, offering gifts, and there was an aquatic dance in which the Lights and the Darks vied with one another to distinguish themselves.

I kept apart, with Sabine and our friend. We watched everything through the hanging branches of an ash-tree. In spite of our anxiety, the festival was not without interest for us. All of a sudden, at the moment of the greatest animation, two men emerged, not far from our retreat. Had they perceived us? Had they been spying on us for some time? I don't know—but they advanced toward us. It was the young chief again—except that he had a smiling, friendly expression, and his gestures were full of tenderness.

He spoke a few words to our companion, and then, drawing away, looked at Sabine. The equivocal avidity of his gaze made me shiver.

They returned to the lake. Then our friend, shaking his head, allowed his disquiet to become clearly evident. He made signs telling me to watch Sabine carefully, and indicating that he too would be on his guard.

The night was troubled. Glimmers of light moved over the lake and through the foliage of the isles. Strange music was heard; groups of swimmers were glimpsed in the water.

The Moon was on the wane. The star rose, three-quarters eaten away, at about 11 p.m. It was accompanied by a cortege of clouds, a pale procession that extended across the entire zodiac. Occasionally, the Moon exposed its yellow head in a vaporous window; then it became possible to see the churning of the lake, traversed by large and speedy bodies.

About 1 a.m., the Darks arrived *en masse*, less than 100 meters from our island. The Moon had whitened, it surged forth thinly over a cloudy promontory, tracing a tremulous path over the waves. The poplars were sparkling softly; in the background, a sheet of vapor dissipated, allowing a metamorphic light to ooze through. The light appeared to trace out a gap, a pale crater, clear at the edges, dappled with white plush and pearls.

The human company contained its aquatic dance. The water began to sing delicately, in a crystalline fashion. Voices were raised in invitation; young people from our island went to join the nocturnal fête.

How charming and exciting these scenes would have seemed to me without Sabine's presence! What a joy to be able to study the mores of these survivals of an ancient aquatic race which might once have dominated entire continents!

Sometimes, I let myself go, and savored the poetry of the spectacle to the full—but my doubts returned very quickly; and there certainly seemed to be a lack of trust between the two races, perhaps originating from ancient conflicts. Their union seemed more tactical than profound.

Abruptly, the Moon was veiled, attained by thicker clouds, and darkness fell, becoming more intense. I was afraid, and drew nearer to my companion's hut, taking up a position in the narrow doorway.

In the distance, the fête drew to a close. A profound silence weighed upon the waters.

I continued to stand guard. Two or three times I thought I heard the sound of footfalls in the grass, and I did not fall asleep until it was almost dawn.

VII. The Disappearance

Nothing untoward occurred during the rest of the week. Every day, a deputation of the black Water-Men came to our island, and our people visited them on the nearest large island, where they had established their camp. The young people of both races continued to organize fêtes. The animation had increased; the nights were spent dancing, in great aquatic ballets in the decreasing moonlight. The weather remained mild; an invincible sense of the exquisite accompanied the continual apprehension that tormented me. My sleep was troubled, haunted by nightmares. I often woke up with a start, my temples bathed in sweat and my mouth feverish.

I should have been reassured, however, firstly because we were well guarded, and secondly because the newcomers seemed to have forgotten our presence. It was quite probable that the young chief, supposing that he had ever entertained any dubious idea, had abandoned it, with that fickleness that seemed to be one of the characteristics of his race.

I told myself that repeatedly, but I was no more tranquil for it. I was obsessed by a presentiment more powerful than any reasoning. Besides, our friends still manifested a mistrust equal to my own, which made no small contribution to my nervousness. They could not be moved by mere presentiments; they undoubtedly had serious reasons for suspicion!

One evening, at moonrise, the black Water-People arrived in large numbers, accompanied by their old men. They made solemn demonstrations, with numerous exchanges of gifts. I guessed that it was a matter of their departure, and hope slipped furtively into my soul.

The sky was clear over three-quarters of its circumference, especially to the east. Yellow light strayed over the waters. Amphibious animals were croaking on the leaves of the water-lilies and on the long blades of the irises. The whole humid scene exhaled a nervous poetry. The boundless fecundity was perceptible, tender surges of joy stroking the tips of the reeds, the flights of bats and moths and the reverie of the willows. It was one of those days when the eternal rebirth of Creation is a hymn of praise.

The Water-People sensed that; their farewells were a miraculous fête. I had never seen such an adorable ballet, a more harmonious moving dream, in the tiny lacustrian cosmos. Black bodies and light bodies passed by in infinite interlacements, in arabesques full of a subtle sentiment of curvature, in a symphony of trajectories. The play of the moonbeams over all those bodies, emerging and plunging into the depths, turning in crystalline penumbras and pools of mother-of-pearl and aquamarine, was so beautiful that I forgot my anguish.

Everything came to an end at about 1 a.m. The farewell scene was grave; I watched the living fleet draw away. "Ah!" I said to Sabine, who had watched the whole display with me. "Can it be that they're leaving?"

"I think so," she said. Her fearful eyes were raised toward me, inundated by pale moonlight.

I kissed her cheeks with a mixture of fever and delight. "I've been so afraid—for you!"

"If only my father would come back now," she said, with a sigh. "I'm so anxious!"

"He'll come back."

But I was still not tranquil. A vague, unreasoning fear continued to stir within me, and even the arrival of our friend, who explained by means of signs that the others had really gone, could not lay it to rest.

At about 2 a.m., however, I lapsed into a feverish sleep.

I think my sleep was quite heavy at first, in compensation for the insomnia of the preceding nights. Toward morning, I had a nightmare that finally woke me up with a start. My heart was in tumult; I was possessed by a confused, stifling terror.

"Sabine!" I cried.

I got up. I recovered my self-composure. I darted a glance outside my hut. Dawn was breaking. The ash-trees were rustling in the morning breeze. The Moon was still wandering near the zenith. Everything inspired confidence. The last palpitations of the nightmare died away. I stood there for a few minutes, contemplating the gentle uncertainty of the firmament.

How pleasant it would be to live here!

I took a few steps toward Sabine's hut, and was suddenly overwhelmed by amazement, horror and terror.

The hut was empty!

Part Two

I. The Pursuit of the Dark People

My fury woke up the Water-People, our friend first of all. I fell upon him like a tempest on oaks, and implored his aid in delirious desperation, pointing to Sabine's empty bed with reckless gestures. A circle of men and women formed around me in the wan dawn light, and the carbuncle eyes with their broad and rigid pupils gazed at me with evident compassion.

The mists rose with the Sun; the horizon, save for the orient and the occident, acquired a precise clarity, and I was able to see, far to the north, an imperceptibly moving speck, which I pointed out to my aquatic brother. He fixed the direction in his head, ran to the lake and dived in.

I saw him beneath the crystalline veil, enlarged and deformed by a slight undulation, his head pointed northwards. I understood that his vast pupils were gathering slow and distant radiance under the water, and my impatience was complicated by a sensation of prodigy. Finally, he reappeared. His batrachian cry gave the news to his brethren, and he disappeared in a northerly direction with lightning rapidity. A hundred of his companions, armed with helical harpoons, threw themselves into his wake.

The same raft on which I had installed myself with Sabine a short while before, during our excursions on the lake, was fitted out. I took my place therein, armed with my carbine and my knife, and I was soon being drawn along at a surprising speed—but no more considerable than that of the other raft that was fleeing in the distance, bearing my fearful fiancée.

Even so, that speed, and the calmness of the wind and the water, soothed my anguish slightly. I examined the situation more coolly. From everything that I had seen, among the dark Water-People as much as the others, I could conclude with

49

reasonable assurance that the young kidnapper would not use force to begin with. Had I not witnessed their patient adventures and their long courtships, and all the graceful cunning and gentle pleading employed by male lovers to obtain the favors of their chosen brides? Was it probable that the dark chief would behave otherwise with Sabine? Would not the very singularity of the adventure excite the tendencies of the race, which were more inclined toward charm than violence? Then again, mores are not easily infringed among primitive peoples. Even supposing that his tribe had granted him Sabine, the young chief would probably still be obliged to conduct himself according to custom. We were not yet at the new moon, the sole period of Choice—nearly two weeks still remained before then.[9]

II. The Underwater Battle

I could not tell whether or not we were gaining on the raft we were pursuing. I could still see it as a black dot on the horizon, but I feared that it would disappear at the first hint of mist. That happened toward midday. The sky was not entirely clear; large clouds were running across it, and the vapors were condensing.

Still drawn along, without the speed relenting, I had slipped gradually into a reverie, and the vain imagination of fantastic means by which my fiancée might be recovered, when the batrachian cries of the Water-Men woke me up. I raised my head. The raft was 300 meters from a low-lying

[9] Rosny is often exceedingly casual in the consistency of his accounts of the phases of the Moon and its course across the sky, but it is odd that he went to some trouble to inform the reader that the waning Moon was three-quarters dark about a week ago, given that the story now requires it to be in mid-cycle.

island, where poplars rose up in a luminous swarm of foliage. Between the widely-spaced trunks I saw the raft again, still a mere black patch, but much closer, since it was visible in spite of the mist.

My gaze, immediately focused on that point, was soon distracted by the splashing appeals of my crew. They were pointing to the right of the isle, beyond which there was a bed of tall reeds, around which the water was furiously agitated. The raft came to a halt. I raised my weapon, both barrels of which were loaded, and waited for the attack.

The seething around the reed-bed moved on, heading toward us. Then, suddenly, there was an absolute calm. The limpid waters displayed the tops of tall plants in their depths, like a submerged forest, and the divine light descended everywhere upon the arabesques of stems and the lacework of foliage, casting iridescent shadows, and air-bubbles clung to the foliage like globules of mercury. The mud had an indecisive color, somewhere between the leaden gray of clay and the gold of sand. At the slightest ripple, silvery napkins spread out, blue edged with orange, and these pleats in the light rippled through the immersed forest like a supple fabric.

Apart from a few mysterious reptilian slitherings, nothing revealed the presence of the men. They must have been buried in the mud, engaging in a bizarre contest of immobility: the ultimate challenge of their reciprocal skill and speed. A little cloud, however, masked the displacement of a body. Then a helical harpoon flew, tracing a wake, and struck home. I saw a corpse floating up toward me. I deduced therefrom the positions of the rival camps. The Lights were slightly in advance of my raft, the others further away, with their backs to the reed-bed.

In response to the deadly dart that had just killed one of our men, 20 others responded, and I saw, with a sort of ferocious joy, two dark corpses rising to the surface. Then the waiting game was resumed. The clouds of mud dissipated; I was able to see the leaden gray and gold of the lake-bed again, the iridescent shadows and the quicksilver globules, and all the tremulous crystal of the waves.

I understood then that attack was as dangerous as defense, that it was necessary not to emerge from cover for an instant—but how could that tactic be prolonged? I reflected on the subject and clarified the matter. I perceived that the two camps, before having recourse to a battle, were disputing a strategic position, and that the position in question would depend on their ability to remain underwater. Those who found it necessary to breathe would be obliged to rise to the surface, thus revealing themselves. Anxiously, I waited for the critical moment, sometimes turning my eyes toward Sabine's raft, motionless like my own in the far distance.

Fans of fine ripples extended from the reed-bed toward the east and the west, but the battlefield remained sheltered, to the extent that, as my gaze plunged into the frail vegetation, I could see thousands of metallic glints among the large leaves of the multibranchial plants, like silver and gold coins in flight. Then, as the crystalline waves, the silvery naps, the globules of mercury, and everything else quivered and vacillated, innumerable schools of fish invaded the battlefield, and I distinguished a distant music—to which another music immediately responded.

I think that the Darks were trying to put that living rampart between them and the Lights, with the intention of drawing breath behind its shield. For some reason—a pact, a law of battle, or simple respect for animals that offer themselves voluntarily but which violence would render rebellious?—the lives of the fish seemed to be sacred.

This was a gripping episode in the drama, full of grace and wonder. As I watched them maneuvering, discoid or tapered, with their delicately-ringed eyes and their rounded mouths open, the mute play of their gill-flaps, scattering and reassembling, with dark bands on their backs and light dots on their flanks, whirling around to the thin voice of reeds, darting as straight as rays of light through branches, or trembling like leaves in a tempest, they seemed to be the visible notes of a prodigious orchestra, in which the eyes took over all the oral pleasures of rhythm and harmony.

When the fish disappeared, the camp of the Darks showed signs of fatigue. A few of those who had attempted to reach the surface during the deployment of the fish were now floating, with darts in their hearts. Three others were rising up in spite of the danger, and were killed. Then the harpoons of the Darks were launched in hundreds, like migrating swallows, and buried themselves among the plants, lifting slight eddies of mud. Our men did not move, except that two wounded men floated upwards—and, before any riposte was possible, the Darks stirred up a thick curtain of turbulence, behind which they came to the surface to breathe.

Already, the Lights were going through that curtain, taking up positions beneath the enemy. Defeated, their munitions used up, the Darks took flight. Many of them succeeded in getting away, but a large number were killed, and many others taken prisoner. I saw that pursuit would be futile, the rearguard of the runaways separating themselves from pursuers with immense veils of mud.

The prisoners and the dead, taken back to the huts under escort, had been gone for some time when I saw half a dozen light men surface, carrying a dark child, which they deposited on the raft. They signaled to me to look after him, and, as I heard him uttering groans, they pointed compassionately to his left arm. I felt the arm. The shoulder was dislocated, but I paid little heed to it, for at that moment Sabine's raft disappeared into the mist.

We landed on the island. Our troops rested there, without any joy in the victory, but rather with disgust and sadness, accompanied by sudden fits of indignation and violent outbursts of anger. While they were cooking some fish, I wandered around the island. I covered some two-thirds of its breadth. Immense grasses grew there, and I recalled, in the midst of my meditation, having noticed a sort of furrow in which the grass was flattened—but it was one of those observations that did not register, only returning later, as sketchy ideas return in sleep. A few steps further on, the terrain collapsed in a funnel strewn with sharp stones, at the bottom of which was a dark and vertiginous hole.

I leaned over that sepulcher, comparing it to my empty and gaping soul, and I experienced a hallucination. It seemed to me that a plaint was coming from it—a plaint unlike any that could have come from the larynx of a Water-Man, with none of that characteristic moist, batrachian croak, but an entirely terrestrial voice, dry and vibrant, like the voice of a European.

"Sabine!" I shouted.

Was I mad? Sabine was fleeing over the waters. I listened nevertheless. I cocked an ear that was capable of perceiving the flight of a moth in the woods—but I only heard the rumor of dead things, which groans in every cave with the faint cracking of stone and the obscure ticks of the clock of substance.

Then, very thoughtfully, I returned to the camp. The delay was not long, for as soon as the fish had been grilled, we carried them off. They would be eaten underwater, as I had often seen before. I ate my own share on the raft. I offered some of it to my traveling companion, but he refused. In the anguish that I was enduring, his suffering left me indifferent at first, but that refusal of food, his continual thirst and the cries he was uttering finally attracted my attention. Using all my strength, I succeeded in restoring the proper articulation of his arm.

While I was leaning over him to conclude the operation, my attention was drawn to a peculiarity. Without the slightest doubt, the eyes of the invalid did not have the same characteristics as the eyes of the other Water-People. The whites were more obvious, and they were more pronounced in their curvature; the irises, although tending to redness, had no precise color. More than one European possesses similar eyes. Very surprised, I examined the other parts of his body. I realized that the skin, the hair and the tapering of the fingers were not comparable those of the aquatic people among whom he lived.

In the midst of my anxieties, hypotheses and conjectures excited me irresistibly. Had I discovered a mixed race, a hybrid of terrestrial humans and Water-People? Or was this individual, by some phenomenon of heredity, a throwback to terrestrial stock? Was it necessary to suppose that the transformation of terrestrial humans into aquatic humans had taken place so rapidly that a few centuries had sufficed? Scraps of memories of things I had read reminded me of the affirmations of ancient authors regarding the extraordinary ability of some individuals to live under water. An experiment carried out on kittens had demonstrated that, if immersed in warm milk immediately after birth, they could remain alive therein for hours. Might not our existence, entirely aquatic before the first emergence into the daylight, be gradually accommodated to an amphibious state?

The kidnappers took care to multiply the obstacles in our path, disturbing the waters over vast extents, and my companions were only able to follow their trail by means of skilled searches. Imagine my joy, therefore, when, at about 2 p.m., the mist on the horizon lifted before the efforts of the Sun and I saw Sabine's raft again.

From that moment on, my finger pointed toward the moving patch, and we slid through the water at an increased speed.

We were visibly gaining. As each quarter of an hour went by, Sabine's raft became more distinct, and I uttered a cry of supreme delight on seeing the blurred silhouette of a woman outlined against the sky—but anguish bit into my heart at the same moment. Rather than abandon Sabine to us, would not the young chief drag her down into the depths of the lake?

Oh! Let her not be dragged into the heavy sheets of moisture: that poor body softer than the body of a bird; that airy being with the beauty of a creature made to populate the fragile gardens of the West!

At even closer range, the adorable silhouette became sufficiently distinct for me to recognize Sabine's little winged cloak. I was standing up; my heart no longer seemed to be within my breast but expanded through space. I no longer had any but the merest impression of the sunlight on the lake, the gentle breeze, and the exclamations of my friends; among these things my body felt like a tree in a forest, while my entire soul precipitated itself toward the raft, from which scarcely 500 meters now separated us—and that distance was decreasing constantly.

Standing on my raft, surrounded by strong and handsome swimmers, in the wind, on the sparkling lake, amid the waves on which a world of light capsized and the hectic song of my Water-Men, was a vertiginous experience. Hope and impatience contested in my breast like cavalry regiments in the thick of a battle. I saw Sabine, but she could not see me; her head was turned to face the open water. How were they forcing her to do that? Why was her adored gaze not seeking mine?

The vague preoccupations of a lover, puerile in the heart of a drama.

When we came within 300 meters, my free swimmers launched themselves in the direction of the raft. At the same moment, a man stood up beside Sabine. My heart gripped by fear, I saw him seize the young woman around the waist. She resisted, fighting him. He tried to drag her sideways.

Oh, I retain the trace of those minutes in my flesh; for years, my heart weakens tremulously at the thought, and several gray hairs have been mingled with my own ever since.

The accursed act was completed before my eyes. Sabine was flung into the waves. The force of distress tore through my being; in veils of obscurity, amid the fall—it seemed—of immense fragments of the world, I threw myself into the lake. Heavy, slow, as impotent as a fly in amber, I swam toward my beloved.

I understood almost immediately the futility of the effort—the futility of any effort on that wretched terrain—and, ceasing to struggle, I let myself sink into the depths.

III. The Water-Child

I recovered consciousness on the raft. It was motionless, and I was alone there. My injured companion had disappeared; I searched in vain for my swimmers. The lake, quite clear, was continuing its great splashing life in the sunlight, transporting gleaming fish in every direction, toward the horizon or towards me, according to the breeze. Luminous trails encircled heavy plates, as shiny and hump-backed as bottle-glass, like the overlapping scales of a pangolin, blue networks bordered with orange alternating with little waves like crystal bells, with ripples so slender and so pale that one might have thought them floating sea-biscuits with luminous stairways climbing sunwards, and silken irises placed flat on the water.

I occupied myself with these things in a sinister bewilderment, the recent drama now relegated to the utmost depths of my being. An interminable time went by, and then my gaze became aware of the presence of someone in the lake. I saw him confusedly, for he was swimming at a considerable depth; he was not moving with the usual speed of his kin, but rather in a prudent and unhurried fashion.

He surfaced. By his trailing arm, swathed in linen, I recognized the child captured in the reed-bed. In his usable hand he held a shiny object—my knife, of which he had gone in search at the bottom of the lake. I helped him to take his place beside me again, but all these occurrences had reawakened the atrocious memory, and, my heart tormented by a terrible certainty, I fell into a wordless despair.

I came out of it in response to a pressure on my shoulder. The injured boy was standing up, with a compassionate expression, making signs of negation to me with a singular insistence, accompanied by a mime whose meaning escaped me. That went on for some time, then he seemed to get discouraged and stopped—but he retained an expression of anxious reflection. Finally, with a curt gesture, he grabbed the knife and detached five pieces of wood from our planks.

There was a certain mischief in his face while he presented the following curious little performance to me. First, holding one of the pieces of wood to his breast, he lavished signs of the most avid tenderness upon it; he even obliged me to do the same, and I wondered what fetishistic ceremony he was trying to signify thus. The second piece of wood he placed on the water, simulating a vessel—but while the first piece of wood was laid down beside me, the third ran toward it, took possession of it, and carried it to the raft.

My interest was awakened, for it became clear that the poor child was telling me the story of Sabine. He observed my attention, and his faced expressed consolation and hope again, while he continued.

Now, this was the moving scene that I witnessed. The raft bore Sabine away, then landed on an island. Sabine got off, conducted by the black chief…and the fourth piece of wood took Sabine's place on the raft.

I experienced a flash of enlightenment. The injured child laughed, and continued his story, now followed with a more feverish excitement than any Shakespearean drama. While Sabine and the chief remained on the island; the fourth piece of wood continued its journey on the raft—and then the fifth piece of wood surged forth, seized the fourth, and precipitated itself into the lake along with it!

The child laughed again, and this time I understood exactly why he was laughing, as well as his consolations and his hopefulness.

Sabine was alive! The penetrating certainty filtered into my soul, more gently than the rays of dawn through the branches of some dark African forest. She was alive—but where? Could I obtain any indication of that from the clever child?

Not only was I able to do so, but with details that surprised me. We had found a language and, every success calling forth further ones, the language soon expressed quite delicate sensations, and even a few abstract ideas.

Thus, I learned that Sabine had initially been taken to the island near the reed-bed. The child told me—although I would certainly have guessed—that there was a cave there, into which Sabine had been taken down.

My supposed hallucination had, therefore, been true; the plaints emerging from the dark and silent hole really had come from my unfortunate fiancée. From that cave she must have been transported to the homeland of the Dark Water-People—which, the child indicated to me, lay to the west.

IV. The Channel

Determined to catch up with Sabine, I racked my brains to find a means. With my knife, I fashioned one of the small tree-trunks of our platform into a scull, and, having been familiar since infancy with that kind of oar, I contrived to travel at 14 or 15 meters a minute. At that rate, to be sure, it would take many hours to reach the invisible shore, but action cost me less than inaction; I was happy to exert myself for my beloved, and I already felt rewarded for the effort, in the advent of hope.

Throughout the rest of the day, my scull turned in the water.

The Sun was declining when I perceived the first hills and treetops of the shore. Undecided as to where to moor, I woke the child. He showed me a point marked by the fleece of a great forest, about a kilometer to the right. We soon found the entrance to a broad channel, and, on the child's orders, I took the raft into it. The waters were so sluggish that they seemed to be emerging from a lake rather than descending from a mountain. To the right and the left, on the banks, trees sprang out of the stream like colossal pillars, forming gigantic colonnades. A chilly impression fell from branches opening out like vast hands.

The setting Sun hung over the depths of the channel, the waves bearing a few bloody stains on their crests. Under the water, tree-trunks were visible within 15 feet. Large blind fish were drifting there, along with enormous crustaceans green-tinted by algae, and abundant cephalopods of an unknown species, with immense eyes. Everything advertised a life in shadow, pale and feverish, the blanched fecundity of plants and animals that had renounced the light. Admirable algae carpeted the shallows, trailing their disorderly hair, several meters long, in the direction of the current; lichens, coarsely sculpted, extended in bizarre strata; and insects like tortoises with enormous oval carapaces were grazing everywhere. A spider as big as a fist, suspended from the branches by a thread, dived to seize soft prey; huge white flies were hovering over livid mushrooms. My scull disturbed a duck-billed mammal, and there were flocks of bats in the air.

The further we went, the darker it became. The channel's banks became steeper, its trees bending over, and I was subject to a grandiose horror, impassioned by these terrible things that had nothing in common with my desire to see Sabine again. The child had gone back to sleep. The last bloody draperies folded themselves away into the waves. Absolute darkness veiled my route. I took up a position at the front of the raft and paddled through the darkness for a good part of the night.

V. The Luminous Forest

I suppose that it was about midnight when the child woke up. His shoulder was much better. We were hungry, but he succeeded in discovering some edible nuts. After the meal I fell into a light sleep.

When I woke up again, the Moon must have been somewhere over to the left, for a spectral light was coming through the trees from that direction; there were vague images of muslin, a nebulous floating whiteness, like a light frost in the forest.

A cavernous darkness reigned in the gaps in the colonnade, illuminated only by the phosphorescent backs of a few fish. I started paddling again.

Taking every precaution, I advanced with an extraordinary slowness, with the result that in three hours I had not covered two kilometers. A sort of dark cliff then loomed up in front of me, while a strange brightness came from the left. Was that really the Sun already? Was the dawn light now filtering through the forest?

I steered the raft toward the light. Ten minutes sufficed to turn the corner, and a vast landscape appeared, brighter than a moonlit snow-field. Neither the Moon nor the Sun was illuminating it, though.

An errant luminosity, with broad moiré patterns, lay upon the river, which now broadened out to the proportions of a lake. The waters, which were lost in the far distance in a flooded forest, were shallow, for initial bifurcations of tree-roots were visible. The light was coming from these roots, in dense circles which became fainter as they extended—but it was shadowless, like a colossal sheet of flat flame, and everywhere the light was moving: undulating, fading, reviving, rippling. It ran from bushes in rutilant miniature cascades, scattering in the breeze like wasps of light, and oscillating broadly in the rare places where the water was able to reflect it. A vast, stupefying silence reigned over everything.

I remained motionless on the threshold of that enchantment. My most distant childhood took control of all my actions. At that age, I was capable of naïve admiration and mysterious terror, curiosity regarding the invisible, and a prickling sense of the occult. I thought that I was confronted by some legendary city beneath the lake, which the Water-People had found a means of illuminating. I imagined that new humankind, inaccessible to my weakness. I, the representative of superior races, had the fearful, melancholy and resigned impression of vanquished races. Innumerable things crumbled within me, including the certainty of belonging to the most advanced human race. I understood the slide into the abyss experienced by our poor rivals, life taking refuge in dreams, confused theories and the consolations of Nirvana.

The phenomenon was, however, complicated by the presence of a being. In the distance, on an islet, there was a man, whose silhouette moved against the background of light. That giant silhouette reached all the way to the first branches of an ash-tree, three meters from the ground. He was very thin, and I soon saw that his height was entirely due to his legs.

Three or four other men of the same kind appeared on the islet; then they went into the water, which came up to their waists. They headed toward us at a rapid pace, and I woke my companion.

Alarmed, and dazzled by the excessively bright light, he shaded his eyes with his hand in order to see better, but nothing in the exclamation he uttered was expressive of surprise or fear. Meanwhile, the men were coming closer. Their torsos were exposed to a greater or lesser extent, according to the depth; sometimes, even their legs were not fully submerged. I had time to realize that those excessively thin legs were matched by exceedingly long arms, stiff and as slender as lianas, covered with yellowish scales, with no trace of hair. Their torsos, by contrast, were hairy and white; their chests were narrow, their heads small, with large, cold, excessively mobile eyes.

The child seemed to take pleasure in their presence—a pleasure mingled with mockery. He spoke to them from a distance. I listened avidly to their reply. They did not have the batrachian voices, moist tones or splashing lips of my Water-Men; on the contrary, the muffled sounds were clipped before emerging from their throats, the syllables further chopped by the movement of their jaws.

With grave expressions, they surrounded our raft. Their entire being gave the impression of a sad race, confined to sterile lands. In the half-light, they manifested the pallor of subterranean life; their pale hair was the color of ash, the hair on their breasts paler than that on their backs.

I don't know why their presence made me feel pity; perhaps it was the protective attitude of the child, perhaps an instinct that showed me these narrow-headed people as pariahs.

I imagined them as having failed in their metamorphosis. Driven back by powerful Mongol nations into these marshlands, inaccessible to the rest of humankind, they had been obliged to live prudently and discreetly. The perpetual effort of finding their nourishment in the marshes and pools had, over the centuries, elongated their limbs. Then new populations of the same provenance had arrived; either a firmer sense of purpose had impelled them as far as the great lakes, or, time having made the region more hospitable, the latecomers had been able to choose a bolder and more successful adaptation, in becoming amphibians, leaving these sad precursors far behind, reduced to the frequentation of shallow sub-forest waters.

I understood that the child was asking them to push the raft, and it seemed more an order than a request. Stupid and gentle, they obeyed in a melancholy fashion—with, I believe, an awareness of their weakness.

Our raft glided through the luminous forest. The scene was dream-like. The ripples of our passage raised radiant wave-crests in the distance like beautiful gleams of mother-of-pearl, but the place where we passed was a rip in a silver cloth, leaving behind a dark wake, while condensations of light traced long furrows to the right and the left. I studied the waters attentively; I plunged my hand in, then drew it out again, flamboyant, and I realized that little vegetable cells, which my subsequent studies permitted me to recognize as animate algal zoospores, probably in their reproductive phase, were moving in a manner similar to that of tadpoles—and were, moreover, phosphorescent.

After hours of travel, the channel began to narrow again, and the water soon came up to the necks of our poor breathless waders. They swam for a few minutes, then, exhausted, abandoned the raft and climbed up on to the bank. As they drew away, my interest in them increased; there was nothing more humble and pitiful than their sad skeletons; whether they were folded up like bizarre marsupials or stood erect, they had the melancholy appearance of being too frail and too long. The last time I saw them, they were trotting along beneath the branches, and their procession of mortal pallor seemed to be moved, like the severed legs of spiders, by a mysterious desolation.

I started paddling again. The water was getting even deeper, the trees sparser, and I was able to see my way through the darkness. I think the child had gone back to sleep. All my sensations then became dreamlike. It seemed to me that a black hole was sucking in the raft, that I was about to sink into some dark abyss, and that I would never again experience the sweet sensation of my lips on my beloved's hair. My courage weakened, although I recalled the moments, almost as bitter, that I had patiently endured in the course of our long journey. Then, however, there had been Devreuse's energy, the presence of Sabine and our European companions; above all, the perils had been foreseen, the struggle had been undertaken against cataloged forces. Now, in the solitude, with the possibility of ambush by men infinitely different from and more powerful than us, and the darkness of the interminable forest, there was a dreadful anticipation in my failing heart of some further prodigious adventure, in which it seemed that my reason was sure to be unhinged.

My paddle was now only beating the waves with intermittent and ineffectual strokes; the darkness trembled vertiginously before my eyes. There were periods when I was not exactly sure whether I was still paddling or whether I had stopped, others when I sometimes thought that I was wandering through urban side-streets, and sometimes that I was sitting on top of a lighthouse—then I shook myself in order to rediscover the river, the night, the rafts, murmuring words that had no connection with the time or the place.

Finally, I sensed that I was definitely falling into unconsciousness, and I remember that my last effort was to reproach myself for the probable wreck of the raft, and to perceive the light of dawn, like a white speck in the channel.

VI. In the Storm

When I came to, the raft was moving at a good speed; we had passed through the channel and were in the open water of a lake. It was terribly hot. Immense clouds were alternately covering and uncovering the Sun.

I looked around for the boy. I saw him at the back of the raft, immersed, pushing it with his good arm. He smiled at me, and pointed at a region of cavernous hills to the north.

"Is that where we're going?" I asked.

His gesture said "yes," and he pressed his hand to his breast—which, in our language, signified "Sabine."

"Sabine!" I said.

I invited the child to rest. He refused. Then I took the scull and paddled. Large drops of sweat bathed me. A heavy electricity was coming from the low clouds. Although there was not much wind, the waves were turbulent and choppy. To our right, the somber mass of the forest became darker and darker, and through a gorge, further away than the cavernous hills, in a sort of desert, whirlwinds of sand covered the entire sky.

I felt the anguish that one experiences in crises, and also a strange sense of rivalry—that of man against the elements. The child was pushing forcefully, while I plied the scull steadily; our combined efforts were bringing us closer to the shore.

We were no more than 100 meters away when the storm burst. Its insensate fury immediately covered the lake with frightful waves. A waterspout lifted me up, swallowed me, and returned me to the surface, and the liquid whips of the rain lashed me, blinding me.

The entire landscape had disappeared into the grayness. I huddled convulsively, clinging to the logs of the little raft, whose ropes were giving way; I foresaw the moment when I would be left without support. The child had disappeared; I suppose he was two or three meters underwater, laughing at the storm and keeping watch on me. How could he have done otherwise, since the tail of the waterspout, with one last effort, had pulled my raft apart? Hurled far away from any support, I was seized and dragged toward the shore.

The child became fearful at the first claps of thunder. These rumbles, stifled at first beneath the low and irregular clouds, soon became a frightful din, as the vault of cloud became higher and more homogenous. Lightning-flashes bit into the waters in brief zigzags, which lit up as soft and large as electric Moons. The waves were visibly hurling themselves at the sky, while the clouds were descending, slowly and capriciously at first—but soon the entire lake was covered with flames and uproar. The child's terror woke me up. I told him by means of signs to take shelter at the bottom of the lake, and that I would wait for him. He accepted, leapt forward and vanished beneath the enormous agitation.

Left alone, I proudly braved the lightning. The indefatigable torrent ran over me like a stream over a mountain. I took off all my superfluous clothing, and, naked to the waist, attempted to explore the surroundings. Visibility was restricted to five meters when the sky was devoid of lightning-flashes— but that was rare; the lake and the sky, clashing in electric tension, populated space with phosphorus reptiles.

Twice I was knocked down by shocks; twice I got up with a snigger. I thought that I was in the utmost depths of adversity, in the black voluptuousness of desperation. The storm—its threats, its infernal tumult, its rain, falling upon me like insulting lashes—gave me the soul of some fanatical Hindu, or some holy martyr of the primitive Church.

Through the fumes of the sodden and overheated soil, through the railings of the rain, I glimpsed the caverns, and drew gradually nearer to them. When I was 50 paces away there was a magnificent lightning-flash, and I fell full-length on the ground—but it was not the electric shock; it was the sight of Sabine on the threshold of one of the caverns. She was sitting on a large boulder watching the storm. There was no one with her.

I did not get up again; I crawled stealthily. As I did so, I perceived that she really was alone. As she closed her eyes at every lightning-flash, she did not see me. Still crawling, I wondered whether I ought to go into the cave. Might not Water-Men be hiding inside?

Suddenly, I felt certain that, like my traveling companion, Sabine's abductors had gone into the water for fear of the thunder. Then, surprised that Sabine had not thought of running away, I perceived that her hands and feet were bound.

My joy was so prodigious that I remained breathless for a good two minutes, amid the unleashed horrors. Finally, I was able to leap forward and throw myself recklessly at my fiancée's feet. She recognized me, and tried to reach out to me, but her weakness transported her, and I received her head on my breast as she fainted with joy. She revived under my kisses. Merely by seeing her blue eyes, her pure mouth, and the grace of her forehead, I knew that she had escaped any outrage, and my lover's heart was large enough to hold the world.

When Sabine was freed, we left in the rain. Everything in the universe seemed good to me, and the terrifying thunder-bolts over our heads were outbursts of victory and joy. Sabine, her sweet face streaming with rain, smiled at me. She sheltered her beloved body against mine, in a frisson of exquisite fever. Her impermeable hood protected her head and her breast, but I remember that once, as she hung on to my shoulders, hugging me tightly, the hood fell back. The blonde tresses of her hair drowned my heart with delight; for as long as I live I shall have her eyes and her charming head before me, the delicate nape of her neck, and the sacred youth of her flesh beneath the indefatigable downpour. I pressed her against me, deliriously, and—in the midst of a thunderclap that made the ground shake, I kissed her feverishly. She had already recovered her composure; smiling, she covered her wet head and drew me on.

I held her nervous little hand as a careful child might hold a bird, and we ran to the place where I had left my clothes.

The child surfaced and came out of the water; although he manifested extreme terror at every lightning-flash, he came to us. Sabine, who had initially taken him for one of our allies, perceived that he was dark, and became so alarmed that I had difficulty reassuring her.

Time was pressing. The greatest obstacle to our flight was the child's terror of the thunderbolts. However, as he succeeded in vanquishing it sufficiently to accompany us, I was obliged to be grateful for that circumstance, for it guaranteed me freedom from pursuit for the duration of the storm. Besides, I saw that the child was infinitely reassured as soon as he took my hand, and I had the intuition then that his malaise might be more physical than mental, contact with my hand easing the veritably electrical undulations that were causing him to shiver. For some reason that escaped me, his body conducted the fluid better than ours, or at least reflected the atmospheric conditions in his nerves—but the cause of that conductivity or nervousness was appeased by my contact, to the extent that he was able to guide us.

We accompanied him in silence for half an hour. Then, to my extreme surprise, I found that we were going into a cave—or, rather, a spacious grotto.

"Where are you taking us?" I cried.

The child looked at Sabine, as if begging her to speak.

"Didn't you come here through a grotto, then?" the young woman asked me.

"No," I said. "We came via a sort of river."

"I was led through immense subterranean workings!" she said.

"Can we risk such an adventure, my dear Sabine?" Addressing myself to the child, I indicated that we wanted to take another route. He gestured that it was impossible, and that it was necessary to go into the grotto—but he seemed sure of himself, as if he had been that way before.

I trembled as I looked at Sabine; she had understood.

"Since there's no other way," she said, "isn't anything preferable to the risk of being recaptured?"

She gave me her hand. The child took my other hand, and we advanced into the darkness.

VII. The Subterranean Journey

In the grotto, the muffled and confused rolls of thunder extended in infinite echoes. It was terrifying in itself to march through vast dark corridors, but the thunderclaps added to that the perpetual fear of a collapse. The danger was not imaginary. Once—when, I suppose, the mountain was struck externally—everything trembled, and after the tide of sound faded away into the depths, with unspeakable terror, we heard a rocky mass fall, a fragment of which struck me on the shoulder.

We went on. I felt Sabine's little hand shivering. We advanced without talking, in a silence in which anguish and hope were mingled as intimately as mistletoe and an oak-tree. An hour went by. The child was still moving, and I explained his confidence to myself by imagining a single corridor without lateral branches—but I was undeceived when we arrived at a sort of crossroads. One of the routes—which we were not following—had a quicksilver gleam at the end.

"How is the child finding his way among so many others?" I said to Sabine.

"I wondered the same thing," she replied, "when they were bringing me through these interminable tunnels—I can't see any explanation for it, unless the Water-People have a better-developed spatial awareness than us, as homing-pigeons do."

"Yes, my dear Sabine—their skill in movement and the long journeys they undertake under water might have given them the sense of which you speak over a long period."

"I think they can also see better than us in the dark…"

After two hours of walking, the tunnel broadened out. In the distance, a motionless bronze gleam advertised the presence of water. The gleam increased, becoming greener and unsteady. Then there was a tentative dawn: one of those feeble vertical shafts of daylight that fade away at cave-entrances. A vast space, whose height our eyes could scarcely perceive, enclosed a subterranean cavern. The water extended in the distance into a gallery, to the right, and the light was coming from there, reflected from the waves on to the wall, and from the wall on to the waves. Several large birds fled as we approached, and we could see them flying along the immense tunnel for some time.

Sabine and I were immobilized by the grip of the light; we experienced the wordless joy of people emerging from a nightmare. The child's face brightened in response to our happiness. He made signs bidding us to rest, and we obeyed, while he plunged into the subterranean water and was lost to sight. Sabine huddled close to me. Our two hearts, in spite of all the weariness, were singing the mighty song of the spring of life.

"Sabine," I said, "we will love one another all the more for having endured so many perils and prodigious adventures. Our love will retain the trace of our terrible emotions. We will never forget this grandiose vault, these magnificent and heavy waters in the semi-darkness."

She rested her head on my shoulder, and adorable minutes went by in which my arm enveloped her, with a gesture that was proud and tender at the same time. The dark galleries spoke of indefatigable passion, of the spirit of renewal in which the nests of sticklebacks and the hearts of men are built, of the sovereign beauty of delicate loved ones who summarize the grace of the world.

VIII. The Interior Lakes

After initially following a narrow path, we soon climbed though a dark passage that must have taken us over the subterranean water, for we perceived its dormant reflection through a crevice in the rock. We marched for about two hours, more light-heartedly than in the morning, even though the darkness was colder and damper, and the corridor narrower. Finally, we emerged into the bottom of a valley. The light was dazzling. The storm had eased; a few blue gaps were opening among the soft clouds, where snowy giants were drifting over cotton-wool mountains.

The valley was a part of the grotto whose roof had collapsed in some cataclysm. The walls, sheer to a height of some ten feet, were covered above that height by a crazy vegetation in which reptiles and lianas disputed with the hard skeletons of bushes. At the base there was the debris of the landslide, a petrified flux of immense stone blocks, sculpted by the rain into monstrous teeth and crude animal figures.

We followed this valley for some time, and then went underground again, only to find, after 20 minutes, another valley. Two hours passed in this fashion. We went from darkness to light, from pretty verdant valleys to stupefying caverns. Finally, we emerged into daylight for the last time into an immense dale filled with water. In the distance, we could see the steam that alimented the gigantic basin; it was a waterfall more than 70 meters wide and 15 or 20 high.

We were struck then by the child's joy. He drew us on rapidly, doubling a cape of high rocks, and human dwellings appeared, similar to those of the Water-People. In response to cries uttered by a number of women, an entire amphibious people emerged from the waves and ran toward us.

They were similar to the child, their hair long and fine, their fingers rather stout—in sum, bearing a closer resemblance to us. I realized that they were, in consequence, inferior to both the light and dark Water-People—and that explained their relegation to the subterranean lakes and rivers. It is worth noting that their inferiority stemmed from their lesser distance from our type, which constituted an evolutionary retardation here. My initial hypothesis, by virtue of which I saw them as late arrivals in the country, did not hold up in the light of subsequent research; it seems, instead, that they belonged to one of the first waves of immigration, which occurred several centuries after that of the Wading Men. The latter had defended the marshes and shallow waters forcefully enough to oblige the newcomers to retreat into the interior valleys, where the depth of the lakes rendered them amphibious. Now, it remains equally probable that the dark Water-People are merely a separate branch of the race of the high valleys, improved for aquatic life, while the light Water-People seem, on the contrary, to have come directly from the western plains, through the marshes, and to have adapted themselves to the new life purely by imitation.

Crosses between the various species of aquatic humans are very rare; although traces of fusion are discovered between the differently-colored Water-People, there is nothing to indicate that there has ever been any marriage between the amphibian species and the Wading Men, the latter being regarded as an inferior race fallen into a melancholy decadence, diminishing by the day.

Having Sabine with me freed me from anxiety to a great extent, and I abandoned myself enthusiastically to many marvelous discoveries. I saw the humanity beneath this new form of direct adaptation, scorned because of our infatuation with the brain. I promised myself a long sojourn among the aquatic populations, and had high hopes of penetrating their mystery, not only from the historical and ethnographic point of view, but also, and even more so, in terms of the modifications they might bring to our notion of living beings and things in general.

A sadness took hold of me, however, at the thought of other expeditions following ours, and, perhaps colonies of terrestrial humans arriving, ferociously destroying the admirable work of centuries, annihilating the various forms of lacustrian humans. Then I told myself, with that sincerity in regard to ourselves that is the most notable achievement of positivist philosophy, that it would be better for these poor folk if we were all to perish.

Then I shivered, in thinking about Sabine, and so I sought some consolation in the near-impossibility of crossing the marshes where we had so nearly perished; I hoped, at least, that many years would elapse before the surrounding populations, so sparsely scattered, would decide to confront the dark perils of emigration—and that, within a century, the organization of the Water-People would permit them to resist. In order not to accept the yoke of a great nation, they would defend the integrity of their territory vigorously. Their cleverness in assimilating our language was an excellent omen. Finally, these regions, although admirable and perfectly healthy, remained nonetheless essentially lacustrian, and thus relatively inaccessible to terrestrial men.

The welcome we received was most hospitable. According to the custom of these people, after a delicious meal, they held a magnificent aquatic fête in our honor. With an incomparable agility and a great resistance to asphyxia—even those abilities were less outstanding than among their flat-eyed rivals—their maneuvers remained infinitely curious to us. After so much fatigue, we enjoyed the calm and well-being like soldiers after a long march.

Dusk came, and the mantle of night was drawn over the valley. Sabine, worn out, went to sleep with her head on my shoulder. The friendly people, the beautiful twilit waters, and the vast sky into which the last vestiges of the storm were disappearing in cotton-wool threads, generated such tranquility, and such a tempting promise of happiness, that I decided to spend the night there with Sabine.

IX. A Night of Anguish

Before the last rays of sunlight were extinguished in the valley, Sabine was installed in a cabin. I bedded down across the doorway, and the child was lodged outside, beneath a wickerwork canopy. Looking through the cracks in the door, I ascertained that the men of the village were also mounting guard, and I went to sleep confidently.

I think we had been asleep for about five hours when a great tumult woke me up. In addition to the tranquil stream of moonlight, there was a blazing fire outside. I opened the door prudently. Some 20 old men were sitting round the fire, and with them, young men whose flat pupils, stringy lichenous hair and dark skin signaled my adversaries.

Besides, the dark athlete attracted my gaze almost immediately. A jealous rage swelled my chest at the thought of his pretensions. I think I would have found a great relief in engaging him in single combat, but that would be to risk Sabine becoming the prize of victory. I resolved to employ all the diplomacy that prudence inspired in me, and only to have recourse to violence when all other means had been exhausted.

The meeting seemed to be a Council of the elders of the host tribe, and the racket was coming from the young men, visibly attempting to intimidate the council-members. At one time, they broke the circle around the fire and rushed toward our cabin. More than 100 men of the valley were ranged against them and they were forced to change tack. It seemed to me then that they wanted to resume the discussion, but the most imposing of the elders dispersed the firebrands with a kick and spoke angrily for some time in the moonlight. A truce followed, during which our cabin was surrounded by the entire population of the village, while the intruders retired to make camp of the lake-shore.

Sabine was asleep. I drew closer to her. A broad white moonbeam fell upon the loose blonde hair spreading around her head; her mouth exhaled a peaceful breath, and I felt close to fainting with tenderness at the sight of that peaceful sleep, amid the adorable living silk of her tresses. I left her to sleep and ran to the door.

Nothing had changed. The kidnappers, sitting beside the lake in the distance, seemed to be waiting for daylight. Disturbed by their presence, I opened the door. The multitude looked at me silently, in what seemed to me to be consternation. My good friend the child was weeping. I called to him. He came, but—alas!—he could not make me understand what was worrying the crowd and making him cry. All that I could grasp was that neither Sabine nor I could leave the cabin, and that the dark men were awaiting reinforcements.

What could I do? Would the proud council of a short while before, which had obviously refused to surrender us, yield to the reinforcements? Why were the dark athlete and his companions camping by the lake undisturbed? I watched, lugubriously. My fiancée's slumber seemed to me to be similar to the sleep of a prisoner awaiting execution. Most of all, I was keenly aware of my impotence; I felt that any attempt to use force would not save me and had every chance, on the contrary, of dooming me.

I had spent a long time in such dismal reveries of misery and uncertainty when Sabine woke up, with a smile. She read the desolation on my anxious face.

"Robert! Are you in pain? You're not ill?"

I explained the situation. She came as far as the door, observed the presence of our enemy, and then, when we had gone back inside, said: "So you think they'll give us up, Robert?"

"Probably."

The scant moonlight coming through the roof was enough to illuminate us. I could see Sabine's eyes, wide and wild, like those of a hunted beast. She threw herself against my breast. I hugged her with such boundless passion! I kissed her forehead timidly. She huddled close—very close—to me, her heart replying to mine; her warm mouth was next to my cheek, and she rendered me almost mad with pain, pride and love by telling me that she did not want to belong to anyone but me, that she would die before any offense. Our souls vibrated in divine accord, and those minutes remain beautiful in my memory, in spite of the sad events that followed them.

We were hugging one another in this manner when the murmur of the crowd drew us to the door. Dawn was approaching; the light of the declining Moon was still bright, but a line of shadow was already trailing across the lake. The light still cut out the silhouettes of the grand old men—and another silhouette, which we recognized as that of the Water-Man who had saved us from the bog!

We opened the door then, and amid the sympathetic murmur of the crowd, with our hearts lifted in hope, we went to meet our friend. His face expressed affection and joy, and all the other faces cleared as he smiled. Save for the dark group on the edge of the lake, the multitude was delicately moved by our gratitude and his generosity—but it displayed a veritable enthusiasm when I took the Water-Child in my arms and introduced him to our first savior.

X. The Return of the Lights

We stayed with the old men, our benefactor and the Water-Child, waiting for the dawn. The Moon brushed the heights of the valley with its pale gleam, and the stars began to fade. Soon, the flower of the aurora reached the Orient, and a delicate daylight fell upon the lake like a scattering of hyacinth petals. The Sun had not yet raised its august face above the hills when a formidable wave rolled along the stream and thousands of bodies fell with the cascade into the lake.

Sabine pressed close to me, but I could see by the smiles of our light friend and that of the child that we had nothing to fear.

Meanwhile, the swimmers were coming ashore, and two distinct groups of light Water-Men and dark Water-Men immediately formed on the shore. The Council of the Subterranean Water tribe spontaneously reunited on a mound, and the tribe arranged itself solemnly around the mound. Then the dark athlete, with three old men of his own race, took up a position in front and slightly to the left of the council. Our savior and three old men of his own people placed themselves to the right.

I then had a clear intuition of the events of the night and the causes that had changed the crowd's consternation and the child's grief into joy and enthusiasm. A few words made Sabine party to my conviction. The council of the Subterranean Water tribe, called to legislate, weak and fearful before its powerful rivals, would have had to hand us over to the dark athlete had it not been for the arrival of the light Water-Men.

We observed the solemnities. Not only did it appear to us that the judges welcomed the speech made by our savior, but that the tribe of dark Water-Men, presumably weary of conflict, approved of the speech. The athlete, confronted with this disfavor, went away and all his companions let him go. We were handed back to our dear initial hosts. And the population of the valley gave the most touching evidence of their sympathy.

The child did not leave our side, caressed by Sabine, by myself, and our aquatic friend. His shoulder was still troubling him slightly, and his feverishly shining eyes looked at us with extraordinary affection. His suffering explains why he could not take part in the utterly marvelous aquatic maneuvers in which the three tribes rejoiced.

Our light savior was the first to disappear under the lake, and although Sabine and I made every effort to make him out among the others, and although nearly all the swimmers surfaced from time to time to wave to us, we were never able to pick him out. We hardly noticed that singularity at the time; we were so happy, so certain of a fine future of love and glory. We were thinking about rejoining Devreuse and the remainder of the expedition and returning to Europe.

Two hours went by in that fashion.

We were still chatting, while holding hands, when I was thrown to the ground with irresistible force. Sabine was grabbed and carried away like a leaf in a whirlwind. When I got up, the dark athlete was fleeing with Sabine in the direction of the stream.

In order to do that, he had to go around the lake along a path, one of whose edges was a steep drop into the lake while the other was a sheer wall of rock. The child was running after him. The man paused momentarily to round fiercely on the child, telling him to go back. The latter began screaming. I was already going after him, racing along the path.

When he saw that there were two of us, and that the entire lake was in commotion, he stopped again. Our gazes met. In his flat eyes, so different from ours, I read jealous hatred and also the terrible fatality of passion—something simultaneously profound, dolorous and savage.

There was a narrow ledge a few feet above us, which could be reached by an unsteady lump of rock—one of those boulders held in equilibrium by chance, which a vigorous effort would displace. Sabine's abductor obviously planned to get up on to that ledge, but, burdened by the young woman, he was overtaken by the child, and I was arriving at top speed. He shouted something that I did not understand, and the poor child made a reply in which I could only divine intrepid anger. Then, after a brief struggle, the child was thrown from the path, smashing his head against the rocky wall.

A formidable clamor of hatred was raised, and my heart, slowed down momentarily by the odious murder, swelled up immediately afterwards with an immense rage. I hurled myself upon the redoubtable adversary, followed by the vengeful crowd. Already, though, the Dark Man had leapt up, scaled the unstable rock and deposited Sabine on the ledge. With a prodigious effort of his legs, he launched the huge stone into the air, thus cutting all communication between him and us for a quarter of an hour.

The narrow ledge went up toward the stream. The opening of the tunnel into which the wretch would soon vanish was visible, and I had read in his expression the resolution of desperation, the dishonor and death of Sabine, and any other abomination! I bloodied my hands in vain trying to go after him. As it fell, the stone had left a gap in the path that made it impossible to reach the ledge.

Extremely skilful as they were in using their harpoons under water, no one dared make use of such a weapon here, for fear of an error that would cost Sabine her life. The man was still running, no more than ten paces from the opening now. I was seeing my fiancée for the last time in the light of this world!

Ten arms seized me as I was about to throw myself into the void, gripped by an insane despair; and, as happens in catastrophic moments in which sensation outlasts rational thought, my hearing perceived a singular rumor beside the lake, immediately followed by a rifle-shot, and then another.

Up above, my rival let go of Sabine, simultaneously clinging desperately to a rocky projection—and then I saw him fall on to the rocks, into which his body smashed limply. A glance toward the lake: Jean-Louis Devreuse, the leader of our expedition, was standing there, sternly, and the second-best shot in the party after me, Cachal, had the barrel of his rifle raised.

After returning to the lake of our first friends, we lived there for more than a month, in peace and abundance. The Dark Men did not show themselves again, nor the Men of the Valleys within the caves. Devreuse told us about the role played by our savior in the events I have just described. Sabine and I could not forget the death of our gentle and heroic Water-Child, and we mourn him to this day.

The expedition commanded by Jean-Louis Devreuse returned to Paris in the early days of May 1893 with precious documents that will provide the material of an important work. My marriage to Sabine was celebrated in June.

At present, we are happy in the glory and comfort of old Europe—but often, in the dreamy hours of dusk, as we huddle together against the cold, we miss the admirable countries where our young love was accompanied by the palpitation of a prodigious drama.

THE DEPTHS OF KYAMO

It was evening in the African village of Ouan-Mahlei, on the eastern edge of the Kyamo forest, one of the largest on the mysterious continent.

In the firmament, the waning crescent moon was floating amid scarcely-visible clouds—long and frail clouds in the form of skiffs, all departing, slowly fading away toward the same horizon. The plain extended in leisurely undulations, with palm-trees on the ridges. In that verdant month, the confidence of perfumes, sweet on the whispering breeze, seemed to be the profound and penetrating language of plants, the hymn of their love, their ardor to grow and multiply.

The wind strengthened and died down alternately. It was as sad and gentle as the sky behind its thin covering of clouds. It lifted up the long grass and the lacy foliage in a rhythm of movement and music for the eye and the ear. Insects were humming; at intervals, the roar of a lion was audible, and, more distantly, the roar of a second lion—then screeches and barking sounds, imprecise rumors. All of that, like the breeze, was punctuated by magnificent silences.

The natives were not asleep. Many of them were standing around the central hut—the chief's hut—where three Europeans were contemplating the night and chatting, between themselves or with the natives. Others were building a large cooking-fire for a celebratory feast, a colossal meal in honor of the gusts. Two of the three travelers—the Austrian, Kamstein, and the Frenchman, Hamel—were fervent explorers, enthusiastic to travel through unknown regions to describe them accurately. Brave to the point of heroism, they preferred the peaceful approach to the conquistadorial methods of Stanley.

Even more so than them, Alglave was a traveler of noble lineage, highly curious, repulsed by useless sacrifices and the inconsiderate murder of animals, an adherent of the system of zoological philosophy that saw animal massacres as both a

81

danger for the future progress of humankind and a diminution of Earthly beauty. He was fervently interrogating one of Ouan-Mahlei's old men about the forest of Kyamo, and the latter was telling him mysterious, perhaps legendary, things that were infinitely interesting and poetic.

Kyamo was as long as 40 days march across the plain and 20 days broad. It was incredibly old, going back to the dawn of time, and the natives never went into it in large numbers. The lions intimidated them, having been expelled from its surrounds. As far as ancestral memory stretched, in the tales of dead epochs, Kyamo had been the uncontested possession of the grand old man of the woods, the giant black gorilla, who had retained it imperiously and victoriously.

This story excited Alglave. A marvelous and profound epic had swelled in his brain alongside the keen curiosity of the scientist.

"Have you ever seen the man of the woods?"

"I've seen him. I've been into Kyamo. The man of the woods is taller than we are, and especially stouter. He has the deep chest of a lion; his arms are invincible. More than one warrior has gone into the great forest, alone and without weapons. If he is humble and mild, no harm comes to him...but the wrath of the man of the woods is terrible!"

"Are there large numbers of the men of the woods?"

"Yes, they're certainly numerous; the forest contains many hundreds of villages."

"But they don't live in groups?"

"No, each man lives apart, with his wives, in close proximity to other families. Villages and tribes sometimes gather together, for expeditions. They can choose chiefs then."

Alglave lowered his head thoughtfully. His dream was heartfelt.

In the hermetic vastness of Kyamo he saw a majestic vestige of the very ancient history of being. In that virgin domain, the intelligence of a species that had been a rival of man had retained traces of a superior estate: rudiments of organization, a strong and considered system of defense, and considerable vital energy. Here was a living analogue of what human-kind had been in the Tertiary epoch: an animal which, for mysterious reasons, had been checked in its development while its rival had succeeded. Here was the genesis of human-kind before humans were endowed with speech—one of the most moving, if not *the* most moving, of *ready-made* epic poems that the human mind could perceive.

Alglave was firmly determined to go into Kyamo, to witness the life of these creatures, to see them going about their business in the intimacy of their refuges.

Meanwhile, a great fire was lit at the edge of the village. Its light blotted out that of the Moon and even outshone the stars. The natives uttered joyful cries.

On the plain, the astonished wild beasts fell silent, and then resumed their clamor of hunting, terror and love. The smoke dissipated the exquisite aroma of the plants. Soon, a buffalo and antelopes were being roasted over the flames.

The pensive Alglave felt that his determination to pene-trate into the depths of Kyamo was growing stronger by the minute.

The forest of ages past! More venerable and more virgin-al than any Amazonian forest or any Australian bush, popu-lated with trees that were thousands of years old, and yet pierced by vague pathways and primitive trails. Alglave had gone into it alone, in accordance with the repeated affirma-tions of the savages that the men of the woods would unfai-lingly destroy those bold enough to penetrate in pairs or in groups.

Surprised by the paths that ran through the immense dis-order, he marched for four hours. The heavy atmosphere, the semi-darkness, and the overabundant and excessively menac-ing life all weighed heavily upon his imagination, filling him with anguish. Occasionally, some large animal had fled before his approach, amid the multitude of smaller organisms, which every powerful respiration put on alert.

Nowhere had he perceived the great anthropoid ape, the king of this prodigious arboreal fatherland. There had, however, been traces of digital imprints, and his heart had beaten faster, while his hands went involuntarily toward the revolvers hidden in his pockets. He searched the shadows with a gaze that was too attentive, too feverish. Several times he had had brief hallucinations, thinking that he could see the broad black face, relatively hairless skull and the enormous hairy arms of a gorilla; but in reality, there was none.

Exhausted, he sat down on a giant root and lost himself in thought. In spite of the nervous malaise of the forest, and the sensation of being as far from all help and all humankind as if he were 1000 leagues deep in the heart of a desert, his resolution had not wavered. Quite the contrary, in fact. Being descended from men whose ardor was awakened by every obstacle and whose determination was redoubled by dread, he felt a more indomitable desire, a more extreme curiosity to know the mysterious realms of Kyamo. For the simple plan he had initially formulated of finding and observing a few gorillas in their habitats, a more extensive idea was slowly substituted: to live among them while Kamstein and Hamel went around Kyamo, to be one of them for a season, to admit himself voluntarily to their population.

By what stratagem or by what action he could succeed in doing that he had no idea; he thought about it with his head bowed and his brows contracted. As always, though, with those who, having had many adventures, had experienced their vicissitudes, he finished up hoping for one of those strokes of luck from which only men of determination and flair could take advantage.

While he was thinking about these things, a distant clamor made him shiver. He got up with a start and looked around.

In the uncertain, greenish and tremulous light, among the branches, lianas and boles of centenarian trees, he could scarcely see 200 paces. That narrow horizon added to the impression of hectic vitality and dark and occult power, as if ancient souls were floating in the heavy atmosphere, as if an infinity of organic forces, dead or in formation, were electrifying the Earth where the forest had reproduced itself, perhaps 10,000 times over, since the Tertiary Era.

The clamor continued, vaguely reminiscent of the noise of a human crowd. With his ears pricked, Alglave tried to analyze it. Although he was not without apprehension, some unknown force attracted him irresistibly. Mechanically, he began to walk, muffling his footsteps. As he drew closer, the clamor became louder, less comparable to human chatter. It was more of a bellowing, like that of buffaloes, a baying like that of large dogs. It sometimes died down, only to break out again louder than before, forcefully.

Alglave hesitated momentarily. How could he calculate the peril? Perhaps it was mortal—and how could he escape it, if he got too close? Vain reasoning! His curiosity was becoming excessive, almost morbid. He was certain that he was approaching a mystery, a scene unknown to all the scientists in the world, and which was, moreover, connected with the great anthropoid ape.

He advanced, therefore, in spite of himself, in spite of all reason and all wisdom. Through the branches of a baobab, he saw a company of black, hairy creatures of large size, but still unidentifiable. He *had* to get closer, he *had* to see. Abandoning all prudence, his curiosity became an intoxication, an autosuggestion; nothing could have made him retreat. He looked for a vantage-point. He spotted an enormous tree-trunk, hollow and riven with fissures; his botanist's eye told him that there were other fissures on the far side, revealed by the effects of light, by means of which he could observe the strange pandemonium.

How could he pass unnoticed? How could he make sure that the anthropoid apes did not pick up his scent, even if their sight and hearing did not perceive his presence?

He dared to hope. He told himself that the very crowd that they had formed, with its strong animal odor, would hide his feeble white man's scent, further diminished by his clothing. And, without reasoning further, he abandoned himself to the adventure. Creeping from stump to stump, plant to plant and from trunk to trunk, he drew nearer to the hollow tree. He got more than half way there in that fashion. Suddenly, his heart began to beat faster. Silence had fallen.

I've given myself away! he thought.

Flat on the ground, he waited resignedly, knowing that he could not get away, but nevertheless hiding himself carefully.

At any rate, there was no further doubt: the large black creatures, crouched down as if holding a meeting, were definitely the giant men of the woods, the terrible gorillas of Kyamo.

Two minutes went by; then a voice roared, and others followed. With a profound joy, Alglave realized that he had not been seen. Their mastery of the forest was sufficient for them not to be easily alarmed. How great their sense of security must be, after so many centuries of domination! Lying motionless, he admired them. They were colossi, superb muscular organisms. Some of them were three times as heavy as a human, although their height scarcely surpassed the human average. Their legs were short, their chests enormous, profound and Herculean. Their arms could have strangled lions and felled rhinoceroses.

Alglave felt a singular pride. He was glad to recognize in these athletic creatures the prototype of primitive human beings; he was glad to tell himself that our ancestors had not, in the beginning, been the weak, naked, helpless animal of the old theories but a redoubtable physical adversary of large wild beasts. Our ancestors, prior to the power of speech, had possessed powerful muscles, formidable in hand-to-hand combat, before dominating the world with their brains. Without affirming that their power of immediate combat was at the same level as their intellectual victory, or that they were sovereign among beasts, they must at least have been among the strongest animals.

While haunted by these reflections, in the midst of his excitement, Alglave had resumed crawling toward the hollow tree. He arrived there without further incident. As he had anticipated, the tree had sufficient fissures for him to be able to see everything that the gorillas were doing. He slid inside it, insinuated himself into a dark corner, and contemplated the extraordinary scene that he would later call "the great council of the men of the woods."

An extraordinary spectacle indeed. In a clearing some 10 or 12 acres in area, the floor of the forest was almost bare, covered with a few mosses and a few meager plants, and that elliptical space, under the branches of the surrounding trees, which intercepted a considerable fraction of the light, formed a sort of natural auditorium.

A multitude of men of the woods was squatting there—about 400, all adult males. A kind of order governed their grouping, and also their attitudes. They made regular gestures one at a time, which all the others followed attentively. These gestures were accompanied by cries, which were evidently significant, either of approval or disapproval. On seeing the play of their features and the repetition of certain movements, Alglave did not doubt that he had before him a kind of council meeting of these singular creatures. During the pauses, there was a visible concentration of thought, and mental contention—all the aspects of a human assembly engaged in some important discussion. The faces were, of course, almost canine, the jaws enormous and prominent, the brow receding and hardly ample—but none of that detracted from the relative intelligence of the assembly; Alglave remembered often having encountered Africans as distant in appearance from the human type as these anthropomorphs.

What were they discussing? What peril had to be avoided, what expedition or communal endeavor undertaken?

Alglave could not form any sort of hypothesis, but the matter in dispute must certainly have been important. The key evidence of that was an indication of direction. In fact, the hands and faces frequently turned the same way, in a vaguely southerly direction. Was it an enemy, a phenomenon…some fortunate or unfortunate occurrence? How he would have liked to know!

In regard to deducing it, however, Alglave soon became convinced that there was little prospect; to acquire an elementary knowledge, the language of the men of the woods would require a long period of study. As to doubt that it was a language, he had none. The naturalist, an expert in the subtleties of life, observed with certainty the recurrence of certain combinations; it was a very simple mathematics of arms and fingers, compared to the sign-language of human deaf-mutes, but savant and complex by comparison with anything observable among the superior mammals.

Oh yes, he would have been interested to know what it meant. What profound information regarding the origin of language! What a page to add to the beautiful book of prehistory inscribed in the strata of the Earth!

I shall be one of them, Alglave resolved. *Whatever sacrifice of dignity I have to make, even if I have to be the humblest of their servants…their property…their slave…I must know!*

That was easy to say. But how could he do it? By surrendering to them, voluntarily becoming their captive? Would they even consent to that? Might they not tear him apart, especially if he dared to present himself during the doubtless sacred hour of the council? Or, if they disdained to put him to death, would they not chase him ignominiously out of the forest?

These reflections ran through Alglave's mind in a disorderly fashion. They did not discourage him. The scientific autosuggestion, the hypnotic state of Pliny perishing in the eruption of Vesuvius, had him solidly in his grip. He scarcely gave a moment's thought to retreat, solely preoccupied with overcoming the obstacles.

As he was thinking and scheming, he heard a slight scratching sound close by. He turned round and saw, in the semi-darkness, a kind of black child: a little anthropoid ape staring at him with round and fearful eyes. Where had it come from? What was it dong there? He did not have time to wonder; the infant had just uttered a cry—a fearful cry provoked by a movement of the naturalist's head.

Immediately, there was silence around the circumference of the council. The child repeated its cry. The men of the woods got up, and a dozen of them hurled themselves toward the hollow tree.

Alglave did not wait for them to surprise him in hiding; he wanted to greet them in broad daylight. He came out of his shelter, having gently moved the anthropoid child out of the way, and stood there in a placid and resigned stance, avoiding—as he had been advised by the natives—meeting the eyes of the new arrivals.

Suddenly, he felt himself lifted off the ground, choking in an irresistible embrace. He thought his last moment had come, and put his hand into his pocket mechanically to search for a revolver. Howls went up, and the formidable grip relaxed slightly.

Between his half-closed eyelids, Alglave observed. He was surrounded by an agitated, curious multitude of black heads, which contained powerfully-toothed jaws, and which, for the moment, seemed ferocious and sanguinary. His life was hanging in the balance. Whatever he tried to do, his efforts would be miserable, pitiful and futile. His extermination by the hands of a single one of these giants would take no more than half a minute.

He then had the singular sensation noted by Livingstone in the claws of a lion: an alarm so great that it abolished terror, an *impossibility* of any pain resulting from the peril.

He heard and saw a debate engaged in regard to him; a few muscular hands were advanced menacingly, but then there was a respite. A man of the woods, a colossus among these colossi, came forward. He made a few calming gestures to the crowd, and spoke at length. Calm was restored. The one holding him prisoner carried him into the clearing; he was deposited on the ground.

Gradually, he recovered *lucid* emotion, apprehensive as to what would happen now.

He saw that he was the object of an intense curiosity. No similar creature had every appeared in the Kyamo forest. His blond hair, his pale face, his pale gray clothing and his double-peaked cap made him an extraordinary and mysterious beast from the gorillas' viewpoint, unknown throughout eternity in their sylvan shade. Negroes were familiar to them; they had fought them and kept them out of their domain, considering them rivals less redoubtable than lions. But what was this? How had it got here? Was it a threat to the security of the race? Anxiety appeared on their ponderous faces.

Was it or was it not necessary to sacrifice him? Should they kill him, chase him away disdainfully, or keep him in servitude?

These questions were raised—doubtless along with ill-defined arguments—but were finally settled; that, at least, was Alglave's supposition. Eventually, a man of the woods approached, seemingly intent on delivering some supreme violence. Thrown down, with his arms pinned, Alglave felt utterly helpless. He closed his eyes and waited.

No blow fell. The individual that was threatening him was shoved aside by his companions. On reopening his eyes, the naturalist understood from the general attitude that, provisionally, his life had been spared. He was transported out of the clearing and laid down between the tree-roots, under the guard of two anthropoids, and his limbs were bound with some kind of rope made from lianas.

In the distance, he heard the council continuing its session. His uncertainty was profound, his sadness bitter, and yet he still did not regret having undertaken this tenebrous adventure; his scientific curiosity persisted, becoming more complex, with the tenacity of illusion that has always characterized fecund researchers.

It is morning. The rapid and resplendent dawn has passed; the star of life has scaled the firmament, and broad daylight has arrived. The forest seems to have come to an end, but that is an illusion; the vast river that extends, in breadth, almost to the bounds of the horizon, pierces Kyamo but does not limit it; its vast vegetal life continues in the distance. Monstrous crocodiles can be seen on the banks, huge vultures are soaring in the blue heights, hippopotamus floating heavily in the greenish waters. Another life, sly, parasitic, hidden, opulent, beautiful, sinister or joyful is evident amid the fecundity of the vegetation.

On one of the inlets of the shore, the anthropoids have made camp. Their number is considerable; there are perhaps 1000 of them—and among them, humble, here is the man from Europe, the pale prisoner.

Alglave is naked; his clothing has been torn away. He is hungry, for he has scarcely been fed as much as he eats on fast days. He is tired, for he has been allowed little rest, his sleep being continually disturbed. The king of terrestrial beings is humiliated, crushed by the splendor of the anthropoids, by their colossal force, by their hatred, but not by their scorn.

On the first day of his captivity, after life had been definitely granted to him, his masters were more curious than cruel, disdainful of his weakness—but by some of his movements, gestures and attitudes, he inspired an anxiety in them. Their instinct divined by some means that he, the unknown, belonged to an upstart race that they had never encountered. They watched him more closely, full of mysterious suspicion. Every day it became more uncertain whether they would finally decide to destroy him. At the same time, they hid themselves from him; with respect to their important actions, they removed any possibility of his being able to observe that for which he had made such a terrible sacrifice.

Alglave pondered these matters miserably. After a short morning march, he and his masters had just arrived on the edge of the river; there they had met a new company of anthropoids at least as numerous as their own, which seemed to have been waiting there for them. From the hubbub of the meeting, the gestures and attitudes, Alglave understood what had brought these creatures to this corner of the forest. In the distance, about 100 meters from the shore, an island was visible, very long but mediocre in width; silhouettes were gesticulating there, calling out to the anthropoids on the bank. Alglave recognized the latter's kin. They seemed to be suffering, thin and in distress—especially the females and their children.

The drama of the great council was explained—the summoning of gorillas through the forest, the meetings, the expeditions—simultaneously revealing a human organization, a solidarity between the various groups of men of the woods, which increasingly discouraged confusion between them and vulgar gorillas.

But what misfortune had led to an entire tribe of creatures standing on that island in the middle of the river—creatures which evidently did not know how to swim, or the most rudimentary elements of navigation?

That problem excited Alglave, making him forget his suffering. He analyzed the surroundings, attentively following the discussion of the gorillas on the bank—for, in their own excitement, they forgot to keep watch on him. Two important characteristics guided his research: a large rock, seemingly freshly broken off at the summit, emerging from the river-bank, and another rock on the island.

Was there a bridge? he wondered.

A bridge? Constructed by them? No—a freak of nature, probably; a natural bridge…and, among the anthropoids, a centuries-old habit of crossing it to reach the island—the habitat of a small tribe or a temporary camp?—then, a cataclysm…the collapse of the bridge…

He refrained from making a gesture, in order not to attract attention, and murmured: "Yes, yes…a hundred times yes. I have it—it's the solution to the problem."

The expressive mime of the gorillas seemed to confirm his conjecture. Then, a vast and tender hope entered into his heart.

What, in fact, did the men of the woods want? Toward what end were they going to devote their efforts? Evidently, to attempt to rescue the others over there, to find some means of communication.

And they surely won't succeed, Alglave said to himself. *Ignorant of the art of swimming, incapable of comprehending skiffs, rafts or tree-trunks—for if they were not, the ones over there would have escaped—they'll never reach the isle...but I could. I might earn their gratitude...win my right to live with them freely...*

His heart raced. He observed the anthropoids anew. His over-excited intelligence interpreted the most frequent of their present gestures: a confused mime, and evaluation of the distance between the two rocks...

A bridge! They're thinking about a bridge! Poor devils!

He sat down and waited. Two hours went by, the gorillas having set to work. They had uprooted the tallest tree in the vicinity—a tree more than 60 meters high. Slowly and awkwardly, they had hoisted it to the summit of the rock.

Oh, the children! Alglave said to himself. *They're going to try to get the other end over to the island.*

Simultaneously, he was moved to pity by their ingenuity, and found them marvelously intelligent for apes.

They're true men, after all...for the idea of a bridge exists in them...and what does it matter that they don't know how to calculate the width of the gap?

The tree was stood on end, but without any apparatus—with no employment of levers or liana-ropes; by simple traction on its enormous roots and the indomitable vigor of the laborers. Then, slowly, having pointed it in the right direction, they let it fall. It fell, collapsing into the river. There was a roaring furious clamor, followed by a bleak discouragement, a dolorous taciturnity

Then Alglave came forward.

He advanced toward the group that had just failed in their task, and toward their chief—the one whom, during his sojourn among the gorillas, he had recognized as the most intelligent.

With an expressive gesture he pointed to the island three times, then pointed to himself, and began again; he established a coordination of gestures between himself and the island, and made it vaguely understood that he wanted to do something for the individuals over there. Curious, and also somewhat suspicious, they all looked at him. He persisted; then he marched up to a fallen tree, found a pointed stone on the bank, and set about stripping its branches.

There was a series of gesticulatory conversations among the gorilla, and the impression to which Alglave had tried to give birth—a vague hope—spread.

When he had detached the first branch, he succeeded in obtaining a certain amount of help; he struck and chipped, and the Herculean gorillas tore and twisted the branch. He worked in this fashion for two-thirds of the day, and then found that he had some 50 branches—which, together with a few willow-trunks, might be used to make up a raft. He was delighted, full of hope; his apprentices had rapidly become more accomplished than at the outset. In addition, he had been given nourishment.

Then he went in search of lianas. Immediately, he had hundreds of assistants. Then he tied together the pieces of the raft, having had the branches and the willow-trunks brought. That lasted until three hours before nightfall—and the raft was constructed.

Then, making a great gesture of delight to the anthropoids, he began again, obstinately, to point to the island.

At this point, the crucial difficulty of his project presented itself: to persuade one of the anthropoids to accompany him on the raft—for to depart alone, to introduce himself to the stranded individuals without an intermediary, would excite their suspicion. Why should any of them decide to take a risk that none of their brethren on the shore had dared risk to come to their rescue?

Alglave tried to explain that. He was not understood. Then, having had the raft put in the river—not without difficulty, and not without the risk of misunderstanding and maltreatment—he began to maneuver it with a crude scull. He drew away from the bank and then came back. A glint of understanding seemed to appear in the minds of some of them, and Alglave pointed alternately at the island and the raft 20 times over, miming the action of the scull and the advancement of the skiff over the waves.

Once again, he achieved a vague comprehension. The most intelligent of the anthropoids seemed to be considering running the risk, but his profound terror of the water was evidently holding him back. Climbing on to the raft again, Alglave maneuvered, left the bank and came back, demonstrating the safety of the primitive vessel 20 times over. Then, slowly and hesitantly, with evident anguish and the shivering movements of a child dipping his foot into the water, the gorilla chief got down on to the raft.

Ah! Finally! Alglave thought.

A feeling of pride mounted to his head—the satisfaction of a scientist who has triumphed over rebellious matter. While he launched his vessel again he smiled, thinking that he had been able to turn the opportunity of which he had dreamed inside the hollow tree to the advantage of his project.

Slowly, the raft approached the island, without too considerable a deviation. Alglave's companion, nervous, agitated and tremulous at first, was gradually reassured. His intelligent eyes observed the human's movements, establishing a relationship between those movements and the progress of the skiff. A sympathy also arose, born of what was, for the gorilla, an extraordinary adventure. Alglave sensed that he had acquired a comrade, a protector, and perhaps a pupil.

Finally, the raft ran aground, and while it was being moored in a creek, a crowd of emaciated, feverish and impatient individuals crowded around.

No more worries, Alglave thought. *He's the one who'll explain the whole thing.*

Indeed, his companion started haranguing his fellows with gestures. A solemn silence was established. In the thin faces, the dilated eyes fixed themselves upon him with an intense acuity. The scene did not lack grandeur. It seemed that these unfortunates had been somewhat refined by suffering; they had a more rapid understanding of everything that related to their rescue. That which was human in them was more pronounced in those that had known horror and distress, and the fear of abandonment. Their souls had passed through the supreme stress from which an animal extracts new ruses or more refined ideas.

In less than a quarter of an hour, a dozen of them had decided to be the first to return to the shore. Alglave arranged them carefully in the center of the vessel, and cast off with infinite precaution. An attentive concentration accompanied the departure. The passengers, apart from shivering with fear, were submissive to the instructions of the gorilla chief. They made their way toward the bank without haste.

A quarter of an hour went by. The water was placid, almost smooth, the pitching of the raft very slight. The bank was reached easily.

Then an immense rumor rose up: a savage, joyful, frantic brouhaha. Alglave was surrounded, caressed by colossal hands, subjected to amiable embraces. All hatred and mistrust directed against the pale beast who had saved the stranded men of the woods had disappeared.

The beginning of the night. A vague and vast Moon has just appeared on the horizon. At first, it is reminiscent of a globe of red linen, then one of polished metal, and then a sharp disk, gilded and silvered. Alglave is dreaming on the edge of the river. His wishes have been granted. He has become the sacred guest of the anthropoids, a respected and admired individual who has, perhaps confusedly, become an object of worship. He can study them without anxiety, and without haste—and what an adorable book is gestating in his head as his observations are augmented! Through him, the marvelous poem of Tertiary humankind will be revealed—not a poem of the imagination, however beautifully it might be conceived, but the noble, religious and divine truth. Through him, people will be able to infer what the ages of cerebral infancy were like, when one creature was chosen among others to take its place at the head of all the beasts.

And that dream is full of happiness, full of tenderness; he loves these brothers of our prehistoric precursor; he loves their powerful savagery, their proud struggle against extinction; he fervently desires to find some means of preserving the depths of Kyamo from the invasion of explorers, from the conquistadorial rage of Europeans.

He loses himself in that dream; the Moon climbs, shrinking as its light brightens. Animals lament in the depths of the forest; the rumors of the river are reminiscent of a vast and intermittent respiration.

And Alglave feels himself invaded by a serenity as calm, as delicate and as charming as the tremor of the moonbeams amid the foliage of the willows.

THE WONDERFUL CAVE COUNTRY

To Ed. Picard [10]

The boat ploughed through the darkness.

Along the immense virginal river it went through the forest, a pale orange-tinted gleam blued by the semi-darkness. Near to the bank, where the boat was moving forward, the glimmers of light were braided, woven and tremulous, sometimes into faint pools, sometimes into magical networks with fine mesh, like coats of mail. In the distance, the light fell with divine serenity, and the open water, seemingly tinted at first by phosphorescent vapor, slowly faded toward a pale steel-blue, a scintillation of millions of blades.

Fecund and monstrous life was detectable in the river. Sometimes, an alligator slid along the bank, alarmed in its sleep; sometimes, a tapir fled from an enemy into the depths of the kingdom of the waves. As for smaller life-forms, they were frightful in their number and mystery.

All in all, however, there was a semi-silence over the stream. Because of these rumors, the forest seemed extraordinarily powerful, beautiful and sinister. Eternal warfare was ongoing there, the furtive conjunctions of love, carnivorous ambushes, pursuit, terror, the genius of attack and defense in formidable freedom—and, above all, the fundamental need of the weak and the strong alike: hunger, for pasture or for prey.

The electrical boat glided with a singular gentleness, scarcely a slight palpitation of its mechanism. It explored its

---

[10] The Belgian jurist Edmond Picard (1836-1924) was the founder of *L'Art Moderne*, a significant periodical supporting the Jeune Belgique movement; he also served as a socialist senator in the Belgian government.

surroundings with a long beam of white light. Three men were standing in the prow; a fourth manned the tiller.

One of them—a short, thickset man—murmured: "Well, the old cacique was right. After the almost-insurmountable navigational problems of the early stages, here we are in broad and beautiful waters, only occasionally obstructed."

"Profound and abundant—whereas back there, at the confluence with the Amazon, the river is considerable in actuality, but poor in flow."

The man who had replied presented a round-shouldered silhouette, with long arms and a bald head, which gleamed with reflected moonlight. His voice was muffled and hoarse, made for whispering in the silence of study-halls.

"Do you remember what the old man said?" the third put in. "*The river comes from lakes that lie in the sunset. At first it is vaster than the Mother of Rivers, but the Earth drinks it with huge mouths, and the water diminishes every time...*" This one, tall and barrel-chested, with a long, narrow head, further elongated by a silky beard, spoke loudly, with forceful gestures and rapidly-moving eyes.

"In that case," said the round-shouldered man, "we must already have passed one of these *huge mouths* that drink the river without seeing it."

"The one that's invisible, no doubt," said the man with the long head, "but *the second opens in a rock*—it's a cave."

The thickset individual said, with a hint of irony: "They're probably allegories! Wasn't the only man slyly giving us a course in Indian cosmogony? Anyway, we're losing nothing by it—we're in virgin territory, beyond all known geography."

"Personally, I believe it," said the man with the long head, with a kind of anger. "I believe in this strange land of subterranean waters, where the cacique's great-grandfather nearly perished."

"We'll see, Alglave."

"You're forgetting the prisoner that the cacique gave us!" Alglave replied. "The captive from the tribe that lives underground."

"Well, the prisoner hasn't recognized the landscape thus far."

"Patience! We were told that he wouldn't recognize it until we're near the *second mouth*."

Alglave started intoning some mysterious Indian incantation, and the boat continued its journey along the great river. The Moon was higher now, and bright; it was visible above the foliage, as if its edges were more clear-cut. The immense battle continued to rage in the vastness of the forest.

Then, two of the interlocutors went below decks to sleep, while the man with the long head remained alone with the helmsman.

Alglave stood in the prow, exploring the river with eyes as profound and sure as those of a condor. A reverie as mysterious as the night of this virgin country drifted through his mind. His intense desire was that the old Indian's legend should be true. His entire being was excited by it and attached to it—for, man of action as he was, full of practical strength and foresight, he was more of a poet than his companion explorers.

He repeated the vague but lovely legend to himself:

"There are lands under the Earth, where long rivers run, and grasses grow, with pale beasts, blind birds and white vampires. Sometimes, there is a faint moonlight, which moves, and dies out after a time—then everything is in darkness again…"

Why should the legend be a lie? Are there not subterranean rivers, even in the old countries of Europe? Are there not still strange and little-studied animals? Here, were everything is immense and free, why should subterranean lands not have an analogous scope? And what delectable mysteries, what magnificent poems of life beyond the life of the surface, what a wonderful dark territory of marvelous fauna and flora might be preserved in the bowels of the Earth!

He recalled another legend that had been told to him eight years before by an old chief in Ouan-Mahlei. The African's predictions had been marvelously realized; why should those of the Red Indian be deceptive? One doubt haunted him, however: could such rare adventures befall the same man twice? Would the old Earth offer him twice over the delightful spectacle of an unknown refuge of large animals?

Why not? he said to himself. *Have I not been traveling the planet relentlessly for 15 years on the run? Is it not the reward of my eternal wandering, and also of my obstinacy in pursuing to the end the meaning contained in the aboriginal legends of every land?*

While he thought about these things, he scrutinized the banks continually, hoping to see the *Mouth of the Earth* appear there—but he saw nothing but the sinuous shore, the forest, and the indecisive forms of large carnivores and herbivores.

Night must be harsh, alone out there in the terrible struggle for existence: jaguars...anacondas...rattlesnakes!

He shuddered with relief at the thought of being safe on the electric boat, so well-designed, well-provisioned and comfortable—not that he did not love adventure, or had any lack of reckless bravery, but even the most heroic of men likes to feel safe in confrontation with a magnificent poem of anguish and fear.

The slender point of an islet appeared in the moonlight. Alglave concentrated all his attention on giving instructions to the helmsman. As the boat drew nearer, more obstacles appeared, in the form of debris and the trunks of uprooted trees, maintained by dense fluvial vegetation. The passage became difficult, and it was necessary to slow down.

The Moon illuminated a solemn perspective: the islet, with its tall trees leaning over the water, the lianas and reeds of its edges, all the detritus of an indomitable vegetation, and extraordinary profiles set against the fragments of a silvery firmament, with cavernous gaps, huge palm-trees taller than the tallest crowns on the bank, floating in the lukewarm ether; the water, reflecting those confused splendors, gently lapping against the frayed bank, carrying away clods of Earth and roots. With all that majestic semi-darkness, the moonlight filtered by the treetops, an indefinable menace expanded: a severity of nature intimating to humans that they ought not to advance any further. And, indeed, the passage became increasingly awkward.

At first, it was relatively easy for the slender prow of the boat to carve out a route through the obstacles, but an inextricable tangle of aquatic plants and large dead tree-trunks soon rendered further progress difficult, and perhaps perilous.

Alglave gave the order to reduce speed; it became evident that he was assuming a great responsibility in acting alone. Primitive nature seemed to be full of ambushes; as far as the pilot's eye could follow the beam of the electric searchlight, there was an uninterrupted sequence of vegetable remains floating on the river. On some of them, aquatic monsters were asleep or moving slowly. A flock of night-birds was perceptible; the murmurs, sighs and grunts of nearby beasts were audible, mingling with the slow susurrus of the waters and the foliage. Moreover, the boat had drifted; it was now no more than 20 meters from the shore of the islet, in the shadow of enormous trees leaning over the water.

As Alglave brought the boat to a conclusive stop and decided to summon his companions to a council of war, a shadow bounded on to the deck: a large silhouette. The helmsman uttered an exclamation of fright.

Revolver in hand, ready for attack or defense, Alglave peered into the indecisive gloom. He saw a human being, of rather small height but very thickset. Once the first shock was past, the helmsman also drew his revolver and took aim at the man.

"Hold your fire!" said Alglave. "He doesn't seem to be aggressive."

Indeed, the human being struck a supplicatory pose, pointing at the river with a fearful gaze. Alglave followed the direction of his gesture.

On a kind of islet, caught in a ray of moonlight, stood a monstrous and splendid jaguar. Taken by surprise, the beast remained motionless, evidently torn between the desire to pursue its prey and fear of the electric lantern. But for that, nothing would have been easier for it than to reach the boat by means of a few bounds over the tree-trunks with which the river was littered.

Alglave took advantage of the beast's momentary hesitation to take out a rifle from a sort of locker close to the prow. He made a sign to the fugitive, telling him to have no fear, and, with the rifle shouldered, paused to admire the beast. With proportions equal to those of an ordinary tiger, with slightly shorter legs, it represented the regal forces of nature, the magnificent effort of a life of conflict. At ease in its supple skin, half-crouching, its entire attitude was expressive of speed, ferocious and graceful skill and the habit of victory. Almost inaccessible to terror, Alglave did not squeeze the trigger immediately, not liking to kill such superb beasts, poems of vigor—but the savage came closer, touched him, and pointed to the right of the islet. The explorer saw three more jaguars.

Oh, damn! he thought.

This time, his heart beat faster, sensing a profound peril. At the same time, he was astonished to see several of these large beasts together; they usually hunted in couples, not in packs. Whatever the reason was for the anomaly, though, the danger was there, terrible in these forests, where a few tribes of ill-armed and wretched indigenes had not given the jaguar any sense of the power of human beings. The same animal that the proximity of bellicose tribes or white men had rendered circumspect, and even cowardly, in other regions was here a perennial victor, certain of its strength, its incomparable superiority over all creation.

In a strident voice, Alglave sounded the alarm, and then took careful aim at the large jaguar, between its eyes. While he still could not decide whether or not to fire, however, another shot rang out. It was the helmsman. Terrified by the sight of the wild beast, he fired his revolver: three shots in quick succession.

Slightly wounded, the furious jaguar leapt to the side of the boat. Gripping with its claws, with a thrust of its hips it arrived on the deck, four paces from Alglave.

You asked for it! the explorer thought.

Swiftly, he fired—but at the exact moment when the beast pounced on him. Instead of penetrating the skull, his bullet broke the jaw of the beast, which fell upon him like a thunderbolt.

His friends, who came up on deck at that moment, thought that he was doomed. He rolled on the deck, but sideways, hardly touched. As rapid as his frightful adversary, he found himself facing the murderous claws. Then, with two or three of those movements that the naked eye cannot capture and only photography can separate, there was a skirmish, the hammer-like blow of a rifle-butt—and they saw the jaguar lying still, while Alglave stood up. A revolver-shot finished the animal off.

"It's not over!" cried the victor. He pointed at the other jaguars, menacing on the islet.

One of the explorers turned the beam of the electric searchlight on them; the blue-white beam frightened them.

"They seem intimidated!" said the bald man.

"They are, Fugère," Alglave replied. "Quite probably, if no one shoots and wounds them, they won't dare to attack us!"

As he spoke, two shots rang out, by courtesy of two crewmen who had arrived on deck at the same time as the explorers. One of the jaguars—a female—was wounded, and bounded directly at the boat, furiously, swiftly followed by her mate. Alglave stopped the female dead with a bullet in the skull. The male stopped with a mighty *miaow*, then leapt again. A fusillade peppered the water around it without hitting it, and it appeared abruptly on the bridge, with prodigious speed. One man was knocked down on to the deck, beneath the colossal paws.

"At the head!" Alglave shouted. Practicing what he preached, he aimed his revolver—then hesitated. The prostrate man screamed in terror, while the monstrous beast hesitated too, seeing itself surrounded by adversaries, and amazed. It was dangerous to fire, for fear of hitting the man.

Meanwhile, with a visionary courage poignant in its awkwardness, Fugère had crept close enough to fire. His bullet went clean through the beast's neck—and almost simultaneously, he was knocked over in his turn and shaken like a rag. They saw his breast penetrated, beneath his lacerated clothing, by dagger-sharp claws. Hypnotized, he did not defend himself, feeling infinitely weak—so weak that he resigned himself to his fate, experiencing no fear.

His friends raced forward, though, and the animal, peppered with bullets, rolled over the scientist, crushing him with its weight.

"Dead!" cried Alglave, sending one last bullet into the head for safety's sake.

Rapidly, they liberated Fugère. His wounds were quite deep, having ripped one of the pectoral muscles, but not dangerous. "I had a lucky escape!" he said, smiling.

The explorers and crewmen looked at one another, astonished by the drama; until then, their boat had been an absolute safeguard against the animals of the river and its banks.

"The fourth jaguar has disappeared!" Alglave said, while carrying out an attentive examination of his friend's wounds.

"Yes," replied the third companion. "But we were in serious danger, all the same—which could have been avoided if no one had fired. The searchlight would have been enough to keep the beasts away."

"That's true, Véraguez," Alglave replied. "But what has become of the man who brought us the adventure?"

"There he is!" said one of the crewmen.

The savage advanced, invited to do so by a gesture. They saw a sturdy man with a nyctalopic gaze, a broad, grayish face, a sloping forehead and an enormous chin. He pronounced a few guttural syllables.

"That's the same dialect as our hostage!" said Véraguez, who had keen polyglot faculties.

"And he's the same physical type," Fugère added. "Let's bring them together."

"I have a feeling," said Alglave, with a hint of irony, "that the old cacique wasn't just giving us a course in Indian cosmogony."

A few minutes later, the Indian handed over by the cacique was brought forth. As soon as he saw the other one, he manifested an extreme joy, which was mutual. The two of them launched into an extensive conversation.

"Is he one of your race, Whamo?" asked Véraguez, in an Akatl dialect.

"He's one of those who go into the caves in the rainy season."

"From your tribe?"

"No, but a sister tribe."

"Ask him whether we're far from his homeland—and tell him that he has nothing to fear, for himself or his relatives."

"Yes, master!"

The dialogue resumed, in the midst of universal interest. It was a hoarse, vague exchange with plaintive intonations of astonishment.

"We're two days by canoe from the caves that open into the Underground Land," Whamo said. "The tribes have dispersed into the forests now, and will only go back to the caves when the leaves are old."

"Would the man of your race care to take us there?"

Whamo continued the interrogation; acquiescence and trust were observable in the other man's gestures.

"He can do it, Master! His life belongs to those who have saved him from the jaguar's claws—but it's necessary to go around the other side of the island, for passage is impossible here."

All night long, the boat sailed on placid waters on the other side of the island. After a short rest, Alglave had come back on deck, with Véraguez and the two Indians. The great peril of the night before seemed like a dream. The proud and slender boat was scornful of all ambushes, invincible on the open river, in the blue light. Finally, dawn broke over the forest. It rapidly drowned out the light of the sinking Moon, and the vast rumor of diurnal life succeeded the terrors of the night.

The island disappeared behind them, the river broadening out further, and rocky crags appeared on the horizon. Then, the Indian they had saved raised his arm and murmured a few words. Whamo translated them: "The Mouths of the caverns open over there!"

The explorers' hearts beat faster, an intense curiosity awakened in their inner being. In the light mist, the rocks were reminiscent of a herd of colossal buffalo that had come down to the water to drink. Then the river appeared to become a large lake, dilating into a circle surrounded by the rocky chain. The boat got closer rapidly; it soon reached the first hills.

The spectacle had a severe and tranquil magnificence; the vegetation stopped almost dead; great arid spaces extended on the bank opposite the rocks; charred debris, lava and vitreous stones told of an ancient cataclysm, a plutonian tempest.

"This is definitely the mysterious region," said Alglave. "The land of dark and beautiful legends!"

A new gesture from the Indian interrupted him; in one of the highest rocks, they perceived a prodigious portal, the peristyle of a temple of giants.

"That's it!" said Whamo.

The river could be seen pouring into the immense opening, and they glimpsed enigmatic colonnades and profound vaults, into which the sunlight penetrated obliquely.

Véraguez and Alglave contemplated the spectacle with a sort of mystical respect. "Look!" said the latter. "The water's going in slowly—and Whamo, like the cacique, claims that it's deep! We're not taking much risk, in any case, by going in there, ready to renounce the enterprise at any moment…"

"Let's go!" Véraguez replied. "In any case, Fugère has agreed to run the risk with us."

The Sun was already dissipating the pale veils of mist. The rocks stood out with somber authority, a majestic aridity, and the plain on the opposite shore, with its harsh desolate and dazzling antique wreckage, was like one of those accursed regions in which religions often see divine wrath.

Slowly, the boat headed for the cave.

The subterranean stream was, indeed, tranquil and profound. At first, the searchlight illuminated uniform sides, pale stalactites, gray rocks strewn with bright sequins of crystal or metal. An infinite darkness reigned there; the electric beam generated troubling penumbras; something confusing, fantastically alive, seemed to be crawling slowly along the moist walls, with vegetable patience. The water was jet black, indecisively reflecting the furtive forms sketched out by the searchlight.

Beneath the high vault, amid the cold odor of a cistern, in motionless air saturated with vapor, the souls of the companions were penetrated by a great and noble melancholy, a religious curiosity, an august sense of the unknown—and also by an invincible apprehension: a vague presentiment that occasionally rendered their chests heavy and tight.

After two hours sailing, the landscape—if these phantoms of banks glimpsed in the cold gleam of the searchlight could thus be described—was transformed.

The sides, at first quite narrow, broadened out. A very pale and frail filamentous vegetation, composed of a kind of stringy lichen and thread-like mosses, marked out matt silver gardens with filigree foliage the color of hemp and white meadows. Here and there, pale animals fled from the cone of light: marsupials with pelts the color of marine groundsel, giant rodents, rapacious nocturnal birds flying smoothly with fleecy wings, and a few large-sized insects that looked as if they had been dusted with chalk.

At the same time, the temperature rose by a dozen degrees, climbing slowly from 20 to 25, and then to 30.

"Should we get off?" Véraguez asked.

"I don't think so," Alglave replied. "I think we should extend the reconnaissance as far as possible, to begin with, observing the broad features of this marvelous terrain. Later, when it's necessary to mount a series of expeditions, we can proceed to detailed studies."

"That's fair."

In spite of his wounds, Fugère soon joined his friends, and they spent entire hours admiring the miraculous subterranean country. It grew, and it developed. The vegetation, though still pale, became more vigorous.

Chlorotic ferns raised elegant fronds along the riverbanks, forming virtual forests; gigabit rodents showed themselves: rats as large as leopards, which did not flee when the light reached them from a distance. It was necessary to move closer and send forth an intense beam, as hard as metal, to make them retreat. The marsupials seemed scarcer, as were the nocturnal raptors. On the other hand, increasing curious varieties of bats flew skittishly over the ferns in pursuit of insects. It seemed strange to see animals that humans only knew in dark colors—russet, fawn and brown—as white as ermine. Quite tiny at first, they grew in size, attaining the stature of the vampires that live in the vast Brazilian forests.

The temperature was no longer climbing; it leveled out at 32 degrees—but in the humid, unrefreshed air, that heat was nonetheless oppressive.

After dinner—dusk must have fallen outside, on the countries of the surface—Whamo announced, on behalf of his companion, that the tribes of his race had never been so far underground, and that he was forced to forsake his role as a guide. He also made allusion to a legend that the river ended up falling into an abyss, where there were countries even more mysterious than those through which they were passing.

"That's good," said Alglave. "For myself, I propose to continue."

"Until the end?" asked the injured man.

"Until the end," Véraguez repeated.

And, indeed, neither the soul of a poet nor the soul of any scientist in the world would have been able to resist the magical attraction of those shadowy lands, with their promise of extraordinary sensations and discoveries. There was an immense perspective now; on the left bank there were abrupt declivities, a hectic succession of cavernous rocks, hard red granites and basalts hollowed out into cyclopean staircases, with overhanging summits, seemingly ready to collapse: an eerie necropolis pieced by tunnels, long corridors that lost themselves in the bowels of the Earth. To the right was a veritable plain, a forest of ferns punctuated by phantasmal mushrooms as tall as trees, forming striking silvery clearings in which the rodent fauna were augmented by albino lemurs, sadly perched, whose soft plaints were sometimes audible, and by owls as white as swans, alternating with livid vampires as big as eagles.

"Wonderful! Marvelous!" whispered Alglave, as he wrote his notes.

Even the crewmen were stupefied with admiration and superstitious terror.

Then, suddenly, a new miracle was added to all the rest.

In the distance, a sort of violet light emerged, which seemed to expand like a dawn, although no original source could be seen. It increased rapidly, tinting the pale plain, and its animals and plants, with a fairy glow. It settled on the rocky shore in a vague enchantment, in which all the shades of violet were blended.

Dark at first, it brightened, and soon had the softness of a ray of moonlight filtering through glass faintly stained with indigo. As some animals retreated, others emerged, and the white vampire bats mingled with other huge bat species the color of lead.

From then on the view extended to the limits of the subterranean horizon, about a kilometer away. A startling beauty emanated from fields of snowy lichen, mysteriously-opened penumbras, and mushroom clearings arranged in colonnades as tall as old bare-created willows on the edge of fish-ponds. Pallor was everywhere! A pallor full of silent life; a pallor emerging in the gentle alternation of darkness and lunar light; a supernatural pallor telling a tale of prodigies, of patient conflicts far from the Sun that nourished the world above; a pallor conserving forms of fauna and flora that had once lived in the pride of coloration!

"Shall we get off, now?" asked Fugère.

"Let's go on further!" said Alglave, feverishly. "I think even greater surprises are in store for us."

Meanwhile, the two Indians pricked up their keen ears and displayed a certain anxiety.

"What can you hear?" Véraguez asked.

"We can hear running water!" Whamo replied.

Alglave, whose ears were almost as good as an Indian's, listened in his turn. Soon, it seemed to him that he could hear the sound of white water: the turbulence of rapids or a cascade. "Watch out!" he said. "I believe that legend will prove correct once again, and that we're about to reach the abyss." He shouted "Slow down!" to the engineer.

Anxiously, the explorers kept a careful watch on the current, directing the searchlight, whose beam was brighter than the mysterious light. Two hours went by in this fashion. Soon, they could all hear the sound of a cataract quite clearly.

"Stop!" shouted Alglave. "Drop anchor!"

"And this time, let's get off," Véraguez added.

Within a few more minutes, the boat was anchored, and then solidly moored to the bank on the side of the plain. Six of the 12 crewmen were chosen to accompany the explorers, along with the two Indians; the other six remained with Fugère, who having acquired a slight fever, did not feel strong enough to go with his companions. Well-equipped and armed, furnished with battery-powered electric lanterns, Alglave, Véraguez and their escort got under way.

The ground underfoot was soft and slightly damp. The friction of livid conifers and ferns generated a slight apprehension even among the most courageous, including Alglave.

As the little troop came out into an uncovered space, four or five of the rats whose colossal proportions had surprised the travelers appeared. They stared at the humans with their reddish eyes, and did not recoil, being masters of this domain, whose tigers or lions they were. They hesitated, though, seemingly disinclined to take the offensive, surprised to see these enormous bipedal newcomers.

At that moment, one of the men in the escort raised his rifle. Alglave knocked it down again. "Don't fire without our orders!" he said, in an authoritarian tone. "If no one had fired at the jaguars last night, they wouldn't have attacked us—and we wouldn't have had the pain of seeing our companion wounded. If you attack these rodents, they'll almost certainly fall on us, along with hidden relatives that will be attracted to the battle."

He had stopped, and he looked at the strange beasts. "They bear a certain odd resemblance to large peccaries. You know what solidarity those animals show—they sacrifice their lives to the very last if anyone touches one of them rather than let the aggressor escape. These appear to be very strong and well-equipped with teeth. Look, they're increasing in number!"

Three or four more rodents had, in fact, joined the troop—and they certainly presented a formidable appearance, with the stature of wild boars, solid jaws and sharp teeth.

"They don't seem to be determined to attack, though," murmured Véraguez.

"They'll almost certainly leave us alone," said Alglave. "We're too astonishing—but that's mutual. Let's go!"

The hesitant rodents let them go without following them. Marsupials made off. Silky wasps brushed their faces. The bats sometimes came close, and were especially inclined to follow them, as if curious.

"What astonishes me most," said Véraguez, "isn't the animals—it's that the giant ferns can sustain themselves!"

"Yes, that's unusual. A naturalist wouldn't admit it, any more than a physicist would admit that light! Can't we suppose that the light—whatever its source may be—was once stronger, and that the vegetation has adapted to its infinitely slow diminution over the course of millennia, utilizing rays that are scarcely utilized at all on the surface? That, combined with the constant temperature, perhaps particular magnetic conditions, and perhaps...but what good are chimerical causes, where the reality is in front of us!"

The noise of the cataract had increased in volume. After an hour the sound had become deafening.

"We're getting closer!"

Suddenly, Whamo and the other Indian, who were marching some way ahead, stopped.

An echo of thunder shook the vaults. Animals were rarer here, especially those of large size. The current was calm and uniform. Its bed broadened out over a declining slope. All the torrential fury was some distance away, at the falls, which were revealed to the ear but not the eye.

Whamo raised his arms and shouted, but his voice was lost in the din like a swarm of insects in the wind.

Véraguez and Alglave hurried forward, and then—motionless, open-mouthed and prey to vertigo—they stared into the gulf.

The immeasurable pit! First, the furious sheets of water, the battle of waters as resplendent as the summits of the Himalayas, resounding like a herd of storms, with the gracefulness of lace and the ponderousness of granite—and the pale rain of spray leaping up above that subterranean Niagara. The legions of the torrent ran over four ledges: four steps of a staircase, each one 20 meters high. And from top to bottom, the stream-ing, the leaping, the ruptures, the rocky islets, the oblique en-counters, and the infinite play of the light, symbolizing the violent force, the irresistible force, the unconscious fury of the element with 1000 nuanced delicacies...

And yet, it was not the cataract that exercised the greatest dominion over the imagination of the voyagers.

More grandiose and even more unimaginable were the surroundings: the pale gulf that was a pale country. Beneath vaults that retained the same height, there was an immense territory down below. Life there appeared to partake of a supe-rabundant splendor: vast sylvan extents, mossy plains, marsu-pials and giant rats, and, most especially, an extraordinary quantity of bat—this time of an absolutely unprecedented size, as powerful as the largest Andean condors. Oh, those giant bats, flying majestically over the cataract, and soaring over the plain! All the grace of birds was in them, with something more—some mysterious intelligence of movement, marking a race of superior mammals.

They're the kings of this creation, Alglave thought. *An attempt by Nature to make—who can tell?—a flying man.*

The strange structural resemblance between bats and humans, which had often struck him, came to mind.

A voice shouted in his ear, however: that of his compa-nion, seemingly intoxicated by the unknown: "Let's go on! Let's go on!"

"Yes, that's it. Let's go on!"

It was not difficult. Beside the cataract there was a per-fectly accessible downward slope, which the troop set about descending.

They had scarcely begun when numerous flocks of vam-pires came toward them and then hovered, seemingly observ-ing them. They continued to move forward, and the animals went with them; above their heads, in front of them and be-hind there was a swarm of wings, a disturbing, curious—possibly hostile—animality.

When they reached the bottom, Alglave and Véraguez stopped.

The bats were still arriving. Soon there were several thousand. Many of them settled in niches, on ferns or on trees. And everywhere, other animals made way for them, with a sort of respect, as for a victorious species.

"What shall we do?" shouted Véraguez.

"Keep going!"

And on they went. For an hour they followed the course of the river without the country varying much, without any animal attempting to bar their way but still followed, albeit to a lesser extent, by the curiosity of the vampires. Their astonishment was silenced; all that remained in them was the desire to go forward, to keep going: the devouring curiosity of scientists.

Eventually, however, Véraguez said: "Fugère's waiting for us."

"Well," Alglave replied, "let's send him a messenger or two, while we have something to eat and then continue on our way. We can go on for another two hours. We won't leave the edge of the river."

"What if the light goes out?"

"We have our lanterns!"

"So be it!"

When the messengers had been sent and the meal taken, they stubbornly resumed their march.

Symptoms of fatigue were becoming manifest among the companions, save for Alglave and the two Indians. Even Véraguez asked to take a short rest.

As they stopped, they noticed for the second or third time, through a mushroom clearing, bats falling upon marsupials or rodents, then remaining attached to the animals' flanks without the latter putting up any resistance.

"Look, Véraguez!" said Alglave. "Doesn't that seem bizarre? These vampires nourish themselves on the blood of quadrupeds, and the latter submit to it meekly."

"Yes," Véraguez replied, in a dull voice. "The slow jaws...that's surprising..."

"Well, I have an idea that these beasts are *domesticated*...I'm increasingly inclined to believe that these immense bats are possessed of superior intelligence, have been able to tame the rest of the fauna, and that they only take the ration of blood that each animal can donate, as we take milk from cows...or as ants take the sweet secretion of domestic mites."

"Certainly!" Véraguez's tone astonished him, as did the attitude of two of the men of the escort, who were huddled on the ground and seemed to be trying to stop themselves going to sleep.

"What's the matter with you?" he shouted.

"I'm sleepy," Véraguez replied, dully.

"Sleepy?"

"Yes." And he curled up like the two men.

Anxiously, Alglave looked around. It seemed to him that the light was getting dimmer—that a mist was descending on the clearings, the lichens and the water. He felt his own eyelids growing heavy.

"What's happening, then? That's strange!" Seeing his friend lying down, he shouted: "Véraguez! Get up, Véraguez!"

Véraguez was asleep. Two of the men were also asleep; the others—even Whamo—were struggling painfully against torpor. Only the Indian they had saved was resisting successfully; he and Alglave exchanged an anxious glance.

"What is it? What is it?" Alglave repeated, with increasing anguish. He was terrified by the notion that the mysterious sickness might be mortal: a subtle poison or an asphyxiating gas. He shook his companion again.

"Véraguez! Be brave, my friend!"

Véraguez remained inert; soon, Whamo and the others were obliged to lie down, succumbing in their turn.

"But this is frightful! Death, perhaps...futile, cowardly death...without having been able to study these mysteries..." For, in the depths of his disturbance, the stubborn curiosity of the scientist still remained, the immense regret for a scientific treasure that would be lost if their expedition perished.

At that moment, he felt someone touch his arm. It was the Indian, who plucked at his sleeve and pointed to a sort of mound. Mechanically, Alglave followed. His anguish sank into torpor; with difficulty, he reached the mound. There, within a minute, he recovered his strength and the lucidity of his gaze and his mind.

"Thank you! Thank you!" he said, shaking the savage's hand.

The latter signaled to him to wait, and, rapidly going down again, he ran toward the group of sleepers. Soon, Alglave saw him return, dragging a body—that of Véraguez—awkwardly. He ran to help him; they succeeded in towing the explorer to the top of the mound. Only then did Alglave reflect on the intelligent significance of the Indian's actions. A cave-dweller, he must have compared what had happened, by analogy, with asphyxiation by carbon dioxide.

He was more intelligent than me!

Successively, taking the rest necessary to dissipate the numbing effect that followed each excursion, Alglave and the Indian towed all their companions to the mound. Strangely and ominously enough, though, although their respiration was normal and their pulse-beats regular, none of the sleepers woke up, in spite of shouting and shaking.

It's not carbon dioxide, then? Alglave thought, despairingly.

Standing on top of the mound, he no longer felt the numbing effect; his companion showed the same endurance. Sadly, he studied the landscape. He observed instinctively that his conjecture regarding the vampires seemed to be correct; everywhere, they were falling upon quadruped animals and sucking their blood, with the tranquility of owners exercising incontestable rights.

But why are the animals resistant to the sleep that vanquished us?

As he asked himself that question, he observed that some animals were, indeed, preparing to rest. Everywhere, rodents and marsupials were lying down on the lichens and mosses. And again, Alglave perceived that *the light was getting dimmer.*

Was darkness falling, then? Was there a correlation between that and the sleep? But that morning, when the boat had been moving through the gloom, they had seen animals fleeing the glare of the searchlight.

This isn't the same region. That was above the cataract—up above!

The light continued to get progressively dimmer. Soon there was nothing but a confused, spectral penumbra in which the vampires were flying. Then, Alglave thought he ought to light one of the battery-powered electric lanterns—but he turned it over and over, pressing the switch, without any result.

"Damn!"

His anxiety increased when he had failed with a second lamp. He tried the others, one after another—in vain.

This is definitely some electrical phenomenon correlated with the extinction of the light—which might itself be electrical in origin.

Desperately, he began to shake his companions again—still in vain, alas, but also without discovering any alarming symptoms in their sleep. The heart, the pulse and the respiration were still normal—and, surprised, his thoughts wandered over irreconcilable hypotheses, for, if he and the Indian remained awake on the mound, why were they not waking up? What peculiarity determined that sleep, once begun, was perpetuated?

The darkness was still increasing. Alglave could only make out the savage standing next to him vaguely. With a slow, sad gesture—a fraternal gesture of farewell—he took the hand of his companion in misfortune, whose language he did not speak, with whom he could not exchange any definite thought. An amicable and resigned smile appeared on the broad face of the cave-dweller: a smile that touched Alglave's heart.

"Adieu! Adieu!" repeated the voyager.

Guttural syllables replied to him—and they stood motionless in the oppressive darkness, punctuated by the distant rumor of the cataract: complete darkness, as opaque as a wall, humid and sinister; the darkness of slow death.

And in that darkness, they sensed the torpor invading them in their turn.

What are these soft exhalations, these fan-beats passing by in darkness, these sighs, these dull, muffled whispers?

Alglave thinks about that, in a confused dream, for the torpor continues to take hold of him, though infinitely slowly, extinguishing everything, including anguish, in some mysteriously voluptuous nirvana.

I'm going to die...to die!

He is astonished not to be more frightened. His hand searches his surroundings; it encounters silky fur and pulls away with a thrill of horror. He deduces that the vampires are falling upon his companions, and that they will soon fall upon him and feed on his blood. He tries to get up; he puts out his arms—but his weakness is extreme, and he falls back, sinking into a profound sleep...not without having felt, on his neck and his breast, the soft, warm weight and the palpitation of a beast that has no difficulty making the king of creation into its prey.

An indeterminate time goes by: hours of darkness. The men on the mound remain motionless, dead or unconscious. And yet, one of them sighs and gets up, with a murmur. After a few minutes, that one stamps his feet, and shakes the others, making hoarse, deep exclamations—but without waking anyone. His footfalls resound on the mound, drawing away rapidly into the frightful darkness, soon confused with the eternal din of the cataract.

More hours in the vast somnolence of the caves. Even the vampires have been asleep for a long time. Death reigns in the immanence. The darkness, it seems, will go on forever...and yet, here comes a slight noise, the sounds of slender feet, slight cries, gnawing and chewing sounds. An observer would deduce the awakening of creatures, the approach of a phenomenon of delight.

This lasts one, two or perhaps three hours.

Finally, a glimmer of light appears, as feeble as a mist at first, then as soft as the Moon behind a triple layer of violet clouds, then brighter and more beautiful in its marvelous indigo shades. It is the daylight of the caverns!

That daylight finds the men on the mound asleep, motionless, perhaps dying. A flock of bats flies over them, but without settling on them.

Suddenly, one of them moves; it is Whamo, who stretches himself and stands up, still very dazed. He looks around, perceives that his brother Indian has disappeared, and then, dully, begins to shake Alglave.

After a brief interval, Alglave stirs and opens his eyes. "Eh? What? Is it over, then?"

He stands up and looks round. He feels weak, but not to the extent of being unable to walk, His eyes follow the flight of the bats with a vague affection.

"They've *used* us, but haven't *abused* us!" These words are confirmed by the successive awakening of his companions. They are weak, almost incapable of walking.

Stupefied, Véraguez asks: "What happened, then?"

His surprise increases in response to Alglave's explanations, along with the joy of still being alive. "We're too weak to get back to the boat...before having eaten," he says, eventually.

They all have little wounds on their necks where the giant vampires have sucked their blood, but they all have to admit the beasts' moderation—and Véraguez, like Alglave, experiences a sort of gratitude.

"We need to eat," one man said. "But we've exhausted our provisions." With a gesture, he makes it understood that he will go and kill some animal or other.

"Let's be very careful!" said Alglave. "I'm quite convinced that we'd pay for that with our lives. Let's march instead. If the light lasts as long as the first time—and I assume that it's periodic—we can get back to the boat without difficulty...for it had already been light for a long time before the cataract forced us to disembark." He addressed himself to Whamo: "Where is the man of your race, then?"

"Gone!" Whamo replied. "He's gone to seek help—I'm sure of it!"

"Me too. Well, let's get going!"

At first, although the little troop was severely debilitated, all went well. Their progress was rather slow, in truth, but they wasted no time. Stimulated by dread, they all gave their maximum effort. At length, however, an extreme lassitude was manifest even among the most vigorous. Most of all, they felt the need to restore their strength, to regain the blood sucked by the vampires.

Alglave and Véraguez opposed all complaints very forcefully, stimulating their men as much by example as by speech. It was, however, necessary for them to call a halt.

"Sir, I beg you!" said one of the hungriest, then. "Let us kill some animal."

Alglave was about to refuse when Véraguez intervened: "Come on, my friend...if not a rodent, at least we can kill a marsupial..."

Confronted by pleading expressions, blanched, emaciated and feverish faces, Alglave ended up giving in. "All right! But I won't take any responsibility..."

Immediately, four men headed for a dense thicket of ferns, carbines at the ready, and set an ambush there. Two anguished minutes went by; then a shot rang out. The echoes resounded in a sinister fashion. Almost at the same time, a rain of stones fell noisily. A cry of pain was heard, and when the dust had cleared, they picked up one of the four men from the ambush; his arm was broken. As for the marsupial he had aimed at, it had not been hit. It was fleeing, along with other animals—not because of the rifle-shot but because of the rain of stones.

"Do you want to shoot again?" Alglave asked his men.

They bowed their heads, humiliated, while Véraguez examined the injured man's arm. After 20 minutes' rest, the march was resumed. The unfortunates dragged themselves along, demoralized, full of horror for the subterranean country, which no longer seemed—even to Alglave, alas!—to be anything but an immeasurable necropolis from which he would never emerge.

A further incident complicated the disaster; the man with the broken arm, who was continually delaying the others, uttered a sigh of distress, hung on to one of his comrades, and fainted. It was necessary to stop again and try to reanimate the poor devil. Another lay down on the ground then, declaring that he would rather die than continue a futile march. Furthermore, on examining the little caravan as a whole, it was evident that they could not go on much longer. As for transporting the invalids, they could not even think of it, given the state of extenuation they were all in.

This is the end! Alglave thought, discouraged. *We've escaped the narcotization only to perish from inanition!*

His head was buzzing, his sight slow and weak; he did not feel much fitter than the others. He imagined capturing some animal without using firearms, but then ejected the idea on observing the uncertainty of his gait and his movements.

Oh well—so be it! The die is cast!

He sat down, dejectedly. Through his enfevered brain passed the vision of a beautiful and grandiose work, a marvelous account of his voyage into *The Wonderful Cave Country*; then he closed his eyes resignedly, and waited...

A shrill cry woke him up and brought him to his feet. He saw Whamo standing up and making signs—and then, in the distance, human silhouettes.

"The man of our tribes!" Whamo said. "He's coming back with help!"

Alglave was soon able clearly to distinguish the Indian he had saved, with three crewmen. Releasing a mighty "Hurrah!" he ran forward. It was salvation; it was life: provisions, cordials, hope!

Five hours later, they all got back to the boat, and the memory of the marvels they had glimpsed dominated that of their mortal anguish.

At the beginning of autumn, the boat ploughed through the immense river again, this time moving downstream. Alglave, Véraguez and Fugère were standing in the prow as dusk fell—the hour of memory. They were chatting about the miraculous expedition they had brought to a successful conclusion, the difficulties they had experienced in learning to explore the subterranean realms, to surmount or avoid the obstacles. Fugère occasionally re-read his notes, the annals of the fantastic voyage. A strong and sweet pride rendered them thoughtful.

Next to them stood the Indians to whom they owed so much precious service, who had become friends, sharing in their good and bad luck alike.

Night fell: a lunar night like the one in which they had encountered the jaguars. And there was still the fecund and monstrous life, the furtive conjunctions of love, carnivorous ambushes, pursuit, terror, the genius of attack and defense in formidable freedom—and, above all, the fundamental need of the weak and the strong alike: hunger, for pasture or for prey.

And the lunar light spread out in the lukewarm ether with a divine beauty, over the free forests and the immense waters.

THE VOYAGE

By what marvel has this delightful region remained un-explored? What mystery has concealed it from the ardent marches of African voyagers? Horrible at the outset, it is be-coming increasingly easy to negotiate as the days go by, al-though the source of its mildness is still just as impenetrable. Its prodigious forests have successively given way to mosses and leprous lichens, its diluvian waters to the taciturnity of peat-bogs, the enchantment of its savannahs to the sinister horror of the Plain of Eternal Desolation.

The animals and plants here are enigmatic; collectively, they have an appearance of youthfulness and obsolescence, of freshness and venerable antiquity. It seems that one is in some other age of the world's history—a strange future is mingled here with the melancholy of memory. Is it not the wilderness Reserve, the Park in which Humankind, disillusioned with so many murders, will come to demand companions of Nature once again?[11]

Those species whose survival is most precarious, the co-lossi which cost life so much labor, drink in immense herds from the deltas of the rivers. This region combines ten climatic regimes: plateau refreshed by breezes, gentle and fecund slopes, warm plains, and immense torrid valleys—into which we rarely descend.

I have tasted divine happiness here—the great dream of free creation. My escort is numerous, armed as well as neces-

---

[11] This reference is to one of the prose poems contained in "La Légende sceptique" (tr. in vol. 1 of this series as "The Skep-tical Legend"), which sets out a prospectus for the future es-tablishment of nature reserves where animals in danger of extinction might be conserved and man's primal relationship with nature partly restored.

sary to face the largest wild animals effectively, and I possess every remedy against reptilian venoms and plant poisons. Several of our men have the delicate senses and long experience of natural wanderers, and an entire population of sagacious animals also accompanies us, not only familiar with the perils of life but hardened to meteorological phenomena, adept at foreseeing changes in the weather, the soil and magnetic conditions. This is what I wanted. I am one of those who believe in an *effective* future collaboration between men and beasts— one of those who believe that animals will lend their exquisite senses in a more subtle manner to masters more inclined to gentleness.

A dog's sense of smell, a falcon's sight, the magnetic sensibility of birds and insects, bring them infinite amounts of information, a vision of the depths of things that purely mineral matter is insufficient to interpret for us. Animals, even the most inferior—formless larvae, motionless mollusks, meager zoophytes—will one day be the great indicators of science, the most penetrating instruments in our laboratories, not at all the pure experimental flesh of today, but voluntary seekers.

From my own viewpoint, my results are already seductive, but I owe them especially to two incomparable assistants, two taciturn peasants who have a prodigious sense of life, an admirably nuanced artistry, who accustom animals to confide themselves entirely to mankind, to understand him. We have brought swallows, wood-pigeons, night-birds, frogs and, of course, monkeys, cats and dogs. Thanks to special care, they support the various climates, and even, when we do not descend into the immense torrid valleys, appear to delight in that extraordinary terrain, drawing new strength therefrom. Are we, the humans, not subject to some enchanting influence, our nerves alert, our hearts relaxed and strong, our faces rejuvenated?

Not, of course, that the voyage has been easy and devoid of perils, any more than the terrain has always been propitious. Sometimes there is an impenetrable forest, sometimes an arid and empty desert, sometimes marshes with approaches full of ambushes. Whether one likes it or not, it is necessary to descend into gigantic valleys, or at least go along their edges. Then, the reptiles become redoubtable; the carnivores prowl around the camp or lie in wait in the jungle; night falls full of anguish, mystery and horror. Doubtless we are marvelously well-protected, and the slightest peril is anticipated by our animals—but what heart can remain tranquil before the grandeur of such dangers, and in the vast unknown of this territory, foreign to Humankind?

One evening, in the red hour when the swollen star trembles somewhat in the crepuscular light, we stopped among rocks. We were very tired. All day we had struggled against the forest, and the plain had finally begun! It extended westwards, immensely verdant, still becoming more open. A river ran through it, often hidden by monstrous vegetation, spreading out into a marshy lake half a mile from our encampment.

To the north, there was a valley at least six leagues around, to judge by its appearance, and to the south, rather high hills, with an implication of plateau on their summits, linked by gently-sloping passes.

The solemnity of the moment was divine: the beauty of space, the magic of the great firmament through which clouds were rolling, and the prodigious life whose ever presence we felt. The endless forest spread out in the pale light, so soft that one forgot the suffering of its traversal; the valley began to resound with loud nocturnal clamors, and the profiles of the hills became indecisive within their celestial confines. I contemplated the noble spectacle for a few minutes, and loved all the more the fabulous expedition that had drawn me away from the known world.

When the camp was set up and the fires built, we ate the evening meal; then the Moon, vast and red, rose in the Orient. The clouds became lower, heaping up in the west. The night was displayed, clear and murmurous, troubling the human heart. I had no desire to go to bed, but rather to walk as far as the river and watch the water running by starlight.

"Charnay," I said to my second-in-command, "I'm going down to the river..." At the same time, I signaled to Malveraz, the older of my two peasants, and Huriel, the gentle colossus who accompanies me everywhere. Two dogs also followed, and an eagle-owl that kept watch on the advancing dusk.

"Shouldn't you take a few more companions?" Charnay asked. "This place makes me anxious."

I placed considerable value on the advice of my second-in-command, endowed as he was by a delicate prescience, so I took two more men, and we went toward the water. The plain was easy to negotiate as far as the borders of the river, where we found pools of water. It was necessary to search further on for a viable promontory.

We walked for about three-quarters of an hour, and were about to turn back when we encountered a sort of natural causeway, abundantly trampled and strewn with large blocks of granite. The dogs threw themselves on to it with the ardor of their race, and Malveraz muttered: "Elephants pass this way. They don't seem to have been here today...so they ought to come down to drink later this evening."

The causeway appeared to come from the valley, whose edges we could see, raised up above the level of the plain.

"Very well," I replied. "As there's nothing in sight, we can follow the causeway, ready to get away in good time."

When I say that nothing was in sight, I am not being strictly accurate. From time to time, some timid animal passed in front of us—a deer, an antelope or a small carnivore—and moving shadows were visible on the plain, while the clamors of conflict rose ever more frequently from the depths of the valley, the darkness and the forest. Our trained dogs did not launch themselves in pursuit, obedient to Malveraz's expressive grunts. The old animal-handler made no reply, and contented himself with following the causeway.

We walked for some time. The causeway stopped; we were moving into difficult territory. Soon we found ourselves on the edge of the river, and I was just about to turn back when Huriel shouted: "A bridge."

To tell the truth, what he called by that name was an erratic series of immense blocks of stone, but very close to one another—so close that one could often pass from one to the next.

"The arches of a bridge, rather," I replied.

Without making any reply, the colossus cut down a young poplar on the river-bank with an axe. "Here's the decking!"

I hesitated for some time before deciding on the adventure, and when I had finally decided, I had a sort of evil presentiment.

We passed over the river. Our dogs, accustomed to leaping over minor obstacles, followed us without difficulty. If necessary, the robust animals could have swum across the river.

At first, we were walking through a sort of meadow, then it became a woodland, but one in which the trees were quite distant from one another. Eventually, a forest extended to our right, while the wooded grassland came to an end, giving way to ground the color of ash. There were occasional pine-trees growing on hillocks, and islets of giant ferns, but little grass, dry, harsh and discolored. A great sadness emanated from it.

"This place is redoubtable…" Huriel began.

I saw concern on Malveraz's face—but an ardent curiosity impelled me to advance, contrary to all prudence.

"There's nothing to fear from the darkness," I said. "The sky's clear. In an hour, the Moon will be marvelously bright, and provided that we return before midnight…"

Darkness had almost fallen. A reddish light trailed over the crowns of the forest and the solitary pines. The landscape became less sinister after we had skirted a marsh where giant frogs were croaking. Grasses reappeared, thicker and greener, on the savannah. Only confused shapes were distinguishable in the faint pale starlight. We walked for another half-hour; then an enormous copper-colored Moon appeared over the treetops of the forest.

"A trick!" said Huriel.

A granite mass loomed up in front of us, in which a kind of giant doorway yawned. At first we thought we were looking into a cave, but we stopped after having taken the first few steps.

"That's odd!" said Malveraz. "I could have sworn that…"

He had set his hand against the rock. Then, a singular vibration became audible, as if a violin-bow were being drawn over the edge of a bronze plate.

"It's a door!" Malveraz finished.

We saw an enormous block of stone turn on its axis, without Malveraz appearing to have done any more than push a light door, and the shadow of a cave appeared.

"How bizarre!" I exclaimed—and I went into the cave. Malveraz followed me in, while Huriel, with one of my men—by the name of Chabe—marched in the direction of the forest. By the light of my little electric torch, we examined the place. It gave the strange impression of having been *constructed*, without our being able to tell whether or not the cavern served as a habitation for some creature.

We had been there for some time when we heard the dogs barking violently.

"Some danger!" Malveraz remarked.

We left the cave. Huriel and Chabe were coming back toward us. Almost simultaneously, there was a strange roar, which had something in it of the voice of the lion, and that of the tiger, the apparition of a monstrous bounding silhouette, and Huriel's and Chabe's rifle-shots. Then there was a terrible scream. The mysterious beast had just fallen on Huriel and carried him off as a lynx carries off a hare.

I ran forward. I caught a glimpse of Huriel's arm, which rose up clutching a knife, and the animal—struck in the heart, as we later discovered—collapsed.

I was continuing to run toward Huriel when Malveraz shouted in a thunderous voice: "Everyone into the cave! Don't lose a second!"

In spite of the excitement of the moment, we obeyed, so habituated were we to putting our trust in Malveraz's instincts and senses. Huriel, Chabe, the two dogs and the eagle owl came in at almost exactly the same time as us.

"Rotate the stone," said Malveraz.

The colossal stone shook with its strange vibration. We found ourselves in pitch darkness, but only for a few seconds—the time it took to light two small battery-operated torches. Then I interrogated Malveraz. "Why did you call out to us?"

He bent down and picked up a large stone. It fitted almost exactly into a gap between the rock and our cyclopean door. Before he had replied, roars burst forth.

While we looked at one another, the old servant said: "It's a herd of wild beasts. I saw them appear at the edge of the forest. You had your backs to them, and the dogs; agitation didn't warn you, to judge by what just happened."

The roars redoubled, sometimes deep and hoarse, sometimes as explosive as fanfares. None of us was in any doubt as to their significance; it was anger—the anger of a race confronted with the cadaver of the tiger-lion felled by our bullets and Huriel's knife. That demonstrated once again the strangeness of the region. Was it not a vestige of very ancient times, when the big cats—the biggest cats of all—had possessed the herd instinct, now extinct in the lions of the Atlas Mountains as well as the tigers of India.

"What are we going to do?" I asked Huriel.

"There's nothing to fear for the moment," the colossus replied. "We can hold council at our ease, like the defenders of a fortress. Any that get this far will surely perish."

"Can't we wipe them out?"

"We'd need a loophole, for opening the door by a crack would lead to an invasion—these giant beasts would enlarge the opening very rapidly..." He interrupted himself. The impact of paws clawing at the entrance was audible. "You see!" Huriel added.

"Yes," I replied. "I can see that it's necessary to leave our fort as it is for the time being. But hazard might perhaps give us an opportunity to do something to help ourselves. Let's search…"

We searched, aided by the dogs and the eagle owl. Outside, the roars became less frequent, but I had a strong feeling that the danger was undiminished. Our minds were full of anxiety and curiosity. The terrible beasts were causing me more interest than annoyance. I felt no anger against them, nor, especially, any inclination to hunt them. I would greatly have preferred not to kill any of them, and to let such admirably vigorous creatures live. Wonderstruck, I remembered the magnificent bound of the tiger-lion that Chabe and Huriel had killed, its great stature and the formidable ease with which it had carried off the giant Huriel.

As I was thinking about these things, Malveraz cried: "There's a fissure in the door itself! But we can only maneuver the rifles up and down; the cleft is too narrow for any sideways movement."

At that moment, Huriel released an exclamation: "We're doomed!"

"What?" I said.

"The cartridges! In the struggle with the lion-tiger, the cartridge-pouch was torn away."

"In that case," I said, "We have exactly ten shots left to fire—and I imagine that there are a good 60 animals out there."

Malveraz, who had climbed on to a block of stone and stuck his eye to the fissure, replied: "There are nearly 100."

We looked at one another silently. It seemed to us that we were in one of those terrible epochs when humans, so small and wretched, wandered over the plains and through the forests and marshes. Were we not at this moment—we, the sons of old Europe—in spite of our weapons, our machines and our intelligence, no different from some poor family of ape-men hiding in their cave on the edge of a lake or a river, while the powerful *Machairodus* with dagger-like claws passed by in the darkness?

Huriel, who was thinking the same thing, exclaimed: "It's a prodigious adventure, though! And if we escape, we won't regret it at all. What a souvenir of the energies of the world! What a communion with the Earth's immense past!"

I hoisted myself up to the slit. Huriel's words reached my ears at the same time as an extraordinary spectacle presented itself to my eyes. There they were, in the westward-slanting light of a huge red Moon: 100 monsters with phosphorescent eyes, and beautiful bodies built for warfare and murder. They could be seen crouching down, standing up in profile, or leaping, and I had a clear consciousness of them, entirely sure that the murderers of their kin were in the cave.

Each of their movements gave evidence of an intelligence much superior to that of our wretched, fallen wild beasts, and a kind of understanding: the ability to act in concert to attain an objective. And their present objective was vengeance. The race did not want one of its individuals to perish in vain. They had decided to wait until the punishment could be carried out.

That certainty caused a long shiver to pass down my spine. What hope could there be of escaping such adversaries? Like the ancient warrior, I saw once again my Argos,[12] the pleasant land left for the wake of wanderlust, and a funereal melancholy penetrated my soul. All the same, I could not succeed in regretting the escapade completely; a certain joy remained; the passionate pleasure of exploration.

Huriel interrupted my reflections. "I'm hungry," he said. "We mustn't forget, because these infernal beasts are besieging us, to keep up our strength."

It was one of our rules, even when we were only leaving the rest of the expedition for a few hours, to take nourishment

---

[12] The reference is to Homer's *Odyssey*, where "Argos" is sometimes used to signify the homeland of all the Greeks, rather than a part of it.

with us. Chabe, Malveraz and Mandar had brought slices of roast meat, cold coffee and biscuits. Huriel had pemmican, and I had a sort of dried mincemeat that was very nutritious. We ate as heartily as if we had been in the shelter of our oaken carts. As usual, Huriel devoured two kilograms of meat and innumerable biscuits. Then he said: "We'll ration ourselves later. If things don't take a turn for the better, Castor and Pollux"—they were our two dogs—"will furnish us with food for a few days, and even drink."

"I'd prefer to ration myself!" I said. "Besides, we still have two days' food. Only drink…"

"There's a little trickle of water running over the rock," said Malveraz. "We won't die of thirst."

That reassured me more than anything else. "There's a strong possibility that the accursed beasts will get discouraged," I said, "or forget why they've assembled here. If we could only warn our companions not to go forward, and to notify the camp well, I'd feel quite tranquil, all things considered."

"Yes, but how can we warn them?" said Huriel.

Malveraz looked up, his face impassive. "I'll take care of that," he said. "The owl will certainly fly back to the expedition. What it has done many times before it can certainly do again—and the darkness won't inconvenience it!"

"We're stupid!" Huriel added. "That should have been our first thought."

"I thought of it," Chabe interjected, "but it's a futile idea. We'd need to be able to get the bird out, and if we so much as open the door by a foot, the watchful beasts will be on us."

There was no need for him to remind us of that. With every passing minute one or other of the lion-tigers hurled itself against the invincible granite. If the ground had not been so hard, we might have been able to dig a hole under the door, but we could not even think of doing so with our knives.

Malveraz, who had listened to us without saying anything, got to his feet. He went to the back of the cave, where we heard him moving around. He came back after a few moments, seemingly tranquil. "It's possible that there's a small exit back there," he said. Above the trickle of water I can make out a glimmer of light in a kind of natural chimney, which might be moonlight. The chimney is slanting. Our owl can easily get through it. If you'd care to write a note, Monsieur Villars…"

As I looked at him, interrogatively, he added: "Oh, I'll make Nox"—that was the owl's name—"understand what we expect from him."

"Let's try it, then!" I exclaimed.

I wrote a short but explicit letter. Malveraz attached it carefully to Nox's neck, then walked toward the trickle of water. We followed him. When we got there, we switched off the torches momentarily and looked up. As our eyes adjusted to the gloom, we distinguished quite clearly a sort of pale gleam.

In the meantime, Malveraz addressed himself to the owl in a singsong voice. The raptor's eyes sparkled in the darkness. We were too well aware of the power our old servant had over animals not to be far closer to faith than doubt.

Finally, there was a slight noise. Nox went into the opening. We heard him rise up gradually. Chabe, whose hearing was extraordinary, cried: "He's found the exit! He's gone!"

"As long as he arrives in time," murmured Huriel.

"He'll follow exactly the same route that we did," said Malveraz. "As that's also the route that anyone coming to our rescue will take, you don't have to worry about the fate of the message."

"By the grace of God!"

For about three hours we continued chatting, making escape plans or imagining the actions of our terrible besiegers. Then Huriel said: "Since our friends haven't arrived, it's more than probable that they've received the message. Let's get some rest, then. That's the first requirement of war. Who'll take the first watch?"

"Me," I said.

My companions lay down, and I remained in the darkness, pensive, all the more emotional and anxious for being alone with my thoughts. I could hear our adversaries growling and roaring. I studied them occasionally through the fissure; I felt a black sensuality in knowing that I was both so near to and so far away from the most frightful peril. Nothing but that granite door, 50 centimeters thick! But that, however, was sufficient to render us as tranquil as if ten leagues separated us from the wild beasts.

In the morning, it seemed that our enemies had not renounced their vengeance in the slightest. In truth, not all of them were outside the cave, any more than they had been during the night; they were taking turns to go hunting—but there were more than 30 of them asleep next to carcasses that had been devoured to a greater or lesser extent.

We spent a terribly monotonous day. Our anguish increased as it wore on. From time to time, we tried to find some secret exit from the cave, but there was evidently only the one through which we had entered.

Evening came, then night—and still the immense pack of lion-tigers lay in wait.

"This is getting serious," Huriel murmured, as we ate supper. "It's necessary not to count overmuch on the discouragement of these abominable beasts. They're damnably vigilant!"

"The life of our prehistoric ancestors could not have been idyllic in the midst of such ancestors," Chabe replied.

"If the Earth nurtured many monsters of that sort," I said in my turn, "I can't even understand how they were able to survive."

The supper was dismal. I lay down soon afterwards, my watch being set for midnight this time. I slept badly, agitated by nightmares.

I saw again the vast park where I had spent the greater part of my childhood. I ran through the woods, through the mysterious half-light, attentive to the petty dramas of life in-sects, fledglings, field-mice, wild rabbits...

All of a sudden, something unnamable, a sort of hairy hand as large as the boughs of an oak swooped down and took hold of me. I was mad with fear for a moment, motionless in that immense warm hand...and then I woke up, covered in sweat.

During one of the awakenings I saw Malveraz up at the slit, his little lantern in his hand, while the tiger-lions were roaring mightily outside.

"What is it?" I said, getting up.

"Something bizarre is happening," said the old peasant. "The beasts have been gripped by a sort of fear, such as I've seen in mountain chamois, ibex and oxen before an ava-lanche."

I climbed up to the opening and looked out. The large beasts were, indeed, in a state of extreme agitation. They were bounding back and forth, seemingly abusing one another, when they suddenly became still—all of them at once—with their heads turned in the same direction.

"Yes, that's very odd," I murmured. "Evidently, some-thing is approaching, of which they're afraid. A fire? A flood?"

"Listen!" said Malveraz.

I have keen ears, but nothing like Malveraz's. I heard nothing.

"It's a herd of living creatures," the peasant continued. At that moment, our dogs started barking. Malveraz added: "They're heavy creatures...a herd of buffalo, perhaps?"

"That wouldn't explain the anxiety of the lion-tigers."

"Who can tell?" said Malveraz, thoughtfully. "Perhaps there are buffaloes in this strange land that can face up to the big cats, by virtue of their number and their courage, and chase them away?"

I began to make out a confused rumor; then there was a vast trampling sound, which made the Earth tremble; and fi-nally, a bizarre vibrant clamor that we both recognized.

"Elephants!" I exclaimed.

The dogs, almost indifferent throughout the day and the night, showed great agitation, while the tiger-lions filled the air with their roaring. Chabe, Huriel and Mandar woke up in succession.

"Perhaps this is the fortunate turn of events that will save us!" Chabe exclaimed.

"Or doom us!" Huriel retorted.

Abruptly, with common accord, the tiger-lions hurled themselves in the direction of the forest. They remained motionless on the edge for a little while, surely hesitating between flight and combat, but their indecision did not last long. In response to further trumpeting, this time repeated by 50 trunks, they slowly withdrew into the woodland.

"The way is clear," said Huriel.

"For five minutes," Malveraz replied.

He was right. Five minutes had not elapsed when we saw 20 elephants appear. They came on solely, swinging their huge trunks and their gleaming tusks. I recognized neither the Asian elephant nor that of Africa. Larger than either of those varieties, they evidently belonged to an extinct type. They were not mammoths either, but they must have been equally formidable, and we understood why the tiger-lions had fled when others passed by after the first group, and then others—perhaps 300 or 400 altogether; our position was too disadvantageous to allow us to count them.

Suddenly, Chabe exclaimed: "Humans!"

A company of strange men had, indeed, appeared, along with women and children, almost mingling with the last ranks of elephants. The males were tall, their skin-color neither black nor white, but a kind of ashy gray. Their jaws were powerful but not as large as those of Hottentots; their heads were large and their hair quite long and stiff, gathered into drumsticks. They evidently lived on good terms with their colossal companions.

"That's a fine herd they have there," Chabe remarked. "There you are—prehistoric man rehabilitated, at a stroke.

With such servants, they could stand up to the carnivorous monsters…"

"Servants!" murmured Huriel. "Really?"

Suddenly, the march of the herd and the humans paused. We soon saw that they were making preparations for a halt. Some were gathering wood and dry grass, with the aid of elephants; others were attaching morsels of flesh to the ends of branches; the women were helping, or taking care of children.

We found the spectacle interesting. It gave us a kind of joy to see the huge fire lit on the plain by our inferior brethren. We did not come out, however, and Malveraz had long since instructed the dogs to be quiet. Although it had changed its nature, the peril was no less. These humans would undoubtedly be no more kindly disposed toward us than the lion-tigers. Who could tell whether they might not be cannibals? And we might as well be prey for wild beasts as for our own kind!

"Perhaps it's no bad thing that they're camping here," said Chabe. "There's a chance that they've chased away our other enemies for a long time, and that once they've gone, we can get away through the marshes."

As he was speaking, a man came closer to the cave. He seemed to hesitate at first, then he made a gesture of surprise, and then he came up and pushed our granite door.

As he did that, I shivered from head to toe. If he had not done it by chance, it implied a knowledge of the cave and its means of closure. The same thought had crossed the minds of my companions. We looked at one another fearfully.

Meanwhile, the man had pushed again, more forcefully.

"He knows!" Huriel whispered.

We could no longer have the slightest doubt about it. When the man called out, others came running. They started talking and gesticulating, and, with a communal effort, they tried to shift the door. Naturally, it resisted—but we felt the stone wedging it shut vibrate.

"Should we put out the light?" Chabe asked.

"Be very careful!" whispered Malveraz. "If they've seen the light, it's putting it out that will awaken all their suspicions!"

The assailants stopped pushing. They deliberated momentarily, and then two of them went toward the elephants. There was some mysterious exchange of signals between the men and the colossal beasts. Then half a dozen of the proboscideans advanced in their turn.

"Look out!" said Chabe. "This will be a more terrible assault."

Without making any response, Malveraz went to place himself against the closing block, in such a way as to seal it more securely—then, so emotional that we could hear our hearts beating, we waited for the attack.

It was not long delayed. It was terrible. The rock trembled. Two of the mighty animals launched themselves forward, standing up on their hind legs and falling back noisily—but the granite resisted heroically. The sealing block jumped in its gap, but it did no give way.

"Bah!" Chabe murmured. "We're safe. The fortress is impregnable."

As he spoke, one of our dogs, terrified, could not help barking. The assault stopped instantly; the men and elephants withdrew.

At first, there was a sort of silence. Then, the savages started talking and gesticulating, but without the slightest attempt to renew their effort. It even seemed, after a little while, that they had become reconciled to it. Huriel remarked on it.

"I'm not tranquil," said Malveraz. "Thirty men have separated, and I fear some kind of trap…"

"Oh, what can we do about it!" I retorted, resignedly. "We're blocked in. We have no resolution to make, for better or worse. This is a matter that fate alone can decide."

"Let the Mysterious Will be done!" said Huriel. "And let's get some rest. It's your turn on sentry duty, Malveraz."

"It's my turn," the old mountain man agreed, calmly.

Deep down, we were more reassured by his guard than any other. We tried to go to sleep, but none of us could do it. I turned over repeatedly, in an anguish that was no less insupportable for having no immediate target. War-weary, I ended up getting to my feet and joining Malveraz. I darted an outward glance over the plain. The elephants were sleeping, and the humans too. Only four or five individuals of both species were on watch by the fire.

"Everything seems peaceful," I said to the mountain man.

"I don't trust it…"

At that moment, one of the elephant sentries raised its head, and then tapped its trunk gently on the head of a man. The other sentries immediately stood up, striking a listening pose that was as obvious in the animals as the men.

"Bizarre!" I murmured. "Those elephants seem to be as intelligent as our relatives…"

"I'm sure that's so," said Malveraz. "In any case, it's not the humans who are guiding or protecting here. Doubtless they render services to this odd community, but they're more like servant-friends than leader-friends. It's the elephants who are in command, Monsieur."

One of our dogs got up, then the other. They sniffed momentarily, attentively, and then both of them launched themselves toward the rear of the cave.

We were preparing to follow them when we saw them standing motionless in the shadows, as if fascinated. At the same moment, Malveraz cried: "To arms!"

Huriel, Chabe and Mandar got to their feet, and all five of us were getting our rifles and revolvers ready when Malveraz said: "They're coming! Men…the ones who separated from the others…"

"Don't fire until I give the order!" I said, vehemently. "Malveraz—call off the dogs!"

An increasing noise was heard, then a sort of collapse. Then, suddenly, a block of stone fell, and silhouettes appeared.

"Light all the torches!" I said.

Our five little lamps came on at the same time—and we saw, ten meters away, some 20 men, staring at us with a mixture of menace, dread and curiosity. A violent combat began in my soul. Should we attack, terrifying these beings by the discharge of our rifles? Should we try to negotiate?

I adopted a middle way: "Fire a shot in the air!" I said to Huriel.

He fired. The detonation echoed beneath the vault of the cave. The savages seemed to be gripped by a sort of superstitious terror.

"Malveraz!" I said, then. "You have the ability to make simple creatures understand. Try to convince these that we're extremely powerful, but that we don't wish them any harm."

Malveraz marched gravely toward the invaders. He smiled at them and addressed slow gestures of peace to them. Suspicious at first, they were gradually reassured. Soon, they manifested a sort of cordiality and drew closer to him. We took advantage of this relaxation to move closer ourselves. Malveraz did not pause in his gesturing—and eventually, they seemed entirely reassured. At that moment, Huriel turned to me in order to say something—but he stopped, his eyes staring, fearful. I followed the direction of his gaze, and I saw that one of the men, who had slipped around to the entrance, had withdrawn the wedge and opened our granite door. I released an anguished exclamation.

"Too late!" said Huriel, philosophically. "There's nothing more to do but accept our fate."

Indeed, the man had uttered a cry. His companions outside came running, accompanied by their monstrous friends.

"Stay calm!" I said.

This recommendation was unnecessary. My companions were awaiting events with the composure of despair. As for Malveraz, he marched toward the newcomers, followed by almost all of those who had initially invaded our cave. There was a moment of horrid uncertainty. One false movement, of anger or fright, among our assailants, and we would be massacred.

Thanks to Malveraz, and our peaceful attitude, the peril of the initial contact had been averted. Our presence excited curiosity and, it seemed, the kind of superstitious dread that Huriel's rifle-shot had caused the first arrivals. Soon, the cave was invaded. We had the means to get out, to mingle with the whole multitude. For a quarter of an hour, the men, women and elephants contented themselves with studying us, as rare and wonderful creatures. Then, a sort of silence fell, and glances were exchanged among the savage warriors.

"This is the critical moment!" said Malveraz. "Everything will be decided."

One of the tallest of the men raised his club; the gesture was echoed by the others. Suddenly, however, an elephant swept the clubs aside with a casual gesture of its trunk, and Malveraz went on: "We're safe. The elephants don't want us dead."

As I looked at him, stupefied, the mountain man added: "The men aren't the masters here—the animals are. I guessed it some time ago. I'm certain of it now. There's certainly a sort of alliance, but in this alliance, the animals take the important decisions. It's the humans, at the end of the day, who have obtained the protection of the elephants against those monstrous beasts to which we nearly fell victim."

As he spoke, I saw the truth: the humans, cunning, weak and perhaps cruel; the great herbivores, full of strength, courage and gentleness. And it became as clear as daylight that it was the animals who had decided, at that moment, to spare our lives. Half a dozen of the old males had shoved our kin aside and were drawing closer to us. They sniffed us for a long time, and stroked us with their agile and delicate trunks. A subtle instinct told them that we posed no danger, and they were able to make their conviction and their decision clear.

When they moved away, the humans came back to us unsuspiciously, and an understanding gradually emerged; we were able to join the extraordinary caravan safely.

We scarcely slept that night, but it was not because of fear. Sitting next to the fire and our savage friends, we could not tire of contemplating the spectacle, even more extraordinary than that of the lion-tigers, of that herd of elephants sleeping peacefully on the plain.

In the distance, periodically, we heard our former enemies roaring. They must have been camped in the nearby forest, keeping watch on our invincible protectors. Their proximity rendered the adventure even more marvelous.

I sat for long hours thinking about our prehistoric ancestors, and that the story of humankind might have been much less precarious and less miserable than we imagine. Who knows whether the domestication of animals might not have been futile malice, a treason for which the human species will some day pay? Who knows whether it might have been more profitable to reach an understanding with our so-called inferior brethren, and whether living on dairy products, fruits, the superfluity of eggs, plants and delicious secretions might not have been sweeter, more beautiful and more harmonious? There is something ugly and squalid about the present human way of life; it would have been fine and noble for us all to contrive together the Great Being that terrestrial animalkind will one day become.

We left in the morning. Our relationship with our fellows, and especially with our large herbivorous friends, had become more intimate. We intended to march eastwards, to the exact point from which we set out; it would take us about an hour to get there. Malveraz had succeeded, with the aid of some exotic miming, in explaining to our allies that we need to rejoin our companions.

"They might have left, though," Huriel said to me, as we were approaching the river.

"I don't think so," I replied. "Malveraz was quite sure of his owl."

We were marching ahead of the herd, with a few men. Our dogs were 20 meters ahead of us. Chabe pointed to them. "They've scented the camp," he said. "We're getting close."

Scarcely had he spoken than we heard a shot; then men emerged from a thicket on the other bank of the river.

"Our friends!" cried Huriel. "The proof is conclusive."

The dogs were already racing forward, barking, and we recognized Charnay. He had raised his telescope. He recognized us, and made expansive gestures of joy—and also of amazement, at the sight of our formidable escort.

Half an hour later, having crossed the river and found ourselves in the midst of our own people, we told the story of our marvelous adventure. It was supported by the most irrefutable proofs: the 400 colossal companions who assembled quietly around our caravan.

We have concluded our voyage through unknown lands, and it has cost us very little difficulty. We have enjoyed the constant protection of our friends with trunks. Thanks to them, we were spared any grave peril. We have brought back the most magnificent account of living creatures and the bonds that unite them. Thanks to us—and a greater good fortune than we deserve—subtle problems have been resolved regarding the manner in which the relationship between primitive humans and animals should have developed. We have been able to establish that, in the majority of cases, the legend ought to be inverted: the first well-constructed animal societies were not human societies.

In the beginning, humans were secondary organisms; for a long time, they were not elevated above the role of subordinate auxiliaries. It would, in fact, have taken very little for terrestrial civilization to have been made by elephants—and it almost certainly would have been, *if they had been able to duplicate their trunks*. The triumph of humankind was only due to our having two hands; they made him a brain that, at the outset, was no more subtle than that of superior animals.

I retain one delightful memory of that voyage. I obtained a better sense of the Life of the Earth—and I understood, with an intensity and melancholy, that humankind had taken a false path; that it was time to revert to a greater fraternity with our inferior brethren; that our existence would be 100 times more beautiful, more noble and more elevated if we could cease our terrible slaughter and make allies of those superior animals that we presently victimize.

THE GREAT ENIGMA

Dawn was near when we finally reached the arid and sinister Blue Hills, made of granite as hard as diamond. Even the lichens had renounced their conquest.

"Here we are at last!" said my companion triumphantly.

I looked at him, full of suspicion. After three days in the desert, that seemed to me a maddening deception.

"Life is beyond them," he affirmed.

"Beyond them!" I said, bitterly. "And how are we to climb them? They're veritable walls."

He nodded his head with an enigmatic smile. "Man of little faith, haven't I told you that there's a path?"

He started walking to the right. After ten minutes, he showed me an irregular fissure that extended into the shadows.

"There!"

He had already gone into the narrow cavern, armed with his electric lantern. Its violet gleam spread out into silent darkness. The path was narrow, we had difficulty walking— and it lasted for a long time! Fatigued by the tedium and the trials of our journey, I had become incredulous.

Finally, the fissure broadened out; we found ourselves in a spacious cave where a new gleam was gradually mingled with our electric beams. That gleam increased; it became sufficient to guide us.

"We're getting close!" Daniel pronounced, almost solemnly.

The light became bright, then softened again; it was that orange light which precedes the Sun's departure. I could not see anything, however. Involuntarily, I cursed. Then we went around an outcrop, and I uttered an exclamation. The Promised Land was there!

How beautiful it was! An immense Sun, a round copper-colored furnace was mirrored in the waters of the lake. Exceedingly tall trees and enormous reeds were swaying gently in the evening breeze—and I knew immediately that I had been initiated into a great mystery. Strange wild pigs with violet tongues and an odd gait were running toward the shore; hippopotamuses were displaying their enormous muzzles at the surface of the lake or climbing up the bank. They revealed golden-colored torsos and convex eyes.

"*Choerotheria*...and *sivalensis*!" said my companion.[13]

There was a rumbling sound in the distance, however. In the vague horses that were moving alongside a willow-grove, I recognized the characteristics of *Hipparion*. Other animals came running, all galloping in the same direction; turning round, I saw an immense herd advancing, irresistibly.

Far away, in the African wilderness, on the banks of the Niger, or near the sacred Ganges, I had seen comparable herds. I was not mistaken in this instance, though. By their double set of tusks, the lower ones almost straight and the upper ones slightly curved back, and an unspecifiable general aspect, and also guided by intuition, the environment and the presence of other animals, I recognized the mighty mastodons.

They came on like living mountains; their feet were columns, their heads blocks of granite. They came slowly and majestically, in their placid strength.

"That's magnificent!" I cried, gripped by a mystical enthusiasm.

"Yes," Daniel agreed, relaxing. "We've crossed 2000 centuries in the depths of time."

I savored the joy of the world's recommencement. The great love of the past that is within the hearts of men was confused here with an inconceivable resurrection.

---

[13] *Choerotherium sansaniense* is a fossil pig from which modern domestic swine might have descended; *sivalensis* is a common second component of Linnean names, but in this instance it obviously refers to the species known in Rosny's day as *Hippopotamus sivalensis* and nowadays as *Hexaprotodon sivalensis*.

A new episode caused me to shiver. Two creatures had just appeared: two *upright* creatures, palpitating with youth. They were playing. Long dark hair was scattered over their shoulders; their limbs and torsos were covered with brown silky fur, and if their jaws seemed a trifle thick, their exceedingly large, soft and luminous eyes were as beautiful as the eyes of the most beautiful woman.

I contemplated them with a sort of dread, and murmured: "Daniel, are they…?"

"They're children," he affirmed. "*Human children*…exactly like the children of our ancestors of the Tertiary Ages, contemporaries of those mastodons that are drinking from the lake. And you can see how charming they are!"

A roaring sound made us raise our heads. A predatory beast had arrived: a thickset animal with saber-like teeth and an orange hide spotted with mauve patches. It bounded forward. The "human children" stood still, magnetized and paralyzed. Another few bounds and the beast would reach them.

With the same gesture, Daniel and I raised our rifles to our shoulders; a double gunshot resounded over the lacustrian waters and made the mastodons raise their heads. Struck in the head and the gap between its shoulder-blade and collar-bone, the beast spun around.

Fearful that, in its death-throes, it might succeed in avenging its death on the children, we fired again. Then, running forward, I plunged my knife into the beast's side. It released a raucous sigh and collapsed on to the ground. Then I turned toward the "human children" and spoke to them, smiling.

It is the privilege of young creatures to pass without transition from fear to delight. They were laughing, full of boundless confidence, as if they had always known us. The children were already beside me, studying me curiously. I took the younger one in my arms; he allowed me to do so, showing his sparkling teeth in the ruddy light. The Sun set and, simultaneously, an immense Moon rose in the east. The mastodons had ceased drinking; they set off again, and the Earth trembled.

Then a voice was raised, deep at first and then shrill. We turned round. It was the upright animal again, but adult: a fawn-colored human with hair like a mane, his face dull but illuminated and humanized by the same eyes as the children. In his hand he held a heavy staff—or, rather, a pike. Shortly afterwards, a second creature arrived, not so tall and rather thin, carrying an infant on her shoulder.

"Our ancestors!" said Daniel, solemnly.

Perhaps they had been frightened at first, but on seeing that their children were safe, they were reassured and broke into laughter, full of confidence.

How can I depict the religious poetry of that scene? It awoke all the profound dreams of adolescence, all the aspirations that were stirring in my soul, beneath the roots of our native forests, satisfying the fervent need I had always had to go back in time, to relive a little of that primitive existence of which we retain a passionate memory in the depths of our instinct.

Night fell after a brief twilight; the Cross of Cygnus shone in the background of the prehistoric landscape, while a silvery and nacreous Moon moved slowly amid the stars and traced a broad radiant causeway over the lake.

We had lit our nocturnal fire; together, we ate the dried meat that we had brought with us. Our guests were as tranquil as if they had lived with us for a long time. They were innocent beings, even though the man had the strength of the great anthropoid apes and had the stature to measure himself against a *Machairodus*.

I thought at first that they had no language. I was mistaken. Speech had already elevated them above other living creatures. They exchanged signs and a few interjections, adapted to the simplicity of their actions and impressions.

In the beautiful night, in which the ruddy light of the fire mingled with the silvery light of the Moon, they were intensely joyful, like children, full of that delightful confidence that

149

makes it easy to forget the future. I too was full of a supreme bliss. I had the sensation of having been rejuvenated in an inconceivable manner, for myself and for all my ancestors; I reunited the present and the entire past in my bosom.

I remember that one of the children went to sleep in my arms; the slight sound of his breath mingled with the enchanted voice of the breeze and the faint rustle of a distant spring. Wild beasts passed by in the darkness; nocturnal birds were flying in the treetops; the intoxicating odor of the vegetation reached us in gusts—and I held that child against my breast with an infinite tenderness...

Such was the most beautiful and exciting adventure of my life—and the one I most regret. I wanted to relive it. I went back to the Blue Hills, and found the cavern again—but the prehistoric land was no longer there! It had only required one quake, one feeble quiver of the terrestrial surface to swallow up the remains of a world more than 200,000 years old!

THE TREASURE IN THE SNOW

I.

"That's erroneous!" retorted my host. "The last mammoth was not contemporary with the one whose remains were discovered in the Siberian ice and which lived about 10,000 years ago. The last mammoth died on May 19, 1899, precisely. I speak with certainty because I saw it die—and I owe my fortune to it!"

My host displayed a peremptory gravity; I did not doubt his good faith at all.

"Moreover, it was not the only animal of primitive times that survived into our own time, since I also encountered, in one of my voyages, the lion-tiger, and a sort of primitive man. The reasons I had for keeping quiet will be set out in my book on *The Double Origin of Man*. I'm talking about it to you today under the influence of an instinctive sympathy, and also because it's getting late."

At the time, I was wandering around miserably in the polar regions, at the mercy of polar bears, cold and collapses. My companions had perished. I had nothing left but a cracked sled, two dogs, a few furs and a supply of pemmican. My exhaustion was extreme; I expected to quit the world within 40 hours. I kept going in a southerly direction, though; my last chance was an encounter with Eskimos.

The Sun was beginning to retrace its steps when one of the dogs lay down in the snow, uttered a few whimpers and then a long gurgle, and died. The other dog continued to drag me through the terrific wilderness. I was in a mixed mental state that was neither entirely wakefulness nor entirely sleep, when I saw three yellow-tinted shapes emerge on the horizon. The dog uttered a howl of fright, and I, woken up with a start, took the rifle from beneath the blankets in which it was wrapped.

We fled for a good quarter of an hour. The yellow-tinted brutes, which would have seemed white against a brown or green background, hastened in pursuit with a sort of guileful stubbornness. They were bears of the most powerful stature, a male and two females; the male would have slaughtered a lion. Terror doubled the energy of my poor dog, but even so, we were losing several meters of ground per minute.

When the brutes were 100 meters from the sled, I put my rifle to my shoulder and fired two shots—in vain. Fatigue had eroded my skill. The only result I obtained was a slight deceleration of the pursuit. Then the damned beasts began to eat into our lead again. With difficulty, I reloaded my weapon and fired again, with no better luck. The excitement that had sustained the dog faded away. It was losing speed by the minute; soon, it began to stagger. I took the only possible course; I got off the sled and started fleeing on my own. I had not gone 200 meters when I heard the agonized cries of my pitiful companion.

How long did I keep going? Perhaps an hour, perhaps two. At any rate, the moment came when, on turning round, I saw that the white brutes had resumed the hunt, and were following me at a distance of about 1000 meters. I should have shivered in horror, but fatigue, disgust and the habit of expecting death allowed me to envisage the situation in a phlegmatic sort of way. I was fleeing out of duty, to such a degree that preoccupation with the peril didn't prevent me from forming a vague hypothesis about the bizarre locale through which I was moving. It seemed to me to be the result of an earthquake, but that wasn't what surprised me most, for at intervals I perceived the covered debris of grass and tree-stumps.

Impossible, I thought, *that all this can be native* here. *One way or another, that vegetation has come from a lower latitude…*

While I was indulging in these reflections, I found myself confronted by an immense wall of ice.

Conclusively cooked! I said to myself.

Worn out with fatigue, I was about to make a gift of my carcass to my pursuers when I saw a deep crevasse that formed a corridor. The terrain was slippery and full of holes; nevertheless, as the bears had hesitated to follow me, I immediately gained a fairly good lead. My luck didn't hold for very long. In a few minutes, the carnivores were on my heels again. Every time I looked back, I could see their pale silhouettes more clearly, in spite of the semi-darkness of the place.

Meanwhile, there was an increasing glimmer of light at the end of the corridor; it hypnotized me and gave me a measure of hope. Then an exit appeared, toward which I limped as fast as I could go. The breath of the bears was now very close. When I was a couple of strides from the exit, a claw grazed my coat, and I had resigned myself to being devoured more-or-less alive when a strange and strident noise became audible and I caught a glimpse of a colossal form, which was rendered even more mysterious by a hairy trunk and two curved tusks.

The bears leapt backwards, growling. The fantastic beast advanced its granite head, shook its hairy trunk, and trumpeted stridently—a sound as intolerable as that of 100 saws cutting through stone.

Terrified, the white brutes fled.

As for me, I stood there motionless, exhausted, stunned and considerably perplexed. What should I do? In the direction the bears had taken there was no other possible outcome than imminent death. In the direction of the Other, there was a grim enigma. With a single blow of its trunk, it could knock me down; by pressing down with its foot it could reduce me to shreds. I didn't hesitate for more than three or four minutes; my means, if I might put it thus, didn't permit me to! Risking everything, I headed slowly for the exit.

The giant beast placidly stood aside; by that gesture alone, I judged that it was granting me mercy.

We stood facing one another, perhaps equally astonished. It reminded me of the description one of our contemporaries has made of an ancestral mammoth: "Its body was a hillock and its feet trees; it displayed tusks ten meters long, capable of transpiercing oak-trees; its trunk resembled a black python, its head a rock; it moved within a hide as thick as the bark of old elm-trees."

The more I studied it, the more sure I was that I wasn't in any danger. Quite the reverse—it reassured me with its tranquil and positively benevolent gaze. And when after having stared for a while, it moved off, I followed it, carried away by an invincible instinct.

As I went, I was overtaken by another surprise. The locale that extended in front of us was no longer a field of ice, frost or snow. Fantastically green, it displayed itself, all the way to the horizon, as a savannah scattered with trees. Instead of the intolerable temperature of the polar plains I savored the warmth of the month of May in my beautiful native region of Touraine.

A mystical confidence overwhelmed me, to the very depths of my inner being. My fatigue disappeared, as if some hand had wiped it away. I opened the little bag in which I was carrying my pemmican and, having eaten a few mouthfuls, felt renewal infiltrating my feverish veins.

The mammoth had stopped. It was grazing the long grass, tearing up young plants; I felt that an obscure, innocent and profound communion was being established between us.

II.

I remained sitting down for a good hour, plunged into a dream and savoring the warmth, so gentle after the glacial trials that I had just undergone. Besides, I was worn out by fatigue; I could literally no longer feel my limbs, and if I didn't fall sleep, it was because a fever of anxiety still persisted deep within me. All around the strange place in which I had found refuge, the polar desert extended—a desert that had become as immense for me as for our humblest ancestors.

White humankind, for whom the planet has become so small and whose ferocious power has subjugated almost all of three continents, became a distant entity, which I could only rejoin by a miracle. In the region I had reached, undoubtedly, not only had no white man ever set foot, but no Eskimo either. Thus, I was implacably alone, having for my sole resources a revolver, a rifle, a few cartridges, a sturdy knife, a chronometer and a marine telescope. It's impossible for you to imagine my state of mind, unless you've been in an analogous situation; it resembled a kind of death...something like the misery of the last man, at the end of time.

I had not lost sight of my mammoth. It continued to graze the grass and devour the shoots; it was gradually drawing away and seemed to have forgotten me. Because it had unwittingly saved my life, I instinctively considered it as a companion and protector. From its own viewpoint, though, I was only a scarcely redoubtable animal, with which it was no more concerned than any other creature that did not threaten its security or compete with it for food. When it was 300 or 400 meters away, I did not stay there any longer. It seemed to me that the perils I had just escaped were about to be reborn, and I stood up, painfully, my joints cracking, in order to go after it.

Birds were moving through the grass, while others were chirping in the boughs of an ash-tree, and I could see a herd of hinds in the distance. Then a boundless astonishment filled my entire being. What was this extraordinary territory into which chance had led me? How had it maintained its individuality in the bosom of the Arctic wilderness? How, above all, had it been maintained for thousands of years—for the mammoth's presence could only be explained by the long persistence of its ancestral climate. Undoubtedly, that climate had passed through fluctuations, through colder periods and perhaps warmer ones too—if only because of the precession of the equinoxes—but it could never have been rigorously polar, for, although the mammoth had been adapted to resist harsh winters, it must be reckoned highly improbable that it had adapted to the same extent as polar bears. Most importantly, where could it have found its nourishment?

Besides, the herd of hinds that I perceived on the horizon amply confirmed the relative, but persistent, mildness of the climate.

"So," I murmured, as I dragged myself away in order to catch up with the mammoth, "for between 7000 and 10,000 years there has been a fabulous place in which a part of prehistoric life has persisted..."

Even so, the only certain vestige was the mammoth, for the hinds belonged to the same species as our ordinary deer— the red deer, which had also lived alongside the humans of the Magdalenian and Lacustrian eras.

As I reasoned thus, the stag—a fine ten-pointer— appeared around the side of a small hill, and I observed that it was not appreciably different from the deer of our forests. Then the herd moved off at top speed, and the mammoth, ceasing to graze momentarily, raised its trunk. I had the sensation of a *presence*; I moved closer to the colossus as quickly as I could—but everything became calm once again.

I lay down in the grass again. Two or three times I saw hares go by—the hares of my native land. I became drowsy. I had the impression that dusk had arrived—an absurd impression, since I was not unaware of the fact that the daylight would last for another three months.

Suddenly, I started. Some way off, between a small hill and the smaller one around which the stag had come, a slim vertical shape had just passed, as to the nature of which I could not be mistaken. It was a man or a woman.

My heart was beating frantically. The presence of my own kind might be the most precious of good things, but there was also a chance that it might be the worst possibility of all. I inspected the surroundings fearfully. Everything seemed peaceful, and the mammoth was grazing imperturbably. Perhaps, after all, I had been the victim of a hallucination, due to fatigue and drowsiness.

Time went by. The mammoth started to move away again, and I made the decision to stay with it. It was going in the direction of the hillock; I overtook it, climbed the slope and found myself on a small stony platform, which made a fairly comfortable observatory. From there, I scrutinized the landscape minutely with the aid of my telescope, and observed that it was surrounded by a chain of high hills, save for the direction from which I had come. It could not be very vast, not in excess of fifteen million hectares.

For some time my vigilance was extreme. Little by little, it eased. Fatigue was numbing my senses and my brain. I arrived at the vegetative state in which the worst dangers come to seem negligible. After a brief struggle, I suddenly lost consciousness of things, as if I had fainted.

When I woke up, the Sun was higher over the horizon; I must have been asleep for about four hours. The mammoth had disappeared. I decided to go in search of it, and I was getting ready to get down from the hillock when I shuddered; some distance away, a silhouette had just reared up behind a bush. This time, there could be no doubt about it; it was definitely a human being!

A head was sticking out—a gray head, whose features I could scarcely make out, but which belonged, incontestably, to an old man. He was not hiding—or, rather, he was no longer hiding—but staring at me fixedly. The point of a weapon was visible level with his jaw.

I adjusted my marine telescope and examined the individual. His appearance was perfectly original. He bore no resemblance to the Eskimos and was different from all of the human races that I had encountered in the course of my travels. The type he resembled most closely was the pure Basque type—except that his jaw was squarer and his lips thicker. As for his skin color, it was indefinable: a sort of pale violet, which deepened in his cheeks and became almost blue at the

157

temples. His eyes, between their slack lids, retained a great vivacity. What I could see of his upper body was suggestive of a certain vigor.

Thanks to my telescope, I did not take long to make out a second human creature huddled behind a block of stone, who was imperfectly hidden—and then a third, further away than the other two, lying in the long grass, effectively enough for me to be unable to detect any structural details. I was surrounded; I naturally supposed that other watchers must be distributed at a distance; even so, in spite of an attentive investigation, I made no further discoveries.

What should I do? In theory, I could have shot the indigenes, for I was a good marksman—but what then? Others might come who would want to avenge their kin and would be able to vanquish me by cunning or by force. What if I were to succeed in forging an alliance? Nine times out of ten—as I am not the only person to have remarked—one can reach an understanding with savages; the brutality almost always comes from the side of the white man.

I decided to make amicable gestures. The old man continued watching me with those round eyes which, even in certain monkeys, express stupor. Successively, I sketched gestures borrowed from the aborigines of the Brazilian jungle, the Australian desert and the forests of Borneo. It was the last that succeeded. The old man replied to them with vaguely analogous gestures.

After a further inspection of the surroundings, deciding to risk everything, I descended from the hillock and advanced toward the bush.

III.

The old man hesitated until I had crossed half the distance that separated us; then he came to meet me. There was scarcely any surprise in the configuration of his features, which expressed the sentiments of peacefulness and hesitation.

When we were a few paces from one another, he proffered a few incomprehensible syllables and uttered a cry for help. Then, looking back, I saw the other two individuals coming forward and I recognized, with a certain satisfaction, that they were women.

One of them looked old, her face dry and sinewy, furrowed with horizontal wrinkles; she must have been approximately 20 or 25 years younger than the old man. She had slate-colored eyes, and the violet-tinted skin that must have been characteristic of the race.

The other, scarcely emerged from childhood, had a bizarre charm, infinitely more exotic than it is possible to imagine. The violet tint of her skin was fainter, more delicately nuanced; her eyes were wide open, full of a fire that I only saw in her, and a youth that was simultaneously a matter of her own age and that of her race. Black hair ran down over her shoulders, in a manner that was rather seductive; her mouth was wide, with a rich scarlet tint; her teeth were sparkling, formed like little seashells. A photograph would have made her slightly coarse and scarcely harmonious features stand out, but those primitive imperfections were attenuated by a youthful energy and plenitude of life that I can't pin down, and which made her graceful.

All four of us stood there, looking at one another, for some time. Nothing could have been more appropriate to dispel mistrust—even the wildest beasts are reassured by immobility; in the forest or on the steppe, it's rare that an attack occurs when it has been sufficiently deferred at the first encounter. In any case, I did not believe that the old man or his companions would have had any other intention than to defend themselves. More instinctive than me, they were more rapidly reassured than I was, and the man informed me of his state of mind by means of a silent chuckle, in which I thought I could detect joy.

He started uttering syllables again, which he accompanied with an agile mime. The syllables disconcerted me. They were grimly guttural, bristling with aspirates; they seemed to come from even lower down than the larynx. So far as I knew, no language included their like. Their rhythm caused them to resemble a primitive chant. As for the gestures, they undoubtedly expressed benevolence—and, at intervals, pointed westwards.

I replied as best I could. Like all white men, especially those of my own race, I was no great scholar of gesticulatory science and I had little natural talent for its practice.

While indulging in this palaver, I studied the accoutrements and weapons of my aborigines. Their upper bodies were covered by a sort of fur tunic with very short sleeves, made of a light summer fur. The garment hung down to mid-thigh. Their feet were bare. Their hair grew at hazard, although vague attempts at combing seemed to have been made. Their necks were ornamented by necklaces of teeth and small green, red and yellow stones; they wore bracelets on all four limbs.

As for weapons, I had recognized them as soon as I saw them; they were as characteristic of their genre as the mammoth. Firstly, there were flat harpoons made from deer antlers, with two rows of barbs, similar in all respects to those of the era separating the Paleolithic from the Neolithic, otherwise known as the Tourassian epoch.[14] In addition, the old man carried a double-edged throwing-spear and a staff of authority on which a carved image of a mammoth was visible. All three

---

[14] What Gabriel de Mortillet—the anthropologist from whom Rosny derived most of the terminology found in his prehistoric romances (see the introduction to vol. 4)—called the Tourassian epoch, after remains found in a cave called La Tourasse in the Haut Garonne, corresponds to the Azilian period of other classifications; as the text indicates, it was supposedly a transitional period between two major elements of his classification.

had clubs ornamented with designs surprisingly reminiscent of the designs that are found in Magdalenian strata.

If an archeologist were to discover such weapons in a cave, no doubt would seem possible to him: he would declare that he was confronted with remains of the Tourassian epoch. Was it necessary to conclude that my indigenes were entitled, in the same way as the mammoth, to be considered as prehistoric creatures? *A priori*, yes. But they might also be human beings of another time, trapped, by virtue of unknown circumstances, in a territory where a few vestiges of primitive times persisted. Even so, their strange characteristics, their language and their armaments inclined me to admit the former hypothesis.

It soon became evident that they wanted to take me westwards, I gave way to the old man's wishes with a good grace, and we continued miming as we went.

During the march, a kind of familiarity developed in my companions. They touched me occasionally, with a naïve curiosity, sometimes on the arm, sometimes the shoulders, and also the beard; the youngest one then emitted a fearful and puerile little burst of laughter. They also felt my rifle and the sheath of my marine telescope, but more respectfully than my person. They certainly thought me inoffensive, at least so far as they were concerned.

We arrived at a rock-face in which a large cave opened. The old man started talking and gesticulating again; I was able to understand that he wanted me to wait, and I leaned against an outcrop while my hosts disappeared into the semi-darkness. It was not long before they reappeared, laden with dry wood and strips of meat. The old man and the adolescent girl built a fire. The old woman rubbed a flint against another piece of stone, probably marcasite.[15]

---

[15] Marcasite is a kind of iron sulphide, also known as "white pyrites," although the name is also employed more loosely to refer to any kind of pyrites employed as a gemstone.

A few moments later, the fire was well alight on the threshold of the cave—a fire that I contemplated with a pleasure increased by the aroma of roasting flesh; for three days I had had nothing but pemmican to eat. When the meal was ready, it was served on a flat stone, and I was invited to take part in it. It was one of the best meals of my life, and I speak as a man for whom the culinary art is no mere bagatelle. We washed down the roast with water that the young woman brought from a kind of cistern, and then we sat still, looking at one another. The two women were frankly cheerful; the old man manifested a placidity so absolute that he soon closed his eyes and dozed off.

As for me, I was strangely happy. The good meal had given me that corporeal security that no moral comfort can replace. The presence of my own kind dispelled the odious impression of solitude that had formerly weighed upon me like the walls of a sepulcher. Even the sensation of being in a quasi-fantastic environment did not displease me at all; it adapted itself to the invincible spirit of adventure that had orientated my existence. Even so, a certain anxiety was reborn. There were doubtless other humans in the vicinity; would they be as benevolent as the old man and his companions? Might they not be prowling slyly around me at this very moment, ready to kill me?

The two women had drawn closer together. The old one tried to make herself understood, gesticulating frenetically; the young one watched me with her fiery eyes, and I surprised myself by wishing that there might be no other male than the old one in our domain…

The essential components of the world are here! I said to myself. *To populate the planet, one man and one woman are sufficient…*

That idea pleased me, although, in sum, it did not appear to correspond to any reality.

Suddenly, the old woman uttered a faint cry, and the old man woke up. While cocking an ear, he looked around. Heavy footfalls were shaking the ground.

IV.

The approaching footfalls grew louder; rude tusks emerged from the eastern extremity of the rock-face, followed by a trunk, a head like a block of stone and an enormous clay-colored body. It was a mammoth, but not the one I had seen earlier: a ruinous mammoth, balding and wrinkled, with gray hair and a white mane; a mammoth 200 or 300 years old, progressing heavily, its eye vitreous and its limbs stiff.

At the sight of it, the man and the two women crouched down, extending their arms in a manner that did not reveal any great emotion—neither joyful nor fearful—and which seemed to me to be ritual. I thought about totemism. By virtue of having existed long before these aged humans, the mammoth probably represented the supreme totem.

It is good to imitate one's hosts; I copied my companions' gestures.

More footfalls became audible; I was not surprised to see a second mammoth appear, this time similar to the one I had seen earlier—and which, I subsequently learned, was the same one. The ritual gestures were repeated, more sketchily. While I was meditating on these circumstances, the two women got up with a sprightly vivacity. The younger one ran toward the place from which the mammoths had emerged.

It was not long before lighter footsteps became perceptible. A human form was outlined at the angle of the rock, quickly followed by two others: a man, a woman and a child. The man and the woman considered me with indescribable amazement, mingled with menace. The male detached a harpoon and sketched an aggressive gesture. A few words from the old man stopped him; his astonishment became manifestly peaceful. He was a coarse individual, with a hatchet-face, bold eyes and a heavy jaw. His limbs and their tendons testified to the strength and flexibility of anthropoid apes, with a rhythmic quality that those forest-dwellers lack. The woman was better-looking; she displayed a proud torso with no excess weight, agile limbs and the same black fiery eyes as the girl. As for her face, you would have found it neither disagreeable nor seductive.

Like my first companions, the newcomers were of a race considerably superior to our black races; for my part, I preferred them to redskins and yellow people. The child, who turned out to be a little girl, seemed to be about five years old; her complexion was a violet so clear that it seemed almost white at a distance.

I did not know whether to be glad or sorry at the arrival of these individuals. The man gave rise to equivocal impressions within me; he disturbed the dream that I had sketched out. I saw in him a sort of rival and awkward sensations were stirring in the depths of my unconscious.

Having drawn closer, however, the newcomers were examining me, each in a different manner: the man impassively, the woman with a certain interest, sometimes tinged with unease and sometimes with a fugitive pleasure.

There was a conversation. The old man and the old woman spoke in turns; they were, I suppose, telling the story of our encounter.

The Sun reached the low point of its course; the time for sleep had come. The old man went into the cave, signaling to me to follow him. As I went forward, a phenomenon became manifest that was as strange as anything I had seen thus far: the cave was luminous. I had not noticed that from outside, having taken the light for a reflection; it was as bright as moonlight in a clear tropical sky.

Dry grass had been spread around in the depths of the cave. We installed ourselves there, each of us at our convenience, while the mammoths lay down, one next to the western wall and the other next to the eastern wall.

I didn't go to sleep straight away. I was nervous. The phosphorescence, these fabulous companions, my solitude, so many enigmas—everything excited me. My life hung on a caprice: a blow to the head from a club, or a thrust of a harpoon in the heart—I would scarcely have time to perceive that I was being slain. The excess of my weakness was precisely what tranquilized me, eventually. Anticipation became so vain that it was childish. I let myself go, and fell into a sleep as profound as death.

It would be pointless to recount the minuscule adventures of the days that followed. I became accustomed to my hosts in less than a week, and I learned that there were no other humans in the territory. Thanks to the women, whose curiosity was less torpid than that of the men, I learned to speak the unknown language. I had no lack of leisure time; they lived without great effort by hunting and gathering root-vegetables, wild fruits, mushrooms and edible plants. Only the terrible guttural pronunciation cost me considerable trouble; the rest went smoothly; my friends' language presented few refinements. Because her diction was clearer and her zeal more lively, the young woman played a preponderant role. The adolescent girl deferred quite naturally to her companion.

Fearing that the man might become jealous, I tried at first to have recourse to the old man and the old woman, but I soon perceived that I was under a misapprehension. The young male wandered around, hunting, carving flints or antlers, occupying himself with some engraving or design, endowed with the naïve but sure talent of our Magdalenian ancestors. I became convinced that he did not avail himself of his companion and did not covet the young girl. I thought at first that it might be some physical injury, but then I concluded—and was not mistaken—that the sacred instinct did not torment him outside certain seasons. The fact is that he only became amorous in the month of September. I assume, however, that an occasional awakening might have been provoked by a strange female.

These mores found their correspondence in the women. They too, as I was to learn, only became emotional at times prescribed by millenary instincts, but could be abnormally animated by courtesy of an unexpected circumstance.

I did not know any of this at first, and I maintained a reserve that was not without its merit. My mores, alas, had the irregularity—or, if you prefer, the excessive regularity—of men of our era; they did not conform to any seasonal regularity. I am, however, the kind of man who would never betray a friend or a host. The singular individuals who had welcomed me into their company and were sharing their nourishment with me merited my respect. Without their possessing our sentiments in their entirety, I credited those sentiments to them in a certain measure; thus, I assumed that they would not grant the young girl to a stranger and I thought that the male possessed the young woman. I acted in consequence, in spite of the temptations to which the most virtuous among us are subject.

The longer I lived with the young women, the more attractive I found them. The relative coarseness of their features vanished before the extraordinary youthfulness that radiated from them. Any return to Europe seemed to me to be chimerical. That life had an indescribable, and in some respects prodigious, charm. I felt rejuvenated, in myself and in my species. Given all that, it was impossible that my female companions should not become very desirable. How could I have escaped the most natural seductions?

They increased, and took on an intoxicating, sometimes intolerable, acuity. I often found myself alone with one or other of them, especially the young woman. She followed me around; more curious than the others, she was passionately interested in the things that I could tell her, however rudimentary. When we were tired we sat down side by side. She had a tendency to petting, like an animal, which my relative gentleness encouraged and developed. She leaned against me, her face brushed mine; she bit the nape of my neck or my ear, and sometimes I could not help putting my arm around her waist, which seemed to astonish her.

One day, when we were resting in that fashion in the shade of a bush, I embraced my companion more passionately, while interrogating her about the caves to which my hosts retired during the winter. Her fiery eyes misted over, her hair flowed over my breast, and her hips had that rhythmic movement which is so dangerous to watch. I felt for the first time that she shared my disturbance...and I was invincibly drawn to lean over her red lips, when a shadow extended over the grass.

Awah, the male, had arrived. Leaning on his heavy ashwood club, he seemed enigmatic and formidable.

V.

Instinctively, I had cocked my revolver, but I disarmed it immediately. I did not dispute the rights of my hosts, much less those of Awah over the women, and I admitted my culpability. I replaced my weapon in my belt, and awaited events with a fatalism that was a consequence of the singularity of the circumstances.

Awah, meanwhile, remained silent and continued to observe us. There was nothing astonishing in that; the young man was exceedingly taciturn. When he was not hunting or sleeping he occupied himself in carving, sculpting, engraving or fabricating weapons.

After a long moment I said: "Is Awah discontented?"[16]

He was in no hurry to reply, and I continued: "Does Awah not want me to be alone with Touanhô?"

That question doubtless seemed bizarre to him, for his brow furrowed deeply, as if he were carrying out some difficult task. "Why should the ally not be alone with Touanhô?"

---

[16] Rosny's narrator inserts a footnote here: "All the following dialogues are imperfect translations, my hosts' language containing neither verbs nor adjectives; the verbs are represented by gestures, the adjectives by the repetition or special pronunciation of nouns. In the same way, the proper nouns only distantly resemble the correct pronunciation of the names."

he asked, in his hollow voice. "The ally should not go into the Caves of the Dead before having given blood. Then the ally will be a Son of the Mammoth."

I remained silent in my turn, trying to understand. Memories of my vagabond life enlightened me, and I replied: "The ally will give blood."

Without making any reply, Awah took out a flint knife hidden in the folds of his fur garment and headed toward us. His face was impassive but grim. I wondered whether he might have employed a savage ruse, and whether he might be going to kill me slyly. My fatalism had not abandoned me. I stood up and I let Awah raise my arm and plunge the dagger into my shoulder. It was neat and precise; a trickle of blood spurted out. Awah started sucking the wound; then he invited Touanhô to do likewise, which she did without repugnance, and even with a kind of sensuality.

"The ally is no longer an ally," the young man said, covering the wound with leaves. "He is a Son of the Mammoth, like Awah and Touanhô! He may go into the caves."

He did not waste time in talk or in needless actions. Having replaced his dagger in his bosom, he drew away with a gait as flexible as that of a leopard in the forest.

That scene, which had left me almost unmoved, was followed by a sort of vertigo, due to loss of blood. Touanhô noticed my weakness and took me back to the cave, where I slept until the hour that would have corresponded to dusk outside the polar regions. Then I shared the evening meal with the others and went back to sleep.

For several days I was able to find myself alone with Touanhô without feeling any further tender torment. Those days were, moreover, quite charming. Awah, having announced that I had given blood, treated me as an authentic descendant of the Mammoth. The souls of these beings seemed to me so precise that, at times, I thought I had been transported back in time 15,000 years, and I cannot describe the extraordinary sense of renewal and the immortal poetry that accompanied the impression in question.

Because of my weakness, I was dissuaded from visiting the caves.

On the fourth day, I said: "I am strong, Touanhô. Shall we go to the caves?"

She understood, and started laughing, for she had a cheerful temperament. Touanhô went to the back of the cave and said: "It is necessary to push this stone."

The block in question, which was plugging a breach, was wider than it was deep. We pushed it on its smoother edge; it rotated slowly on its axis, uncovering an opening into which we went. The same phosphorescence that illuminated the exterior cave lit the corridor. After ten paces or so, we emerged into a spacious grotto, irregular in form, in which I discerned tools, weapons and carved objects; in places, the wall had been polished and blank but expert hands had drawn the figures of animals, and even of men, thereupon. One of those walls—the tallest—hypnotized me. The designs that it bore must have dated from a more remote era than the others, as was revealed by their appearance, more especially by the fact that they represented vanished animals, including reindeer, a saiga, horses with enormous heads and a cave-bear.

"Touanhô!" I exclaimed, excitedly. "No living being has seen these animals!"

"No," she said. "Wanawanoûm"—that was the old man—"says that the mothers of his mothers never encountered them. That was the time when the Sons of the Mammoth filled the Earth."

"What about the others? Did Awah draw them?"

"No, but some were drawn by Wanawanoûm's uncles."

I do not know whether you can understand the tumultuous sentiments that swelled in my breast, which resembled religious exaltation.

"There are other caves," said Touanhô, who did not understand my silence.

We descended an exceedingly steep slope and a new grotto opened its vast flanks. Far from diminishing, the light had grown brighter. Skeletons, some of them thousands of years old, were drying out on the ground—human skeletons, entire or nearly so, and the fragmentary skeletons of horses, saigas, reindeer and cave-bears. The works of art were scarcer and in worse condition; the walls only displayed sparse designs. This cavern had only been inhabited at intervals, for relatively short periods of time.

In the next cave my enthusiasm was renewed, followed by a veritable ecstasy. As I learned much later, it had communicated once directly with the exterior; a landslide had sealed it off in prehistoric times. It contained even more sculpted and engraved works than the first. A battle between a cave-bear and a gray bear revealed an artistry almost equal to that of our great animal painters.

While I was dreaming, almost moved to tears, Touanhô had drawn closer. On seeing my moist eyes, she threw her arm around my shoulders.

"Is Alglâ ill?"

I took her in my arms, squeezing her waist gently. The gesture did not fail to astonish her, but also to charm her. She leaned against my breast. Her eyes gave off a mysterious gleam; her red mouth was there, half-open over the sparkling shell-like teeth.

I saw myself lost in the night of time, with that woman, so young and so ancient; my lips descended. Surprised, Touanhô recoiled; I embraced her more tightly; my lips took hers, and suddenly, as if by a revelation, she took part in the unfamiliar caress.

In the caverns of ancient humankind, I espoused the daughter of those who carved stone and horn on the banks of virginal rivers on the edge of carnivore-infested forests.

There was one more cave, lower-down and rugged, in which human presence was revealed by fairly scarce traces. I sat down there, in a dreamy lassitude. Eventually, my attention was attracted by a scintillation; leaning forward, I saw a sort of pebble from which a glimmer had sprung. The brightness of the fracture-line was striking; I examined it curiously. Something ardent passed through my flesh: the frisson of a fortune, which resembled the frisson of the marvelous. I was holding a massive diamond—and the walls of the cave undoubtedly contained others.

For a minute I was subject to the fascination of the fabulous stone, and then I started laughing. In that lost land, it was not even worth as much as a harpoon or an axe!

"Let's go see the Sun again," I said to Touanhô.

August passed; the pale stars of September rotated in melancholy fashion in the sky. The temperature decreased.

Awah no longer left me alone with Touanhô. His voice was sharp; his taciturnity seemed to increase. One morning, he said to the young woman: "Touanhô is going hunting with me!"

There was no mistaking his intention. It was the season in which he ceased to be merely the young woman's companion and became her master. She looked at him with her fiery eyes.

"Touanhô is tired!"

A grim anxiety appeared in his face, which resembled dread. Jealousy ran through my breast like a jet of vitriol; hatred made my hands tremble.

Vehemently, Awah said: "Touanhô must come!"

She looked up at me, without suspecting my jealousy—but the sentiment of preference had entered into her soul. Undoubtedly, Awah seemed to her to be superior to me, but she knew that he was rough...

As she did not budge, he adopted his commanding voice: "Touanhô!"

Rage and a frightful distress ravaged me.

VI.

Touanhô had risen to her feet; she was submissive. I was demoted to the second rank; not only was the superiority of

Awah accepted, but it seemed to me that it was accepted without displeasure. The primitive woman was thinking less of secret moments spent with me, than times past, 12 months before, with her master.

Already the couple were drawing away. The scene seemed to me so decisive that all revolt ceased. My recent mentality yielded to ancestral fatalities. What right had I to fight against Awah? I had taken his wife, the daughter of his race, without his deigning even to notice it. He was taking her back at the time when the sacred instinct instructed him to do so; any dispute would have been odious and iniquitous…

My suffering was no less bitter for that. I watched their lithe silhouettes draw away; my arteries pulsed desperately; large tears ran down my cheeks.

One chagrin followed another for days. The fortunate lack of foresight was no more. In that savage life, I was subject to the mental miseries of civilized life. Touanhô scarcely looked at me. Subservient to all Awah's movements, she went hunting with him and sat next to him in the cave. He behaved in a tyrannical and exclusive manner. The same instinct that drives the stag into the autumnal forest filled him with suspicion, sometimes with pugnacity. He avoided me; he was even more taciturn than usual, and no longer carved either stones or antlers.

One morning, when I was sitting on the threshold of the cave, I noticed Namhâ, the adolescent girl, playing with the child. Since being abandoned by Touanhô I found her beside me more frequently. Naturally less familiar than the young woman, she had a kind of passive gentleness that was not without charm. That morning, I noticed a certain mysterious languor in her, and her fiery eyes occasionally became fixed, very wide, full of a "panic" dreaminess. I had never seen her so seductive. She was at the divine age when almost all the daughters of men have their grace, even the ugly, and Namhâ had received the gifts of brightness, youth and suppleness.

I sat there for a while, bathed in the vague sweetness that accompanies nascent hopes. Then I got up, with the aim of going to collect grains, nuts and roots for the winter provisions. Just as I set of into the open at a brisk pace, Namhâ and the child moved sideways and found themselves in my way. Namhâ stopped, looking at me in a strange, almost fearful fashion, and suddenly fled toward the eastern corner of the rock-face.

"Namhâ!" I shouted, in surprise.

Instinctively, I had followed her. She stopped, and turned to look at me again, and then bounded away and started running again.

One might think that she's afraid of me! I thought.

I stopped following her, wondering periodically why she had adopted that unusual attitude. Perhaps, after all, I had made some awkward gesture that had frightened her.

Eventually, I stopped thinking about it. Images of Touanhô and Awah began to torment me again, and I was busy gathering mushrooms in a wooded spot when I saw Namhâ, unexpectedly, standing under a beech-tree, half hidden by the trunk. She was watching me, as before, with that same fearful expression.

"Namhâ!" I cried. "Would you like to help me collect mushrooms?"

She hesitated; then, quitting her shelter, she took a few steps in my direction. Suddenly, she stopped, agitatedly.

"Do I frighten you?" I asked.

I went forward. With a light bound she retreated, then ran away, as nimble and frisky as a goat-kid. That seemed bizarre to me, and I tried to catch up with her. Bushes got in my way, and I decided to abandon a pursuit that might be terrifying her.

While collecting my mushrooms, I continued to meditate upon the adventure. I saw Namhâ again at the moment when she had stopped, quite distinctly, as if she had been in front of me; I analyzed the expression on her face, reminding myself that she had, after all, followed me. New ideas occurred to me, that I dared not develop too far, for fear of disappointment.

When I returned, I met the old women, Howouoï, with the child. "Have you seen Namhâ?" she asked.

I thought I glimpsed curiosity in her wrinkled face and said: "I did see Namhâ. I spoke to her and she ran away."

Howouoï looked at me for a moment silently, and then began to laugh. "Namhâ has become a woman. Perhaps Namhâ followed…"

My heart began to beat faster; any ambiguity as to the meaning of the incident was erased; Namhâ was following an instinct born before humankind, in the forests and savannahs.

"May Alglâ follow Namhâ?" I asked.

"Has Alglâ not become a Son of the Mammoth?" Howouoï riposted.

"What if Awah wants to follow Namhâ?"

Howouoï started laughing again. "Awah is Touanhô's master. There are only two women among us, and there are two men."

Chagrin vanished from my heart like mist from a stream, and I looked at the yellow September Sun with joy.

I did not see Namhâ again until it was time for sleep. In the cave, among the others, the young girl behaved as naturally as usual, but the following day, she remained invisible or only appeared in company. I resolved to catch her, and the day after, I set off on the warpath. I climbed to the top of mounds, hillocks and rocks, slyly exploring the surroundings.

After two hours of vain research, I hoisted myself up on to an erratically-shaped block of stone, from which my view commanded a broad extent. For some time, I could not see anything, and I was about to get down again when I distinctly perceived Namhâ's silhouette, near a wood of beeches and birches. Taking advantage of the uneven terrain, I succeeded in getting to within three or four paces of her without being seen—but then she slipped away and disappeared into the wood.

I ran after her. Once, I was only a few steps behind her, and leapt forward to seize her, when she slid into a bush and buried herself within it. I had no hesitation in following her, but at that game, in which I was less expert than her, I lost ground. When I emerged again, her silhouette was disappearing into the forest.

For more than an hour I tried to pick up her trail. I found it suddenly, by chance. The pursuit began again, ardent and subtle. Every time I was on the point of catching up with the girl, she found some new trick; besides which, her knowledge of the area was superior to mine. Nevertheless, I succeeded in guiding her from the confines of the wood to the plain. She tried to get back under cover, but I barred the way. Then, as if despairing, she decided to flee in a straight line.

She was heading for the cave. At first, she succeeded in maintaining the distance between us; I had, after all, expended much more energy than she had, because she had been able to rest while under cover. After a quarter of an hour of pursuit, however, I had gained ground, and I had nearly reached her when she climbed up on to a block of stone—the very same misshapen block from which I had seen her.

Because the block was only accessible on one side, the maneuver left her at my discretion. I hoisted myself up in my turn. When I arrived on top, she tried to push me away.

"Namhâ!" I murmured, in a supplicant tone.

She was out of breath; her effort weakened; I found myself beside her.

Then a veritable terror appeared on her face. She recoiled to the very pinnacle of the rock, which overhung slightly, and uttered a long moan.

VII.

"Why is Namhâ afraid?" I asked.

"Will Alglâ strike as hard as Awah?" she sighed, shivering. "Awah almost killed Touanhô!"

"Alglâ will not strike!" I replied, softly.

The girl looked at me with extreme suspicion, mingled with disdain. "The Sons of the Mammoth cannot unite with a girl without striking her. Their posterity would be annihilated."

These words did not surprise me overmuch; they were in conformity with the mores of many primitive populations whose customs have been described to us by travelers—but they embarrassed me. All my instincts rebelled at the idea of striking a woman. It was, however, necessary. Namhâ's gaze showed that she would not yield to a man who did not understand ritual violence.

"Alglâ will do as all the Sons of the Mammoth do," I declared.

Then the terror reappeared in the young face and paralyzed me. To gain time, I said: "Let's go back into the wood."

She followed me in silence, doubtless torn between her dread and a sentiment of the inevitable.

A fine affair! I thought. Men who hit women are not even rare in our civilized milieu—and it is still without the consent of the latter.

I was still irresolute when we found ourselves under cover. As before with Touanhô, but even more forcefully, I was intoxicated by the youth of the world. I trembled as I looked at the fascinating primitive and, moved by a sort of ancestral violence, suddenly lifted my fist and struck Namhâ on the head. She released a feeble plaint, and pressed herself against me. I put my arms around her. For the second time, I espoused a daughter of an abolished era.

The days of the long evening were full of sweetness. While the coppery Sun sent forth its impoverished rays, I lost myself in the wilderness with Namhâ. She was my wife, according to customs as scientific as ours; she was charming, in the simple and spontaneous manner of children. In sum, I never loved any woman as much as her. To the exaltation of love was joined a strange sentiment of immortality—the sentiment of an individual who might have lived for 100 centuries and found himself still as full of life as in the epochs when prehistoric herds roamed the immense planet.

Night fell—the polar night, which would envelop us with stars for six months. It did not interrupt our happiness. We took refuge in the deep caverns, where the temperature was almost immutable. It seemed that the perpetual light that shone within them had increased its intensity. Besides, we were not confined to our new abode. Numerous boreal auroras illuminated the territory. We could still hunt and collect seeds, nuts and mushrooms.

The mammoths, installed in the summer cave, went out as we did, even when the night became black. They found their pasture on the plain and in the forests, but they ate less and slept more. It was in that period that I familiarized myself with them. The older one turned out to have been stupefied by age; our relationship remained passive. The other demonstrated an intelligence as quick as our elephants. I won its confidence. Nourishment inevitably played a preponderant part in our initial relationship, but the affection to which the habit of being together almost invariably gives birth, even in stupid creatures, eventually sprang up. The mammoth came to enjoy my presence, independently of any gift of roots or stems—and I tried to domesticate it. I had no definite objective; it seemed obvious to me that the animal might be useful in some fashion.

It was necessary to proceed prudently. Awah, Wanawanoûm and even Touanhô did not like anything that deviated from their traditions; furthermore, the mammoth was their totem. At first, therefore, I kept my attempts secret, and the mammoth already obeyed me in many things while my companions were still in ignorance.

A discovery rendered my task less difficult and less delicate. One day, when I had taken Namhâ to a place where the others hardly ever went, I found a singular engraving on a reindeer antler, which must have originated in the final phase of the Magdalenian Era. The engraving depicted a man perched on a mammoth's back. It seemed to me to be indisputable proof of domestication—perhaps a fortuitous and local domestication, one of those isolated attempts that must often have preceded the achievements of our distant ancestors.

Awah and Wanawanoûm examined the engraving with a greater interest than they usually brought to events foreign to their routines. I succeeded in persuading them that their ancestors had been accustomed to living more intimately with mammoths than they did; I suggested that we ought to imitate the ancestors. They did not contradict that, although they took no interest in the matter themselves—which, of course, I preferred. I gained the advantage of being able to attribute my attempts at domestication to a revival of ultra-venerable traditions.

For my savage companions, as for almost all human beings, it was sufficient to break down certain prejudices for the rest to follow. They were initially astonished by what the mammoth consented to do, but then found it quite natural.

In order to excite less suspicion, I observed the rituals strictly; I did not forget to render the mammoth the same homage as my hosts; I even exaggerated that homage slightly.

In parallel with this work, I learned to make use of primitive implements. My secret objective was to build a sled. Two or three preliminary experiments gave me considerable hope. In the month of December, I set to work in earnest.

Needless to say, I continued to make progress in the prehistoric language. I even succeeded in getting a few simplifications adopted, and a few new terms that rendered conversation less difficult. The women helped me in my efforts and understood the novelties better than the men; contrary to the norm of ultra-civilized societies, they seemed less neophobic than their masters.

By February, the sled was beginning to take shape. I wanted it to be spacious, in order that it might accommodate all my companions and considerable food-supplies. At first, Awah had looked at the unprecedented object with hostile suspicion, but in the end he became used to it, to the point of no longer even looking at it. He had become placid—the season that rendered him aggressive would not reappear for many months—and slept for ten hours a day, as did all the others.

In January, the temperature decreased to a low level, although it remained far superior to polar temperatures, but in the caverns we did not suffer from the cold at all. Magnificent aurora illuminated the domain; I delighted in taking solitary walks.

Then an ominous event occurred.

VIII.

On the day in question, there was a particularly spectacular aurora borealis. Immense sparkling arcs and jets of light like fountains of luminous water lit up the landscape. At the base there was a scarlet blaze, torrents of rubies and carbuncles; at the zenith, a delicate aurora of beryl and aquamarine, which blotted out the petty stars and only allowed the regal stars to shine through. The air and ground were still; all life was concentrated on high, mysterious and tremulous.

I was thinking about the innumerable energies of which we would never know anything, which might perhaps nourish worlds as complex as our own, without anything advertising their presence to us. I have always thought that there is an infinity of coexistences everywhere, that where we only see one Sun and planets there are millions, trillions of systems different from one another, which intersect as if each system were a mere absence so far as the others are concerned.

I was, therefore, thinking about these things while walking on the plain with Namhâ, when we felt a shock so violent that we lost our balance. It only lasted for two or three seconds, and was not repeated—but we felt that it was a redoubtable circumstance.

"Our ancestors perished thus!" said the young woman fearfully. "Mountains fall in that manner!"

I remembered then the tormented locale that I had passed through while fleeing from the polar bears.

We headed back to the caverns; the mammoths had come out, the old one torpid, as usual, the other very nervous, agitating its ears with a mixture of fear and menace. My presence calmed it down; it put its trunk around my body—which was a kind of caress—and gradually resumed its customary attitude.

We went into the caves warily; they did not exhibit any damage. It was only several days afterwards that Touanhô, Awah and Wanawanoûm noticed a few fissures.

While we were examining the ground and the walls, Touanhô came in with her little daughter and the old woman. They were still very frightened. The old woman mumbled incoherent words relating to similar shocks, several of which had occurred in her lifetime.

As Awah and Wanawanoûm had not come back we went to look for them, Touanhô toward the north and the old woman toward the east, while Namhâ and I headed westwards.

Namhâ had become insouciant again—her mentality scarcely took account of anything beyond the present moment—while I remained anxious. My mature civilized imagination painted the future for me in colors that became blacker as my cogitation became more abundant. Similar accidents had evidently reduced that human tribe that had maintained itself in the region since the Tourassian Epoch to a handful of individuals.

We had been walking for about an hour when there was a bellowing to our right, and a large red deer stag was silhouetted by the boreal light. It was a magnificent ten-pointer with a broad breast and a solid and supple back. Its agitation was visible, causing its slender legs to tremble—and it had lost the instinct of self-preservation momentarily, since, instead of running away from us, it seemed to be waiting for us.

My first impulse was to reach for my harpoon, but I remembered immediately that we had sufficient meat in the caves, and it would have been ridiculous to sacrifice so beautiful an animal, not only for its own sake but that of the generations that it might father.

Suddenly, the stag charged, at lightning speed.

"It's furious!" Namhâ cried.

I grabbed my harpoon again, and waited for the animal while Namhâ ran sideways. She was the one the animal went after. In a few bounds, it was close. She fled, but the outcome of the pursuit was certain.

I threw my harpoon, which grazed the animal, and then I drew my revolver—and just as the girl was about to be overtaken I fired twice. The stag reared up convulsively on its hind feet, turned, and collapsed.

Bewildered, joyful and amazed, Namhâ exclaimed: "Alglâ has killed the great stag!"

Soon an anxiety appeared on her face, mixed with admiration. She realized that I had employed a method of combat unknown to the Sons of the Mammoth; she looked fearfully at the weapon I still held in my fist.

"The stag would have killed Namhâ," I murmured. "Namhâ must not tell the Sons of the Mammoth about the fire-axe. If Namhâ mentions it, the fire-axe will no longer be able to save anyone."

"Namhâ will not speak of it!" she exclaimed.

I sensed that she would hold her tongue. The neophobia of Awah and Wanawanoûm had caused me to keep the properties of my rifle and revolver secret; Awah especially might have taken exception to them. I had decided only to make use of the weapons in case of extreme necessity.

"That's good," I said, supportively. "Namhâ will thus be the friend of the fire-axe."

We walked on for another hour. Finally, Namhâ, whose hearing was as delicate as a she-wolf's, put her ear to the ground.

"I can hear Wanawanoûm's footsteps," she said.

Several minutes passed before I heard them in my turn; then the silhouette of the old man appeared on top of a rise. He had seen us; he allowed us to come closer, and then pointed

181

westwards. "The mountain has fallen in the caves that are under the ground!" he said, hoarsely. A deep sadness appeared in his face.

He led us to the boundary of the territory. An entire section of granite ridges had disappeared; the harsh polar landscape was visible through a gap; a glacial wind chilled us to the bone. "It's the end of the Sons of the Mammoth!" the old man added.

And we returned to the caves in a melancholy mood.

Gradually, the excess of my anxiety had disappeared. I told myself that, all things considered, many years might pass before the annihilation of our habitat—and, as is my nature, I formulated projects and conjectures. The sled, which I had hitherto considered as a simple instrument of exploration, became a potential means of salvation. If I could domesticate the mammoth to the point at which I could persuade it to render the services of a draught animal, I could attempt to cross the distance separating us from the nearest Eskimo tribes. If that adventure proved impossible, at least I would be able to place markers in the surrounding wilderness that would enjoin some future polar expedition to reach the territory. Such expeditions could only increase in number; eventually, one of them was bound to follow the route that my own expedition had taken.

I devoted the rest of the winter to finishing the sled and solving the problems of provisioning it. Accumulating the supplies necessary to humans was nothing, but the mammoth required a more considerable volume of food for itself than all of us put together, because that nourishment had to be exclusively vegetal. I imagined various combinations, including a sort of biscuit made from a wild cereal, fairly similar to barley, which my hosts did not exactly cultivate, but the growth of which they favored by ripping out rival plants. I resolved to cultivate it, to the extent that that was possible.

Daylight returned to shine on these enterprises: a pale and chilly daylight that scarcely elevated the temperature for a fortnight. I worked stubbornly. Gradually, I forced the idea of a possible salvation into the heads of my companions, in case further cataclysms threatened our existence.

The women, even the old one, allowed themselves to be convinced, but the men were extremely reluctant to abandon their ancestral land. Awah, especially, listened to me with a discontent that went as far as anger.

IX.

The Arctic spring grew warmer as the Sun rose higher into the sky. Beyond the habitat, the wilderness remained glacially white and sinister. Since the earthquake, it was constantly visible through the breach made in the granite ridges, as one sees a landscape through a window. A keen wind often penetrated from that direction, making the temperature we enjoyed all the more welcome. Its nature remained completely mysterious; it was an emanation from the ground, whose constancy over the millennia far surpassed the thermal constancy of radium.

Aided by the women, I cultivated the species of barley I mentioned as best I could. Our work consisted of strewing seeds on favorable ground and extirpating harmful plants. No further accident having occurred, I became more confident. Primitive life recovered its sweetness.

Touanhô and Namhâ were pregnant. The latter, submissive to ancestral instincts, lived with me as a sister; I respected her wisdom. Touanhô also led a continent existence; even so, one day when we were alone in the winter caves, where I was assembling documents, she suddenly remembered the foreign caress, and her lips sought mine. It was her only awakening until the summer.

It soon seemed probable that my cereal crop would be abundant. At the end of May, it had put forth innumerable stalks. I had some difficulty in preserving our fields from the appetite of the mammoths and wild herbivores, and, in spite of everything, they devoured a substantial fraction of the barley. Luckily, it happened that other plants, which they preferred, were more abundant that year in pastures sufficiently distant from my fields.

The mammoth's education proceeded apace. The colossus allowed itself to be put in harness and we made a few excursions by sled into the polar desert. It drew the heavy contraption along without difficulty, seemingly indefatigable.

At first, Wanawanoûm and Awah observed this new form of my activity with a jaundiced eye; they anticipated obscure perils arising from infractions injurious to millennia-old customs. It was necessary to invent confused pretexts and incessantly to remind them of the engraving of the man perched on the mammoth. As they had little imagination and their logic was obtuse, I easily overcame their objections, to the extent that, the annoyance of reflection coming to my aid, they eventually shut up. The earthquake and the evident imminent extinction of their race had rendered them somewhat inert; they sensed formless threat around them, and, in their better moments, understood that it was not futile to think about salvation. Besides, the women, now convinced, acted with cunning, subtle and effective patience.

One day, when I had taken my excursion further than usual, Awah was particularly irritated. "Does Alglâ want to make the mammoth die?" he grumbled, with an anger that needed little encouragement to become furious.

"It's not Alglâ who will kill the mammoth," I replied, softly. "It's the Earth's depths, which will open up for him, and for us too."

He shook his head, obstinately. "The Sons of the Mammoth will die if Alglâ makes the mammoth die. The white plain is our enemy. The ancestors never went there!"

I turned to Wanawanoûm and asked: "Have the Sons of the Mammoth not been masters of a land greater than this one?"

Wanawanoûm replied, emphatically: "The Sons of the Mammoth have been masters of a land ten times larger than this one!"

"They hunted out there, then?" I went on. "They lived in the direction of the Sun. The land there is no longer white; it is as green as these leaves and this grass. That's where the Sons of the Mammoth lived to begin with. That's where they will find their hunting-grounds and become a numerous tribe again."

Wanawanoûm listened to me in bewilderment; Awah was attentive, and seized on a confused hope.

"Alglâ is right," Touanhô affirmed, impetuously. "There are lands with other animals—animals like those engraved in the winter caves."

That was an excellent idea; I took possession of it. "I've seen vast herds of those animals!" I affirmed. "Do Awah and Wanawanoûm not want to hunt them, as their ancestors did?"

Wanawanoûm nodded his head, conviction dawning. Awah's anger had decreased; a thought had been planted in him that took several days to take form, but which rendered him inoffensive in the meantime.

In June, Touanhô brought into the world a boy of the pure prehistoric race, while Namhâ gave birth to a daughter in whose veins a partly-modern blood ran. At the end of July, we had an abundant harvest of barley, a part of which was put in store, while the other furnished us with our meals and new seed for sowing. We lived more happily than ever. The mammoth was perfectly tame. I had consolidated the sled in such a way as to protect it from the rudest shocks.

Awah, ever taciturn, made no further objection to my singularities; in fact, he ended up no longer seeing them. It was, however, necessary not to think of the voyage until a further cataclysm had demonstrated its absolute necessity. I could, in truth, have risked the adventure alone, but that would have seemed a betrayal. Then again, powerful bonds retained me among my comrades—firstly my daughter, whom I loved ardently, and then Namhâ and Touanhô. Will moralists complain if I confess that I cherished the one almost as much as the other?

In the month of August, Touanhô, who had been absorbed until then by her maternity, became familiar again. She remembered. She found me in the wilderness and in the half-light of the caves; my love was rekindled, as sweetly as in the days when the young prehistoric woman had made my exile an enchantment...

As the polar night approached, the salvation plan became less practicable; toward the end of the month, however, we discovered a new peril.

The weather having been unusually mild on the exterior plains, a few Arctic animals had ventured as far as our latitude. One day, Awah, Wanawanoûm and I headed for the breach, in the vicinity of which there was a great abundance of edible roots and mushrooms. While we were gathering our harvest, we heard a growl. I straightened up, and perceived two fine polar bears. They had crossed the zone separating their territory from ours; they were advancing slowly, with a certain prudence. The configuration of the place had revealed them before they had been able to perceive us. When they did see us, they hesitated, perhaps astonished by our form.

Wanawanoûm and Awah were certainly more surprised than the wild beasts. The bear, very rare in the region, into which they only strayed in consequence of misadventure or exceptional circumstances, had never penetrated into the habitat in which my companions lived. The ones that had pursued me into the corridor the previous year, and which the mammoth had put to flight, had not returned.

"Waô! Waô!" cried Wanawanoûm, in whom legendary memories were waking up. "They're snow bears!"

Awah had his axe and his harpoon ready. Wanawanoûm had his spear, and I waited with my harpoon in one hand and my revolver in the other. After a moment of uncertainty, the bears retreated. Their obscure consciousness perceived danger. The larger of the two—the male—calmly turned to its right and started trotting toward a little clump of ash-trees. The female followed, and within a few seconds they became invisible. The peril had been deferred; it nevertheless remained redoubtable.

"The women!" I cried.

Fear, which I had not felt for myself, gripped my guts at the thought of Namhâ, Touanhô and my daughter.

X.

Wanawanoûm and Awah remained impassive, but they did not waste any time, and we were soon on the bears' trail. The pursuit was not very difficult. We were delayed in the middle of the wood, however, where we were first made to pause by the tracks of a group of hinds that crossed those of the bears, and then by a clearing of hard ground. When we emerged from the wood we could not see the fugitives; they had doubtless gone over a hill that rose up 400 or 500 meters from the edge of the wood, toward which we set our course. When we reached the crest, I released a cry of alarm, while Wanawanoûm uttered a dull exclamation: the bears were chasing Touanhô!

We were too far away to reach her in time. Awah bounded forward like a red deer and I, being an experienced runner, kept pace with him, but he was too late. The male bear seized Touanhô and knocked her flat. With a wild growl, it began to tear the young woman apart.

At that moment, a massive silhouette appeared at the edge of a wood: a mammoth. Unfortunately, it was the old one. At the sight of the bear and the recumbent Touanhô, it came to a halt. Its ancient mummified brain undoubtedly had a vague understanding of what was happening, for it trumpeted, and the male bear, raising its head, was gripped by such amazement that it released its prey. Its mate, which had advanced a paw to seize Touanhô's child, recoiled. Then we howled frantically, brandishing our weapons. The old mam-

187

moth came forward—at which sight the bears made off at a tangent. Only Awah thought about pursuing them; Wanawanoûm and I rushed toward Touanhô.

She was losing blood from two long cuts. I thought at first that she had been mortally wounded. She was almost unconscious. A summary examination revealed that the wounds were superficial and only involved unimportant veins. Wanawanoûm made a dressing with aromatic herbs, which was better than any I could have contrived. The young woman came round.

Awah had returned, not out of fear but by virtue of the prudence that was innate in my prehistoric people as in almost all savages, which dissuades them from needlessly braving perils in which their strength and skill are likely to be defeated.

As soon as Touanhô was on her feet I asked: "Where's Namhâ?"

"Touanhô has not seen Namhâ since she left the caves."

Awah and Wanawanoûm looked at one another indecisively. "We must start tracking the bears again!" I cried.

That was the only possible course of action, as we did not know where Namhâ and he old woman were. My companions did not raise any objection, but Touanhô could not go with us and at least three men would be necessary to confront the bears.

"Touanhô will stay with the mammoth," the young woman declared.

The old mammoth had not been domesticated at all; it wandered at the hazard of its senile fantasy.

"What if it abandons Touanhô?" I objected.

"It's slow…Touanhô can follow it."

That was obvious, and the primitive woman's resilience reassured me. Awah and Wanawanoûm had not waited for my decision; they were already back on the trail. I was long in going after them.

Unless they had been delayed, the predators had to have a long lead. We went into a wood of beeches and birches,

pressing forward as rapidly as Awah's senses and Wanawanoûm's sagacity permitted. In spite of the inevitable pauses,
we moved quite quickly; it did not take us long to reach the
other side of the wood—as chance would have it, the bears
had taken the most direct route. From there, we could see the
granite mass in which the caves were hollowed out.

Awah and Wanawanoûm discovered that the bears had
been on the point of invading our refuge; there were tracks
alongside the rock-face. After a detour, we picked them up
again on the plain. Our enemies were nowhere to be seen; either they had hidden in some thicket or they had taken shelter
in one of the numerous outcrops of rock that cut across the
territory—but their tracks could not escape my companions.

Suddenly, a clamor brought us to a halt and, on turning
round, we saw the old woman. She had spotted the bears and
had hidden among the trees with Touanhô's daughter.

"Namhâ is beyond the Red Hill!" she shouted.

"Are the bears pursuing Namhâ?" I shouted, in anguish.

She made an affirmative sign; she explained that the
young woman had disappeared on the other side of the hill
before the bears could begin their ascent.

We required no more than ten minutes to reach the Red
Hill. When we reached its crest, we finally saw the bears.
They were indulging in a phantasmagorical gesticulation.
Each was crouched at the extremity of a block of basalt; their
heads and one of their paws disappeared periodically. After a
fairly extended movement, the heads and the paws reappeared,
while they emitted furious roars.

Wanawanoûm was the first to understand the significance of the bizarre scene, and called out. A tremulous voice
replied: Namhâ's voice.

As we continued to advance, Awah and I soon understood what Wanawanoûm had guessed. The basalt block,
shaped like a prism, had a cleft cutting all the way through it.
Namhâ had slid sideways into the cleft with her child. The
bears had not been able to follow them; they could only insert
their narrow heads and long necks into the fissure, along with

189

one of their paws, but their upper bodies remained outside. As we drew closer, the scene seemed more ominous. We could vaguely discern Namhâ, standing upright, with the baby in her arms. When the bears reached down it seemed that it would only require a slight effort for them to reach the unfortunate girl.

"Namha should not be afraid!" I shouted. "We're coming to help her."

Before proceeding with the attack we conferred rapidly. It was primarily a matter of succeeding; Namhâ's situation would not get any worse for some time. We had a good chance; in Awah's hands the axe and club were formidable weapons, Wanawanoûm threw his harpoon with great skill, and I had my revolver, loaded with six hardened bullets.

The bears were hesitant. Our presence, which was connected with a disagreeable memory, certainly puzzled them. Perhaps, if we attacked deliberately, they might take flight, even though they must be exasperated by their disappointments—but I thought it important to destroy them. Their flight would leave the peril in place.

If I could only bring the mammoth! I thought.

My eyes explored the surroundings. There was as much chance of discovering the colossus as there was of our running around for a long time without finding it. Wanawanoûm, who must have had a similar idea, took a long look around the horizon.

"Waô!" he said. His extended finger pointed out a distant silhouette.

"Let Awah and Wanawanoûm wait," I recommended. "The mammoth will help us!"

"Awah will wait."

I had already started running. When I was within range, I shouted an appeal. The mammoth stopped grazing, raised its massive head and came toward me. I brought it back to my companions and declared: "Let's attack! It's necessary that the snow-bears should be injured!"

I cocked my revolver and marched toward the male, while Awah made ready to attack the female.

XI.

After a momentary hesitation, Wanawanoûm decided to follow me, persuaded that the powerful Awah could reckon with the she-bear, while he had his doubts about me. I had, moreover, chosen the more redoubtable of the two predators.

Without worrying about the effects of my action on the superstitious mentality of my hosts, I made immediate use of the revolver. The bear, hit by two bullets, turned round with a furious growl and hurled itself forward. However serious its wounds might be, its vigor seemed intact. Within a moment it had covered the distance separating us.

Wanawanoûm, initially amazed by the gunshots, recovered his composure. He threw a harpoon, which sank into the beast's side and deadened its speed, which permitted me to take better aim. A bullet penetrated its yellow breast, and the bear collapsed with a sort of cavernous sigh. It got up quite promptly and resumed the attack, but it was tottering. My fourth bullet struck its shoulder, and I was about to finish it off when the mammoth appeared.

The scene was brief. Seized and crushed by the monstrous trunk, the bear exploded like a goatskin bottle, and was then reduced to a pulp beneath feet like pile-drivers.

Awah had carried forward the attack in his own fashion. After feigning to draw away, he had come back, circling a mound. The she-bear was suspicious; when the prehistoric man reappeared, she began to gain ground. It was the detonations of my revolver that stopped her. In her dim consciousness, she glimpsed the danger to her companion and, I imagine, the necessity of coming to his aid.

At the moment when Wanawanoûm threw his harpoon at the male, I saw the she-bear, which, avoiding Awah, attempted an oblique movement toward her companion in adventure. A new detonation stopped her short; she must have seen the mammoth running forward, and a sure instinct told her what to do: she fled. In the meantime, however, Awah had approached within spear-range. His harpoon lodged in the she-bear's side just as the mammoth crushed the panting body of the male. She turned furiously, hesitated for a second, and then resumed her flight.

Although weakened slightly by her wound, she gained ground. Dreading that she might escape, I uttered a cry that the mammoth had learned to understand; all four of us launched ourselves in pursuit. You would have thought that the mammoth was trotting—and, in fact, it was not moving at top speed. Nevertheless, it was running fast enough to overhaul the fugitive well before she could reach the nearest thicket, and she knew it. She veered sideways toward a small chain of rocks, and climbed up the steepest slope. The maneuver proved disastrous; the other side was perpendicular.

We surrounded the beast easily, and I was getting ready to fire when Awah, gripped by a sudden overexcitement, ran up the slope in his turn and hurled a spear. With a screech that was almost a sob, the she-bear plastered herself against the granite, begging for mercy. Awah thought that she was exhausted—an excusable error in a man who had never hunted large predators. He took two more steps, raised his axe, and struck twice. The she-bear threw herself upon our companion, and rolled down the slope with him.

When Awah got up, the she-bear was dead—but he had a broken arm and a deep wound in his chest.

There was no other notable incident until the day when darkness descended upon the territory. Awah's arm, crookedly healed, had lost some of its strength and skill. That circumstance conferred an authority on me that was all the more necessary because the effects of the revolver had awakened unfavorable ideas in the minds of my companions. My physical condition was the best possible argument. It imposed respect in the women and in Wanawanoûm. Awah also submitted to it, not out of fear—he was extremely brave and did not even fear death—but primitive wisdom.

I became the chief of our fragmentary tribe, the person who disposed the community's resources as he wished, and to whom obedience was due on pain of death. My will became a supreme argument, on condition that it respected the affiliation of the tribe and its sacred relationship with the mammoths.

I was able to dispense with any explanation regarding my revolver and my rifle. That would have been an error, liable to sow seeds of mistrust. I therefore affirmed that the Sons of the Mammoth, when they had lived in the southern lands, had made an alliance with the fire-axe and the fire-spear, and that that alliance would be renewed if we ever saw the hunting grounds of our great ancestors again. The story initially gave rise, if not to manifest incredulity, at least to a fearful—and fundamentally hostile—incomprehension. A second repetition succeeded in rendering it plausible. The females were the first to come round, then Wanawanoûm; Awah took more than a month to accommodate it within his rebellious brain.

The long night passed peacefully until the middle of January. The temperature in the grottoes dropped slightly, but without our experiencing any consequent discomfort; we could, moreover, obtain an agreeable warmth in the deepest cave of all.

Namhâ was pregnant again, but not Touanhô. Both of them showed me a faithful and increasing affection. I asked nothing of the morrow. A perfectly healthy life, a dream-filled insouciance, no servitude, female companions I loved sincerely, and who never subjected me to any of the torments that we owe to their civilized sisters, and nourishment that I found flavorsome—what more could I need to make life seem charming?

In the month of February, when I was returning with Awah, Wanawanoûm and the mammoth from a sort of tour of inspection of the domain, we felt the ground tremble. It was so brief and so feeble, that I would scarcely have given it a thought had I not been on the alert. After the previous incident, the event seemed to me to be very ominous; it seemed no less so to my companions.

The shock was not repeated that day, and if there was any damage to the territory, we could not find it—but a week later, the warning was renewed, with greater force. The caves exhibited numerous fissures and a part of the granite frontier collapsed.

Wanawanoûm issued a pessimistic prediction: "The Earth will open up and devour the Sons of the Mammoth."

The polar day was approaching when a third, violent quake shook the caves and the entire habitat. It was just as we were going to sleep; we woke up with a start. A part of the roof came down in the next cave—and when we went outside, we were not long delayed in observing sinister collapses everywhere.

A few peaceful weeks followed. The Sun rose; its gentle light gave us some confidence—but in the month of April, a feeble shock reminded us of our peril.

"We must get ready to escape!" I declared.

It was the time when the Sun marked midday. The women listened to me with a dread full of hope. Wanawanoûm acquiesced, ready to obey. Only Awah seemed not to hear me. He was by far the most attached to the territory, as to the ancestral traditions, and it was difficult for him to believe that there was anything else outside but the pale locales that horrified him.

I said to him, softly: "What does Awah think?"

He replied, in a bleak tone: "Awah no longer has his strength. Awah is no longer the chief."

XII.

We worked actively in the weeks that followed. With a part of our stores of barley we made large biscuits, to which we were able to add pemmican, dried mushrooms and roots. The rest of the barley was to constitute the mammoth's nourishment.

Salvation presented itself in a disheartening and sinister form. It would probably be necessary to flee before summer, which rendered the enterprise much more difficult and perilous. My only good fortune was that I knew the route, and that my poor comrades in exploration and myself had set up signposts—some of which, however, must have been obliterated by the weather.

We finished our preparations before the end of April. There were provisions for 20 days, and we would doubtless kill some game en route. Moreover, if we succeeded in crossing the desert region rapidly, we would find edible vegetation for the mammoth.

In addition to the natural difficulties, one moral problem presented itself. What were we going to do with the old mammoth? It was impossible for it to make the journey; it would cause us considerable delay, would consume barley uselessly and, after all, would certainly perish one way or another, in conditions which could hardly avoid being embarrassing.

The only reasonable course was to abandon it. Its fate would be no worse, since it could not survive until the annihilation of the ancient pastures. There were, therefore, no grounds for hesitation—and on my own account, I had no hesitation. In this instance, however, my companions' wishes had a capital importance. I did not know what those wishes were; I delayed an explanation that, undertaken awkwardly, might have led to disaster. If, perchance, Awah and Wanawanoûm, not to mention Touanhô, were to demand that the Father go with us, I would have no means of causing my opinion to prevail, save by trickery—for there was no possibility of using force; in totemic matters, my companions would have perished rather than compromise.

I opened myself up to Touanhô first; she had the most flexible mind and knew the mentality of her companions better than Namhâ. I did not ask her advice, of course—that would have opened the way to ominous uncertainties—but one morning, when we were walking in the plain, I said: "The Father of Mammoths will not leave these pastures. He's too old. He won't survive from a day in the snowfields. We would have killed him."

Touanhô looked at me with surprise and disquiet, but she raised no objection. Eventually, she said: "What if he wants to follow us?"

That was an excellent question, in that it furnished me with a perhaps peremptory argument. "If he wants to follow us, he will follow us. The Sons of the Mammoth will bow down to him."

In truth, that was a risk—but I knew that if his companion did not summon him, the old mammoth would not go out into the snows.

I hesitated for a few days more, and then decided to talk to the males. "The Sons of the Mammoth," I said, "will only take the Ancestor if he wishes to follow us. If he prefers to remain in the pasturelands, he might live until their end—but the snow would kill him."

"How can we know the Ancestor's will?" Wanawanoûm asked.

"He will know that we want to save ourselves," I affirmed. "He knows already. When he sees his companion depart, he will choose."

The question was not resolved that day. Awah had made no reply. He lived in a disturbing mutism. I returned to the issue several times, without persuading him to offer his opinion, and I began to fear a redoubtable opposition.

One morning—I mean the hour when we got up—Awah said, abruptly: "The Ancestor will not follow us. He will die in his pasturelands. That is better for him and his son."

He spoke bitterly; I sensed that he envied the beast rather than lamenting him. The mammoth had ended his days; he could no longer be of use to his descendants, animal or human—while he, Awah, was still too young to abandon his race!

Tragic events hastened our departure. There were no more earthquakes, but collapses, which were reshaping the locale from day to day. Grass, bushes and woods would sink in a matter of hours; holes took the place of mounds, even hills. The animals fled recklessly; stags and hinds went to perish in the white wilderness. The birds flew southwards. The granite ring that had protected the habitat for millennia was crumbling all along its length. We camped in the open. I had got everything ready for a sudden departure and, in addition to the provisions, I had packed a cargo of large diamonds that were, in my estimation, worth between five and six million francs.

The caves collapsed in their turn, at the very moment when we were heading toward the devastated zone that separated us from the Arctic wilderness. We were nearly swallowed up several times; chance alone saved us. When we were safe, I turned to take one last look at the singular and blessed region in which I had known the life of freedom that our descendants will never know again.

In the distance, on a granite islet, I glimpsed the massive silhouette of the old mammoth. He was standing still, as if stupefied; I understood that he was rapidly going numb and that that numbness had further increased the inertia of his ancient brain. It seemed impossible that he could survive for more than 24 hours, assuming that he would not be crushed by a rockslide.

My companions had seen what I had seen; a sudden emotion gripped the young women; they extended their arms toward the place where the caves had formerly been. Awah and Wanawanoûm remained imperturbable and taciturn; the old woman moaned periodically.

The journey was painful, even though it was favored by relatively mild temperatures. Furthermore, the air was perfectly still. The wind only got up two or three times in the first ten days. I had taken all possible precautions for the halts; we were buried up to the neck in deer-skins lined with feathers; our tent was very primitive but, all in all, efficacious. The mammoth seemed the most sorely tested, although it revealed an unexpected endurance; it went forward with a rapidity superior to that of dogs or reindeer.

In brief, in spite of acute suffering, no one had died after ten days of travel. I found en route the markers that I had placed two years before; I was, in consequence, sure that we were heading in the right direction. Besides, I recognized the broad outlines of certain locations. Another week, and we would reach the proximity of Eskimo tribes with which I had made alliance—when I say "proximity" I mean, of course, a chance of proximity, my Eskimos being nomads.

On the 12th day, the old woman, who had been manifesting symptoms of lassitude since the previous day, and who had become torpid, suddenly died. We buried her in the snow. I do not know whether her companions missed her much; at any rate, they did not appear unduly grief-stricken. At the most, they manifested a slight increase in anxiety.

On the 14th day, Wanawanoûm was overtaken by a sort of delirium. He talked very loudly, telling fragmentary stories of old times of which no one had any memory. He fell into a coma and died without recovering consciousness.

Our suffering increased, even though the temperature continually became less rigorous. Our strength was decreasing gradually, and the mammoth was showing signs of distress. The young women were dejected; Namhâ's second-born was growing weaker. Only Awah retained all his strength, and, animated by his youth, even regained hope, wanting to see the southern lands where the Sons of the Mammoth had once hunted.

We had three horrible days, although we were beginning to emerge from the murderous wilderness, and encountered occasional traces of vegetation. Namhâ was growing progressively torpid, and the mammoth's speed was decreasing by the hour. It was a courageous beast, though, patient and prodi-

giously resilient. I firmly believe that it had a confused awareness of the situation, and that a profound instinct was bearing
it toward the lands of the South where salvation was to be
found. At any rate, it supported us with an extraordinary good
will, and the more it weakened the more submissive it became.

For two further days, the mammoth struggled on with
grim courage—but on May 19, in the morning, it uttered a sort
of hoarse plaint, turned its head toward me, and collapsed in a
heap.

XIII.

I precipitated myself out of the sled. The enormous body
of the mammoth was palpitating feebly. When it saw me
standing there, beside it, it raised its trunk as if it were an arm
and looked at me steadily. A tragic gentleness emanated from
its brown eyes, with I know not what intelligence and instinct,
more poignant than rational intelligence. No human dolor has
touched me more than the dolor of that immense beast, in
whom the last vestige of a species doomed for millennia
would be extinguished. It did not last long. The pupil vitrified;
the breath faded away; the formidable organism fell into unconsciousness. It took less than an hour to die, and it did not
appear to suffer.

When the mammoth was no longer moving, despair
overwhelmed Awah and the two women. They had seen Wanawanoûm and the old woman perish without any great emotion, but it seemed that their own race was disappearing with
the mammoth.

"The Sons of the Mammoth will be annihilated!" Awah
murmured.

He was so discouraged that I was afraid that he might let
himself die of hunger and cold. Fortunately, I had an idea.

"There are mammoths in the lands of the Sun!" I affirmed. I was thinking of elephants. It would not be very diffi-

199

cult for me to make my primitives believe that they were the descendants of the colossi that grazed the prehistoric forests and savannahs.

"Is that true?" Touanhô exclaimed, always quicker to understand than the others.

"Certainly!" I affirmed. "I've seen them."

Awah took some time to get the idea into his head, but as soon as he succeeded, he was gripped by an extraordinary ardor and he harnessed himself to the sled alongside me.

That day was much harder than any we had yet experienced. We advanced slowly, five times more slowly than with the mammoth, but the temperature was getting steadily higher; we were arriving in a region into which the Eskimos came, and even touching the zone in which I had left the tribe with which our expedition had been allied.

The night was relatively peaceful. The death of our companions had increased our individual shares of the rations and left us a surplus of garments and blankets. We had a copious meal, which gave us back some of our strength and, although bent double, we progressed by 15 kilometers in the course of the following day.

That evening, we were worn out by fatigue. For some unknown reason, it was not very cold, and that circumstance contributed to rendering our ordeal less painful. Touanhô's spirits had recovered; she was now almost as resilient as Awah, who was displaying a magnificent energy. Even Namhâ was battling successfully against fatigue. One might have thought that the young flesh of all three was infused with new energy. As for me, I was on the up again. Without having Awah's extraordinary endurance, I was giving no more sign of distress. All the same, our speed slowed down the following day; we had great difficulty covering 12 kilometers.

The next day, it was even worse. The terrain became difficult. It was continually necessary to make detours. Furthermore, an enormous bear started following us toward dusk, and when we were out of harness it remained on watch, uttering intermittent growls that disturbed us much less in itself than because it might have attracted other predators.

Suddenly, a sharp joy: a group of huts appeared in the coppery light—snowy huts that I knew well, and the sight of which caused me to cry out.

Awah had stopped, full of suspicion.

"It's a friendly tribe!" I told him.

"Are they Sons of the Mammoth?"

"No," I replied, for I knew that the appearance of Eskimos differed too much from that of my prehistoric people, "but I've made an alliance with them."

He remained rooted to the spot, his face hard and stern. I had neglected to warn him in advance, fearful of his prejudices; the proximity of unknown men filled him with grim hostility. His right hand gripped a deer-antler harpoon, his left held a nephrite axe.

"Is Awah going mad?" I said, authoritatively. "Can we fight a tribe?"

We were slowly approaching a village—if it could be called a village. Dogs were barking. At first, we could not see anyone; then short and ridiculously wrapped-up women appeared. They ran away, uttering cries of alarm that were repeated by children of both sexes, while the dogs barked furiously.

"We're friends!" I shouted. "We've made an alliance with your chiefs!"

Other silhouettes appeared, gliding cautiously between the huts. I counted half a dozen, short and stout. In the end, men showed themselves, having been convinced, I think, of our numeric weakness. Five or six angry dogs made as if to attack us. "We do not know you," said one of the men, finally. "Where have you come from?"

I pointed to the North and said: "We've come from out there. Before then, though, I came from the South. I was received by a great chief who became my friend."

"What is his name?"

"Wandrov."

The Eskimos looked at one another suspiciously. As with all savages, circumstances could render them dangerous. Evidently, they felt strong; in addition to warriors they had dogs and a certain number of females skilled in combat.

"We know Wandrov," said the man who had spoken first, finally. "When did you make an alliance with him?"

"It was two summers ago, less than one day's journey from here."

The man exchanged a few words with his companions. Suddenly, two dogs launched themselves forward, immediately followed by the others.

"Into the sled!" I ordered Awah.

I had drawn my revolver from its holster and seized my rifle. I had a few cartridges left. The next minute was agonizing. If the dogs attacked in earnest; I would have to defend myself; it would be war. "Call off your dogs!" I cried, loudly. "We would rather not kill them."

I brandished my revolver, Awah his harpoon. The Eskimos drew their bowstrings.

XIV.

Whether it was because they knew the effect of firearms or because of a concern for hospitality, the Eskimos did not encourage their dogs—which, having arrived in the vicinity of the sled, stopped; they limited themselves to sniffing us, threatening us with their fangs and howling, with the prudence of wolves. Uncertain themselves, the men and women limited themselves to watching the dogs, and us. That game went on for two or three minutes.

"What will you gain," I shouted, "by letting us kill your dogs and causing several of you to perish?"

These words appeared to have some effect. One of the Eskimos sounded a summons, swiftly followed by another.

The dogs retreated, growling, while the same Eskimo said: "Wandrov's guests will be ours!"

We lowered our weapons; the man who had spoken advanced toward us. That was the critical moment. I knew that as soon as we were welcomed, we would be out of danger—for although not all Eskimos can be trusted, those of the region in question had a profound sense of hospitality.

After a brief hesitation, I emerged from the sled and went forwards in my turn. I completed the rituals, with which I was quite familiar, and we headed for the village in the red dusk.

We were given a hut, which reeked of rancid oil and putrefaction, and fed on meat and dried fish. Nightfall saved us from curiosity and intrusion. We slept well in our stinking refuge, but on the following morning it was necessary to submit to the company and investigations of our hosts.

We spent the day negotiating our departure. I was not without resources. First of all there was the rifle and the revolver, weapons well known to my hosts, which inspired a passionate desire in them. I promised them to anyone who would accompany me as far as a settlement of white men—a relatively easy matter, since I knew the route. I had other wealth: there were sparkling pieces of quartz of various colors, of which I had made a provision in our caves, and there were a few prehistoric necklaces, which produced an extraordinary effect.

At the end of the day, we had arrived at an agreement of sorts. It would not be sealed until the next day, because the Eskimos wanted a supplement of crystals, in addition to a staff of authority in reindeer-horn, which greatly tempted the oldest of the men who were present. I did not want to yield without haggling, knowing how important it was for them to be persuaded of the value of what I was giving them.

We were provided with four dogs and given two men for an escort, but our sled, being too heavy, was abandoned. In exchange for the rifle, Oudalano was one of our two guides. Clever and sagacious, he knew how to select the paces where partial melting, which frequently occurred during the middle of the day, would not impede our progress. We had reached a region where vegetation and animals were reappearing; to travel over it by sled required long detours, so we advanced very slowly. All the same, I ended up recognizing, by reliable indications, the proximity of a settlement through which our expedition had passed. A recrudescence of cold gave me hope that we would soon attain that goal. On June 1, I calculated that only one long or two short stages remained to be taken. It was high time. Namhâ was dangerously weak and one of the children had fallen into a disturbing torpor.

Until midday we made good progress. Toward 1 p.m., the sky became very dark and a nasty wind began to get up, soon accompanied by stinging snow. Immediately, we took precautions, people and animals alike piling into the large tent that I had brought from the territory. The wind blew furiously. Even though we were huddled tightly together, we were frozen. The tent clattered under the assaults of the tempest; I feared that there might be a catastrophe at any moment.

Finally, the storm eased—but when we tried to get under way again, it transpired that one of the sleds was broken, in such a way that it was unusable. The other could only carry a part of our company. What should we do? We could not entrust the women to the Eskimos. Awah, on the other hand, would not consent to be separated from them, and I would have considered myself a coward if I had not stayed at my post. It was also impossible to separate the children from their mothers. In sum, there was only one thing to do: to trust Oudalano and his companion. They had no interest in betraying us; we retained the promised rewards. I gave the Eskimos instructions so precise that they could hardly go astray.

"Oudalano and his companion will not only have the promised weapons," I said, pointing to the rifle and the revolver, "but they shall receive an abundance of cartridges, which we will obtain from the white men. They shall also have more shining stones."

The cunning children that my Eskimos were laughed happily, and their sticky little eyes sparkled. They set off with an ardor equal to that of a Carnegie in pursuit of billions.

When they had disappeared, I felt the solitude more keenly. In this wild country, they represented reliably instinct and the wisdom of experience. Awah, Touanhô and Namhâ, in spite of their sharp senses, could not replace them. Fortunately, they had left us two dogs, and in that tragic hour, those humble beasts represented something solid, of which I would not have wanted to be deprived at any price.

XV.

We lived in the corrosive suspense of waiting.

We were condemned to immobility. Setting off into the desert would have risked those who would come to our rescue losing our trail. After 40 hours of waiting, however, I resolved to make a reconnaissance with Awah and one of the dogs.

The weather was clear, no peril probable, and we were only proposing to go up to a height from which we could see nine or ten kilometers. Sheltered in the tent, with the second dog, Touanhô and Namhâ would be able to wait for us in total security. By way of extra precautions, I showed them how to make two or three signals, which Awah would doubtless be able to see with his naked eye, and which I could, in any event, discern with the aid of my telescope.

My companion and I headed southwards. The terrain presented few difficulties. No melt having affected the frozen snow that day, we made easy progress. Although cold, the temperature was tolerable, even excellent for walking. We only had a few detours to make, with the result that in less than two hours we had reached the bottom of the hill. Before climbing it, we looked back; a red flag was flying over the tent—a sign that all was well.

The ascent turned out to be quite difficult. We were stopped several times by crevasses, which we had to go around. The slope was, naturally, very slippery. When we reached the summit three hours had gone by, and we could only count on four and a half or five more hours of daylight. First we assured ourselves that the red flag as still flying, and then we peered out over the long plain that extended southwards.

We could see for a long way. The air seemed even drier than on our departure. For league upon league, the white wilderness extended its bleak monotony. Nevertheless, on the far horizon, we perceived a few green and brown islets suggestive of habitable land.

Animals occasionally passed by: the melancholy Arctic fauna of dismal white birds, hares, foxes and ermines. I had expected that; I knew perfectly well that the American base was out of sight—but in spite of that, I was discontented. Deep down, I had hoped to see the rescue-party, of which Oudalano and his comrade had gone in quest, approaching.

After waiting a quarter of an hour, I said: "We have to go back!"

Before doing so, I planted a spike terminated by a pennant, in order to guide our saviors, if they were in any doubt as to the direction to follow.

Awah watched me silently. His face was impassive, but I understood the expression on his mouth well enough to discern disappointment. Suddenly, he murmured: "Awah would like to look through the crystal eye."

His request astonished me, because of his repugnance for all instruments to which he was not accustomed. By virtue of seeing me use the telescope, he must have familiarized himself with it. I gave him instructions as to how to make use of it—instructions that he understood, because he had often observed my movements while I scanned the horizon.

After a few minutes, he uttered a joyful exclamation. "Oudalano is coming back with four sleds and men!"

It was only after a fairly long time that I began to see confused images appear, through the telescope. They became clearer. In my turn I made out three sleds and, seized by a sort of delirium, I shouted: "Let's go to meet them!"

Awah seemed passably excited. We assured ourselves that everything was in order at the tent and went down the southern slope of the hill excitedly. Even the dog seemed impatient. We trotted for an hour, and made no less than seven kilometers. For their part, the sleds were advancing at considerable speed. Soon we were only a short distance from our rescuers.

The dog had taken the lead; it launched itself furiously toward Oudalano.

When we met up with the expedition, I was so agitated that I was trembling in every limb. With a mixture of intoxication and affection, I saw men of my own race again. They were three Americans of various sorts, all three of whom affected a phlegmatic calmness. The first was a tall Anglo-Saxon with a thin face and a lantern jaw. His steel-gray eyes studied me circumspectly. The second, an Irishman with sparkling eyes, showed an active face that was made for laughter. The third, shorter than the other two, with a ferrety appearance, seemed to be a half-caste.

I thanked them effusively.

"Impossible to do otherwise!" said the Anglo-Saxon.

"Anyway, we were bored," said the half-caste.

Meanwhile, the Irishman offered me his hand, saying: "Did you get close to the pole?"

"I reached the 88th degree," I said.

The three men deigned to smile. "Glorious!" exclaimed the Anglo-Saxon.

Meanwhile, they were inspecting Awah with evident curiosity. "One of your traveling-companions?" asked the half-caste.

"No," I said. "A race of men that I discovered en route."

The Americans did not hide their surprise, which increased the more they studied the prehistoric man.

"Awful!" muttered the Irishman.

"What equipment!" said the half-caste.

The Anglo-Saxon limited himself to shaking his head.

During this brief palaver we had installed ourselves in the sleds; they set off again at top speed. The Irishman, whose name was Murtagh, continued to question me. My intention being to keep a part of my discoveries secret, I only replied with respect to matters whose disclosure did not seem to me to be compromising. Reduced to the discovery of an unknown land full of vestiges of lost times and inhabited by a group of humans with violet-tinted skins, they already seemed sufficiently marvelous to my interlocutor, who deigned to set aside his authoritative phlegm and utter exclamations of surprise.

The fair-haired man—James Warman—listened with equal curiosity but more discreetly.

Meanwhile, we made rapid progress. The Sun sank to the horizon, within an hour, dusk would commence to sow its grayness. The sleds had to make a detour because of the hill, which was inaccessible to them. When we arrived at the bottom of the north-west slope, we tried to see the tent, but a certain unevenness in the terrain rendered it invisible. Even when we reached the uniform plain we could not make it out at first, for the daylight had become feeble. Awah finally discovered it, with the aid of the telescope, but we had to go a further half-kilometer before he could make out the red flag. Soon, the tent became visible to the naked eye, and the slight anxiety that had crept up on me dissipated.

"We'll be there in a quarter of an hour," the Irishman affirmed.

Suddenly, the ground became difficult. Crevasses and holes hindered our progress. It was necessary to make another detour, longer than we had anticipated, and when we arrived in the vicinity of the tent the scarlet Sun was disappearing over the horizon.

Oudalano, who had remained impassive until then, said: "Is there a dog in the tent?"

"Yes," I said, with a slight pang of anxiety.

"It's odd that it hasn't made its presence known," Murtagh put in.

It was also odd that Touanhô and Namhâ had given no sign of life. Awah, who evidently thought so, had straightened up and was looking avidly at the tent.

Our dogs hurled themselves forward, growling.

When we reached the tent, the Sun was hidden. A long coppery light spread over the pale solitude. I was now very anxious, and when the sleds stopped, I ran forward, followed by Awah.

We lifted the tent-flap that served as a doorway.

There was no one inside.

XVI.

Awah uttered an exclamation of rage, while I remained momentarily dumbfounded. Then we tried to figure out what might have happened. It was possible that Touanhô and Namhâ, having become anxious, had set out to look for us— but the removal of pieces of quartz, prehistoric necklaces, axes and staffs of authority quickly convinced us that marauders had arrived during our absence. The ground bore traces of footprints.

"It could only have been Eskimos!" Murtagh remarked.

Oudalano search passionately; by taking the quartz, the necklaces and the staffs of authority, the unknown raiders had stolen part of his wages. Aided by his dogs he searched for the trail. It did not take him long to find that it headed eastwards. In spite of the late hour, the Americans consented to a pursuit, which was facilitated by a full moon.

"On condition that there are not too many of them!" Warman objected, however.

"There are only two sleds," said Oudalano, swiftly. He understood a little English.

Within a few minutes, we were on the track of the abductors. We advanced rapidly, thanks to the two lead dogs; they were unharnessed and followed the trail without difficulty.

"The thieves can't have got far!" observed the half-caste. "It's a matter of catching up with them before they rejoin their fellows."

Oudalano, when questioned, did not think that there was any encampment in the neighborhood, but he could not be sure; it was the season when the Arctic tribes wandered.

"We'll soon see!" said Murtagh.

Warman checked his rifle, a repeater, which I knew that he could use as well as a Boer. The twilight reddened further in the far west; an enormous sulfurous moon rose in the east. The cold was intense.

An hour went by. Our animals, although fatigued by a long run, maintained a good speed. The lead dogs showed an increasing ardor, proof that we were gaining ground. Warman noticed that, and said: "It's quite plausible that these brutes have dog-teams as tired as ours. They've obviously come a long way, since you had no inkling of their approach."

A second hour went by. The teams were showing signs of exhaustion.

"They've had a long day!" Murtagh muttered. "It's time we got there."

"We're nearly there!" said the half-caste.

For ten minutes, Awah had been straining his savage senses; the fixity of his eyes and the flaring of his nostrils were evident. He ended up saying to me: "There they are!"

His hand was pointing eastwards. Warman adjusted his telescope; I did likewise. A confused group of men and dogs was moving in the lunar light. Our approach occasioned an attempt at flight, which was abandoned almost immediately. Barking sounds and howls went up on the plain, uttered by the marauders' dogs and ours. In a short time, we arrived in proximity to the group. We stopped about 200 meters away. Our weapons were ready, and victory certain; the number of our antagonists was no greater than six.

It was Oudalano who called out to them, ordering them to surrender the women and the booty.

There was a brief attempt at resistance; one of the abductors had a rifle—but on seeing Murtagh, Warman, the half-caste and I raising our weapons he understood that the contest was too unequal.

Five minutes later, we had recovered possession of the women and the booty.

Epilogue

"The remainder of our adventure is of no interest," Alglave went on, after a pause, "for we were not subject to any further ordeals of consequence. "I returned to the United States, and then to Europe, where I succeeded in exchanging my diamonds for a sum of 6,000,000 francs, after which I came to take up residence in Kabylie[17] with my prehistoric people. For a few hundred thousand francs, I bought these forests, pasturelands and fields, where numerous humans could live by hunting and fishing. Awah set up home in a cave, with Namhâ, while Touanhô has adapted herself very well to a more comfortable life in my house. She had become my companion, while Namhâ is more Awah's—although he shows no sentiment of ownership except in autumn.

"My life is simple and beautiful; it's the life of our Magdalenian ancestors, save for the luxury of a constructed dwelling, a few items of furniture and a few choice aliments, including coffee and wine. We have a great many children. Awah's are now numerous enough to perpetuate the ancient Tourassian race..."

While Alglave was talking, I saw a young woman coming toward us. She had an exotic complexion and large sparkling eyes.

---

[17] A region of Algeria.

"This is Touanhô!" Alglave said.

She was obviously not pretty in the sense that we understand, but she had a good deal of charm—a mysterious, distant, very youthful charm. I understood perfectly why the explorer had made her his companion.

She pronounced a few words, in an extremely guttural accent, which did not seem to me to be unpleasant.

"I didn't want her to learn any other language than her own," Alglave said. "My dream would then appear less captivating. But here's Awah!"

A tall man with a flexible gait appeared around the corner of the oak-plantation; I was surprised to see that he was followed by an elephant.

Alglave was smiling. "Yes, I had that elephant brought here to make life pleasant for my prehistoric friend. Awah's iron-hard belief is that it's a mammoth, so his totemism is satisfied; he's convinced that he is communing with his ancestors, and renders the same worship to the innocent pachyderm that the ancient Tourassian rendered to the last remaining mammoths."

He fell silent. Touanhô, leaning on his shoulder in a familiar fashion, looked at me with her blazing eyes.

"Now I'll introduce you to our little miracle," my host went on, after a pause. He whistled briefly, and a 12 year old child appeared in the doorway. "That's Raouham, Awah's son."

Alglave caressed the boy's black hair; the latter was smiling softly. Raouham was pleasant to behold; his eyes seemed to devour the form of living beings and things.

"He's an artist...an artist far superior to Awah, who is nevertheless skilful at reproducing the structure of animals. I've encouraged his work, and I've helped him; I've introduced some discipline into it. I ended up enabling him to produce works which demonstrate that the sculptural genius of prehistoric people was equal to that of the Greeks—they didn't have the means to develop it, that's all! Would you like to see?"

Alglave took me into a large studio, with whitewashed walls, where an entire menagerie of plaster castings was on display, along with carved antlers and sculpted bones. There were deer, jackals, hyenas, oxen, dogs and panthers, imbued with a gripping and perfect life.

I looked at them in amazement—and then I remembered something. I remembered a corner of the Autumn Salon where I had seen Rodin and Bourdelle in ecstasy. Rodin had said: "He will be the great sculptor of the next generation."

They had been the same deer, the same jackals and the same panthers that I was now admiring in the savage studio. They bore the same signature: Ram.

THE BOAR MEN

The caravan went into the forest, which became more ferocious and treacherous by the hour. The tree people moved thus in the times when humans were beasts like other beasts, because they had no weapons and had no other foresight than ancient instinct. As the caravan passed by, the predatory beasts immersed themselves in thickets or huddled in their lairs.

Occasionally, a deer ran under distant branches, a monkey showed a sly head or parrots raised their insolent voices, but there was a suggestion of a mysterious and innumerable life; it revealed itself in subtle traces, fugitive effluvia or light rustlings. Infinite mistrust, cunning ever on the alert and inexhaustible patience equilibrated the drama of beasts that devour and beasts that are devoured.

Night fell; the caravan camped in a clearing in the Blue Forest, which was separated from the Red Forest by a river. Fires projected their coppery light, mingling in fugitive waters with the tremulous image of the Moon and the primitive palpitations of the trees. Crocodiles were glimpsed lying dormant on islets, crafty monkeys in the forks of branches—and the senile voices of frogs, croaking among the water-lilies, punctuated the enchanted murmur of the waves.

Suzanne Dejongh was no longer surprised to be on this island, almost at the antipodes of her native land, which was ruled by her people. The death of her parents, the difficult voyage, the new stars, and also her youth, had accustomed her to adventure. She sometimes looked at her brother Lodewyk, full of insouciance, and sometimes at the giant who was in command of the caravan, and in whose house she was going to live; then she meditated on the twists of fate. She was an innocent creature, a passive soul varied along by circumstance as the river carried along blades of grass. She scarcely wondered how she would withstand her new life.

The giant leader, Karel van den Bosch, was descended unblemished from the great Nordic dolicocephali, with bright eyes, a rounded skull and blond hair; he conducted himself with earnest good will, obstinate in his projects and energetic in their execution. His florid beard was reminiscent of the beard of the benevolent emperor Charlemagne. In times of peril, he could as easily recall the King of the Sea that Jean Revel described as "Athlete of life, gladiator of the Ocean, that magnificent adventurer, familiar of the swell, braves the elements and says of the tempest: 'It will take me where I want to go.'"[18]

His voice was as gigantic as his stature, and his Soldanella eyes had a marvelously young gaze. "My house will be your house," he had said to Suzanne and Lodewyk.

She believed him, blindly.

His son Hendrik was there, who no longer had the linen-white skin of the mists of the low countries; there was Lodewyk, on whose face was inscribed the tranquil boldness of sea-rovers. The others, the vanquished, belonged to the ambiguous race of Sumatra, apart from one Mongol-Hindu and a stray Chinaman.

In the middle of the night, two men, whose approach had been signaled by the dogs, emerged from the woods. The sentries recognized the explorers of the wilderness sent forth by van den Bosch.

The giant watched the two men approach: one indigene and one half-breed. The former said: "Master, Bandits[19] are in the Vlugt Gorge. I counted 50 of them."

---

[18] "Jean Revel" was the pseudonym of Paul Toutain (1848-1925), a regional writer famous for his celebration of the culture of Normandy. The quote probably comes from one of the items in *Contes normands* (1901)

[19] The word that I have had to translate as "Bandits" is the much more colorful *Ecorcheurs* [flayers], a designation initially given to gangs of rogue mercenaries active in France in the

The giant shook his head. "Will they dare to attack us?"

"They are getting bolder every day, Master."

The half-breed reported: "Boar Men have penetrated into the Red Forest, two leagues from here."

"That's not possible!" muttered van den Bosch. "During the great invasion they scarcely got past Wittenberg. You must have made a mistake."

A disdainful indignation lit up in the half-breed's eyes. "Matzal's eyes are equal to an eagle's! They do not confuse the tapir and the buffalo, nor fireflies with the stars. Are not the heads of the Boar Men covered in fawn and gray hair? Do they not have pointed ears, fingers shorter than the fingers of other men and the legs of an orangutan?"

"One can't doubt you!" said the planter. "Were there many of them?"

"I counted more than ten—but our forefathers have told us that when they leave the marsh, they march in bands."

"That's true," van den Bosch agreed.

"They have the noses of wolves," the scout added. "Whoever gets too close to them will not see the morning!"

"Matzal is always skillful and always vigilant!"

Astonished by these unforeseeable perils that were gathering around him, the giant remained pensive. There were only two routes: the Vlugt Gorge or the Red Forest. Thirty men could fight, of which only 20 were reliable; van den Bosch's rifle alone could do the work of ten. Because he was feared in the forest and the mountains, although the indigenes did not hate him, they might escape attack in the Vlugt—but they would not know until they had passed through it.

Everything about the Boar Men was mysterious; there was no way of knowing whether they would fight or disappear—and it was possible that they would attack the camp that very night.

14th and early 15th centuries—the name represented their alleged habit of stripping their murdered victims bare. It was subsequently used to refer to any unusually rapacious robbers.

To ward off an assault it would have been necessary to fell trees; the carts did not form a long enough barrier; only the river, as tumultuous as a torrent, was effective. Full of anxiety, the planter turned toward Suzanne, who was asleep on a mat, and Lodewyk, a little further away. The idea that his guests might be in terrible danger while under his protection was painful to a man in whom the primitive soul and the disciplined soul were in harmony.

As he was meditating, Suzanne opened her eyes. She saw the giant, who was looking at her, the fires that lit the vegetation strangely, and the profound Sky, across which the stars of the Southern Cross were moving in the direction of the pole.

"Is it necessary to get up?" she asked.

"Perhaps," said the big Dutchman. Because he did not like indirection, he added: "We'll probably camp in the Infernal Rocks."

"Are we under threat, then?"

"Not yet, niece. We might be. The Infernal Rocks are a hard camping-ground—that's why I avoided them—but it would take 100 men to force a way in!

Sitting up, she scanned the edge of the Red Forest on the far bank, listening to the moaning of the river, the lamentation of the batrachians and, in the distance, an obscure plaint—perhaps the plaint of an animal being eaten alive. "Is it Boar Men?" she asked.

Van den Bosch did not know how to lie or be evasive. "Boar Men have been sighted in the Red Forest, and a band of half-breeds near the Vlugt Pass. The latter undoubtedly won't attack us, and won't be able to for several hours, but we must be wary. I shall, therefore, set up camp in the Infernal Rocks.

The murmur of speech had woken up Lodewyk; other men were sitting up within the flaming circle.

"Should we get up?" the young man asked.

"That would be best. I'll give the order."

Half an hour later, the man and animals were ready to leave.

The Infernal Rocks formed a redoubtable fortress: four masses of granite separated by three narrow defiles, the largest of which overhung the river. Rapids rendered any disembarkation impracticable for 2000 meters upstream and down. The tallest of the rocks loomed up 400 meters; they all had sheer sides and the defiles permitted defenders to fire on aggressors without exposing themselves. To storm the redoubt would require an assault so murderous that only a numerous company would run the risk.

It was a rough spot, the ground bristling with sharp stones and split by ravines. When the carts had been unhitched, they served to render the defiles even more impenetrable. The horses were sheltered in a large excavation, which formed an embryonic cavern, and the men were distributed on three sides.

"It would need 200 men to mount an effective assault," the giant remarked, "and it would cost them dear! Those in the Vlugt Gorge can't amount to more than 150 men, and no one has ever seen a company of 100 Boar Men." He shrugged his enormous shoulders. "Four more hours of darkness—let's get some sleep."

With the fires lit and the sentries posted, the caravan took its rest—but neither Suzanne nor Lodewyk went to sleep.

Toward dawn, the track-beaters reappeared. The news was bad. The Bandits, having left the Vlugt Gorge, were advancing through the Blue Forest.

"They've become very bold!" the planter growled. "What are they hoping to do?"

"Nothing good for us," said Hendrik, who had got up, "but everything depends on their leader."

"Exactly!" his father agreed. "Fundamentally, the race is brave. If we want to get past, Hendrik, we'll have to kill a great many of them!"

"A great many!" sighed the son.

Crouching distractedly beside one of the fires, on to which he threw branches that, being green, crackled before catching alight, van den Bosch remained silent.

218

The stars faded; the equatorial twilight turned to dawn in a moment, and the Sun rose with lightning speed. The father of life, the immense red furnace, was reflected in the rapids, and the fearful animals abandoned themselves once again to the ambiguous joys of daylight.

The Infernal Rocks were succeeded by infertile ground, in which only a few trees took root, the majority of them remaining paltry or perishing, malnourished and deprived of water. The jungle did not begin again for 500 or 600 meters, with the consequence that it was impossible to reach the fort without passing under the fire of its defenders.

Would they dare? The big Dutchman asked himself again.

He doubted it, but had not all his expectations been proved false? Besides which, if *they* did not attack, a siege might prove more redoubtable than combat. Then again, there was the enigma of the Boar Men.

The whole caravan now knew what menaced it, and van den Bosch, going to his niece, said, in a melancholy tone: "Forgive us for having exposed you to danger."

"We're the ones who need forgiveness!" Suzanne exclaimed.

"No one could have foreseen what has happened!" Hendrik put in.

"That's true," his farther said. "We've never seen anything similar before."

The half-breed Matzal came out of one of the defiles. Standing still, with his eyes fixed on the planter, he said: "Master, the Bandits are approaching. They might attack within the hour."

"We're ready," said the giant. Having made sure that all the sentinels were at their posts he shouted in a thunderous voice: "Let those who are afraid to fight make themselves known—but let them be quite certain that no treason will allow them to escape danger. The Bandits do not keep any promises or grant mercy to anyone. We need to hold out for two days. We'll release the pigeons. In two hours, people will know that we're in danger—the planters and the military post will come to our aid."

The men looked at him avidly.

"The river is uncrossable at this point, so the camp can only be reached through the three defiles. There's no cover between the forest and the Rocks; they'll have to pass through our fire. There's no reason to think that they'll dare to attack us."

The men of the indigenous race listened to the immense voice without anxiety; none of them was positively cowardly, several possessed a stubborn and cunning bravery analogous to that of the Japanese. They could also have confidence in white/indigenous half-castes, but the Hindus were passive and the Chinese equivocal.

When the men had eaten their breakfast the daylight was bright; the Sun was beginning to roast the bare rocks. The rocks seemed melancholy to the point of being funereal, bones of the old earth transpiercing a lichenous epidermis.

The camp formed a bristling semicircle, in which the cryptogams and pellitories accomplished their eternal mission; a few wretched trees grew, having drilled their roots into fissures; one of them, crooked and verrucose, eaten away by animal and vegetable vermin, had persisted for more than a century. It stood at the summit of one of the rocks, putting forth branches that were alternately bare and leafy, a sickly victim of the Sun and the weather.

A man, hoisted up there, alternately scanned the Blue Forest, the Red Forest and the river. Obstinate and crazy, life swarmed in the waters and the woods alike; the baroque voices of parrots pierced the silence like myriad drills, and the insects maintained their victorious existence, dominators of predatory beasts, holding in check the ferocious human race.

The man stationed on high, the half-breed Matzal, who had the eyes of a bearded vulture, came down at midday to say: "The Bandits have arrived."

"With the Lord's help, we shall defeat them!" said van den Bosch.

The time went by: a time of expectation and peril. The enemy remained as invisible as if he had been shrouded in profound darkness, but every man in the camp knew that homicidal eyes were on watch in the foliage, the bushes and the tall ferns.

When the Sun had quit the zenith, they heard a resounding voice that drowned out all of the noises of the forest. It was not the voice of a man or a buffalo, nor any beast, although it resembled an immense roaring or a giant's plaint.

Suzanne and Lodewyk had straightened up.

"The horn of the Mountain Wolves!" said the Dutch leader. "I understand the Bandits' audacity." Seeing Suzanne's interrogative expression, he went on: "They're primitive Malays, as savage as real wolves, and very audacious. The *others* would not have dared to take on old van den Bosch, but *those*...!" He made an evasive gesture, discontented at having given way to his ill-humor once again. "If they show themselves," he said, "it's because they want to talk."

The trumpet had just fallen silent. A white pennant appeared above a thicket.

"There's the proof!" said the planter. "These hyenas are aping our customs."

A strident voice resounded at the forest's edge. The Netherlander replied, as loud as a church bell: "The Bandits' envoy may approach. Van den Bosch will answer for his life and liberty."

This speech must have inspired complete confidence, for a man with an ochreous complexion, prominent cheekbones and cruel narrow eyes appeared on the bare ground. Tall for a man of his race, when he appeared before the colossus he looked no bigger than a child. Their gazes met—the extraordinary honesty of the Dutchman's blue eyes and the insectile gaze of the Malay.

"I've never seen you before," said the planter.

"I am To-Tay, the Gray Eagle," the man replied, not without pride, "second-in-command after the chief."

"And what do you want?" van den Bosch asked, rudely. "We're peaceful folk, but we know how to defend ourselves and we aren't afraid of bandits."

"We are not bandits!" the other retorted, standing up straight. "We are free men."

"Who murder and rob other free men."

"Men who have taken our valleys, our forests and our mountains, and who call themselves our masters. Have they not killed our forefathers, and, more recently, our rebellious brothers? We are waging war."

"Fine," said the giant, impassively. "You're refusing to let us pass?"

"We need guns—and money to buy more guns."

"With which to fight us!" said the Dutchman, with a scornful smile. "So, if I promise you guns and money, we'll have free passage?"

"My brothers want you to surrender your weapons and pay 1000 guilder for your ransom."

"Oh! Knaap![20] Your brothers are imbeciles. They must know that if I promised guns and money, the guns and the money would be delivered at the agreed time and date."

"The Mountain Wolves do not know you."

The colossus saw that discussion was vain. "I know the Mountain Wolves. Go tell your brothers that we will not surrender our weapons." The blood was rising in great waves in his powerful body, overtaken by wrath. "Your stupidity will cost you dear," the Dutchman proclaimed.

An ashen pallor invaded the negotiator's face; doubtless he feared some violent action, for he had his kris in his hand.

The giant shrugged his shoulders.

The envoy had already recovered his composure. "We shall wait another hour," he said.

"We're not asking for an hour, or even a minute."

---

[20] A literal (if somewhat euphemistic) translation of this Dutch term of abuse would be "knave."

The messenger withdrew at a slow pace and the planter turned to Lodewyk to say: "We're at war, nephew!"

Lodewyk, looking at Suzanne, felt his heart grow heavy.

The harsh sunlight became as mysterious as darkness; no night could have rendered the enemy more invisible, but the men in the camp knew, and the travelers divined, that the silence and stillness concealed redoubtable traps.

The impassive van den Bosch went from one defile to the next, with vigilant slowness, and sometimes scaled a rock.

"Unless they dig a tunnel underground they can't take us by surprise for as long as the light lasts," he said to Lodewyk, after one such inspection. "Without the Wolves, there'd be nothing to fear before dusk—but the Wolves are more impatient and more aggressive than their allies." The howl of a siamang made him raise his head. "That's Matzal!" he said. "Ah!"

He advanced into the middle of a defile; a thick bush formed rapidly at the edge of the wood, between two teaks. Matzal seemed to spring out of the rock.

"They're going to attack, Master."

"Is it the bush that tells you that?"

"Yes, Master—it's a trick of the mountain folk. The bush is going to start moving."

"Carried by men?"

"Carried by a cart. The men will be invisible—and shielded."

"So they're counting on taking us by storm?"

"They'll try."

Conscious of the anxiety that the stratagem would sow among his men, the leader leaned forward.

The bush, deployed over a width of 10 or 12 feet, had started moving slowly; as it came closer, thick branches became visible among the foliage; a superstitious dread immobilized the camp's defenders.

"Above all, don't waste ammunition!" the leader's thunderous voice proclaimed. "Fire on command, and only once each. Wait! One...two...three—fire!"

Twenty shots rang out. A clamor of defiance rang out behind the bush and in the forest.

"There are wounded, some doubtless mortally," affirmed van den Bosch. "Ready, lads!"

There was a second salvo, and the bush tottered; meanwhile, a further clamor challenged the besieged.

"It's too far away!" growled van den Bosch, who discerned a decrease in the shouts coming from the bush, while those in the forest were still as loud. He waited until the device had advanced for another 40 meters before ordering the third salvo. It was undoubtedly more murderous than the other two, for the bush was immobilized.

"They're still there, boys! Get ready!"

The bush had started moving again. When it was less than 100 meters from the rocks, the planter gave the order to fire for the fourth time.

In spite of the stoicism of the Malays, a few screams were mingled with the vociferations, and the apparatus tottered.

"They're having difficulty reorganizing themselves!" Lodewyk remarked.

"There must be a lot of them, though. If not, you can be sure they wouldn't have risked an attack."

The leader waited until the bush was only 30 meters from the rocks, then shouted: "One last salvo—and everyone take cover!"

The cart swayed; ferocious howls went up; 40 individuals bounded forth, krises in hand. They were all Wolves, come from the highlands, more primitive, more ferocious and more impetuous than the Malays of the lower valleys.

They headed straight for the central defile—the largest and the nearest—imagining that they would be able, by virtue of an excess of speed, to startle the besieged and cut their throats, as they cut people's throats in ravines and caverns. The men in the camp were not unaware that the Wolves were formidable in hand-to-hand combat; trained in fighting with the kris since childhood, they knew the deadly blows that pierce the heart or cut through the entrails.

The fusillade was now incessant; the giant, wedged between two rocky spurs, shot down a man a second—but after eight or ten seconds, the aggressors were in the defile. Without the thick branches and heavy stones accumulated there, the fate of the expedition would have been decided; inferior in hand-to-hand combat, the besieged forces would have been slaughtered like livestock, save for their giant leader, Hendrik and three or four elite fighting-men—but while the Wolves exhausted themselves climbing over the obstacles, and incessant fusillade decimated them; at short range, more than a third of the bullets struck home.

Even so, 20 Wolves got past the obstacles and seven Sumatrans went down stabbed by krises, while Lodewyk fixed his bayonet, Hendrik, a revolver in each hand, continued shooting antagonists down, and van den Bosch, cornered by four Wolves, struck out with an enormous axe, which split a head of a shoulder at every stroke. Then the axe began to whirl, and the planter, carried away by a frenzied rage, all the more violent for having arisen slowly, gave voice to his war cry, louder than the clamor of ten siamangs. Three Wolves gave way to panic, two more were struck down by the axe. Lodewyk skewered a third with his bayonet. Hendrik discharged his weapon at point-blank range.

Then, overwhelmed, the last aggressors stopped fighting. There were five of them. The leader granted them mercy.

Events had moved so rapidly that Suzanne had not had time to form a resolution. She came forward to seize the weapon of a wounded Sumatran while the last Wolves were surrendering.

"We're victorious, and it's sad!" growled van den Bosch. "Men shouldn't die like that—but it wasn't us who wanted it."

Five men from the caravan were dead and seven wounded. Of the dozen surviving indigenes, seven were conducting themselves with some bravery, increased by the victory; the other five were indubitably cowards. They made little attempt to calculate the enemy's losses. In all probability, 30 Wolves had been killed during the bush's advance; 20 had fallen before the palisades, and in the camp itself there were seven dead, six wounded and five prisoners.

"They won't attack again," said the leader. "The punishment has been too harsh, and they don't know our losses. In any case, with the seven men on whom we can depend, and you, nephew"—he turned to Lodewyk—"who fought well, and my son, we still have ten combatants."

"I hope we'll have 11," said Suzanne, softly. "I was taken by surprise—but I believe I would have fought!"

"Very good! Very good!" murmured the planter, tenderly. "Ours is an ancient warrior race—our ancestors dared to fight the great peoples of Europe, and our mariners were able to conquer their share of the world!"

Long, plaintive and sinister howls went up in the forest.

"The clamor of defeat," van den Bosch affirmed. "An attack is becoming more improbable. Only the Wolves would risk it, and they're no longer numerous. You can be sure that the men of the valleys didn't approve of that folly!"

Silence fell again, scarcely troubled by the distant cries of parrots. The presence of the dead and wounded impregnated the men with a black melancholy.

Hours passed; a fugitive dusk preceded the night. On the far bank, a troop of siamangs, like black dwarves, emerged and disappeared again, with cries that might have been cries of joy but which resembled the moans of brutes prey to an immense misery.

Suzanne was on the river bank, her reverie filled with bitterness, pity and disgust. The darkness had grown more intense: the fugitive night of the planet beneath the eternal night of interstellar space; a night still warm from the Sun's heat, enveloped by a night so cold that it would have reduced living beings to a mineral state in a matter of hours.

The siamangs having fallen silent, and the silence making the darkness seem deeper, slighter sounds and distant clamors denouncing slaughter became audible; the red radiance of the camp fires pierced the mystery full of traps set by humans and animals. Under the branches and in the thickets hundreds of diligent and ferocious eyes watched the rocks. The young daughter of Holland sensed the law without appeal that spreads suffering and death untiringly.

After a brief and melancholy meal, van den Bosch had given his orders for the night, adding: "The pigeons must have arrived by now. We shall have help the day after tomorrow."

Lodewyk wanted to take the first watch. Suzanne, alone in a cleft in the rock a few meters from the river, went to sleep, with difficulty.

A noise woke her up.

Flames were running between the forest and the rocks; the camp's defenders had occupied the three defiles; gunshots rang out—and something floating through the air, falling upon the young woman, wrapped itself around her head.

She tried to cry out, but she was firmly gripped and lifted off the ground; she was aware that she was being carried off. The river was rumbling, close at hand; Suzanne divined, by its bobbing, that she had been deposited in a boat, which the current drew away.

There was an abrupt impact and a pause; carried off again, she struggled, full of a tenebrous terror without her imagination offering her any precise account of what was happening.

Footsteps sounded softly on the forest floor.

The immense power of human adaptation began to bring back coherence, and almost self-composure, to the young woman's brain. She assumed that she was in the hands of the bandits who were besieging the camp. The idea of an obscure danger, which had no clear corresponding image, terrorized her. Had Lodewyk and his companions been taken by surprise, as she had been? Had they been put to death?

The anguish became so strong that she could not bear it. She fainted.

227

There was another pause. She was laid down on the ground. The animal skin in which she was wrapped was taken away. Coming round, she saw that she was in the middle of a clearing, in which hideous men were moving back and forth by the light of three red fires. Saurian gazes filtered between narrowed eyelids, shaded by enormous hairy brows. Thick hair bristled on pentagonal skulls. Their teeth were the color of jade; their ears were pointed.

One of them, his torso like the torso of a bear, came toward the young woman and uttered sounds more reminiscent of the bellowing of a buffalo than human speech. The mobile face—uniformly mobile, however—recalled the wrinkles of the faces of certain dogs. His gestures were not manifestly threatening, and Suzanne thought that she was the captive of a strange animal race, intermediate between the great apes and wild boar.

The man continued uttering sounds and gesticulating. The young woman discerned a vague chant, confused articulations drowned in the bellowing; if a bull could talk, its speech might resemble the pronunciation of that monstrous human.

Eventually, he fell silent. What he had tried to say remained as mysterious as the impressions of a batrachian or a reptile. No movement of that phantasmagorical physiognomy resembled the movements of human faces. It seemed, however, that neither he nor any of his companions, male or female—for there might perhaps have been women in the horde—had a menacing attitude. What did they want? Why had they abducted her instead of killing her?

For some time, in Suzanne's hypnotized brain, the external world only appeared in flashes; then her vision cleared, and she saw four bound men lying beside one of the fires. They were natives, perhaps some of those who had laid siege to van den Bosch's camp. They were not moving; they were waiting, with the patience and stoicism of men of their race.

At length, the number of watchers diminished. One after another, they lay down on the ground next to the fire. Soon, there were no more than four men standing, in addition to the one that Suzanne assumed to be the chief. They had set about assembling foliage and long tufts of a silver-colored lichen, whose form was reminiscent of hairy lichen. When they had constructed a sort of mattress, the chief came back to Suzanne; the primitive bed was intended for her. These creatures had some notion of the habits of a humankind other than their own.

In spite of her terror, she was almost grateful for their effort, and because she felt as powerless as a hind beneath the claws of a leopard, she sat down on the green mattress.

Ominous minutes went by. Suzanne was in the same state of mind as someone awaiting the executioner, but nothing happened. One by one, the last wakeful individuals went to lie down.

For a long time she stayed there, sometimes in a hypnotic trance, sometimes gripped by a horror that racked her entrails. The constellations passed slowly between the branches: the Southern Cross marked eternal time over the pole; the snoring of men and the crackle of the fire blended with the sounds of the wilderness, and Suzanne felt as weak, as abandoned and as wretched as a puny animal before large carnivores, until she sank into the quotidian death: the salutary respite that obscure forces have accorded to miserable creatures.

At first light, when she woke up, the fire was reddening. The Boar Men were still asleep. She perceived that while she was asleep, someone had covered her with an animal skin—which surprised her profoundly. As consciousness penetrated the torpid regions of the self, her astonishment increased. These men had done her no harm; not only had they let her sleep peacefully, but they had shielded her from the cold.

She was not reassured at all; she continued to fear death and torture, but in a less terrified fashion. Plunged in a somber dream, through which remembered dawns and dusks passed, she dimly perceived the formidable mystery of the world, in the bosom of energies that create and destroy, which distil joy and spread suffering. She had lived happily in that terrible world; her foresight only extended over a feeble distance; she had had no fear of the future, accepting without anguish the fragile security of the present. Death had seemed to her as distant as the nebulae lost behind the stars. Her capacity for sadness had been suppressed by dazzling fables, by her ability to enjoy herself, and by an imagination in which joyful flames quickly chased away the phantoms that perpetually invade our souls...

In the carnivorous forest, the memories were reborn one after another, posing momentarily in bright light and returning to the darkness. She thought most of all about Lodewyk. Although he was older than her, she felt a maternal sentiment for him, because he had an unstable consciousness, lacking in foresight. The idea that she would never see him again was almost as unbearable as the idea of death itself.

She went to sleep and woke up again several times, until the light of day impregnated the forest. The Boar Men set the quarters of a deer to roast. When it was cooked, the chief removed the meat and sliced it up with a knife made of nephrite—a stone almost as hard as steel. Then, the portions having been spread out on the deer-skin, each man came to take his own and set about devouring it. They ate like wolves, sometimes burying their faces in the flesh, abundantly smeared with blood and grease.

The chief had set aside two portions. He brought the smaller one to Suzanne, growling dully and making enigmatic signs; then he joined the feast, with the same crudity as the others.

At first, Suzanne did not touch the piece of warm meat that the chief had deposited beside her. She was astonished not to be disgusted, but inflexible nature constrained her to hunger and made that coarse nourishment into an appetizing dish. She did not want to touch it and believed that she would not touch it—but then she thought that it was better to give herself as much strength as possible; the precarious possibility of a rescue would be even more precarious if she were debilitated. That argument, more than the temptation, made up her mind.

The Boar Men extinguished their fires very carefully, anxious to avoid a forest fire. Then the troop got under way.

Suzanne was free in her movements; her limbs were not hobbled. When they set off, she had a surge of rebellion, but, considering that she would gain nothing by being tied up, decided to accompany her disgusting kidnappers.

They moved forward without haste. From time to time men detached themselves from the horde and disappeared into the undergrowth; a few came back with small game, and three hunters even brought back the corpse of a deer.

They were well-armed, with primitive weapons: pikes, the points of which were as hard as iron; wooden clubs; green stone axes; bows; javelins of a sort; and harpoons. She could have believed that she had gone back to a time even more remote than that evoked by the Indians of the American plains.

Sometimes, Suzanne's consciousness seemed to dissolve in the forest; everything became vague, distant and animal; then a surge of terror, astonishment and rebellion woke the captive up again. Was it really her, a daughter of low-lying meadows and plaintive polders, where carillons of bells awoke insect songs in the most placid of atmospheres, who was following these men with the muzzles of swine?

Stunned by anguish, she thought of killing herself, but then the love of life rose up within her young flesh, made for joy, and she devoted herself to hoping for an adventure as astonishingly bright as this adventure was somber.

Meanwhile, they went on. The flesh of the deer was finished off at midday and Suzanne took part in the feast with an appetite of which she was ashamed. The meal was followed by a siesta during which no one troubled the young woman's relative solitude. She could almost have believed that she had been forgotten, but whenever she turned round she always ended up discovering eyes watching her from the shade—and even if she had not been watched, these men had the senses of wolves, which would immediately have detected any attempt at flight. At least she was free in her movements, while the indigenous prisoners were still tied up; the Boar Men's instincts perceived that the latter were endowed with both animal and human cunning.

The shadows were lengthening when the Boar Men resumed their march.

They marched for several days, and then reached a formidable terrain—a region of marshes, black and red rocks, and sinister plants, punctuated by islets from which enormous reptiles surged forth, or swarming with primitive beasts.

The horde stopped in a megalithic circle, in which men dead for millennia had accumulated strange formations: upright blocks, funerary slabs, rocky alleyways, the sketches of roofless sanctuaries, which were vaguely reminiscent of Angkor Wat or the columns of Karnak.

Women, children and old men who had stayed in the camp—the oldest of whom seemed hewn from the surrounding stones—came to meet the Boar Men, with raucous shouts and bestial howls—cries of elementary joy unaccompanied by any caress. Then silence fell. An old man stood up and spoke in a singsong fashion; the Forest Chief spoke thereafter in a deep and proud voice; more shouting echoed from the rocks and the waters. A great fire was lit in the center of the circle.

The prisoners were taken to the center, escorted by six men holding jade daggers in their hands. The old man proffered raucous and rhythmic sounds, raising his arms, while the captives were laid out on the ground. Amid the acclamations of the horde, the jade knives cut into the flesh of their torsos, on the left side; red hands reappeared, holding bloody hearts. The old man resumed his chant in a louder voice.

Terror froze Suzanne's vertebrae as she tried to turn her dilated eyes away from the corpses, but an implacable force condemned her to look at them. That was how she would die. Her youth trembled pitifully; her legs would no longer support her; her heart was like an internal executioner.

Further fires were lit, in which the victims' flesh was roasted; the crowd waited with ardent covetousness. Every time a man approached her, Suzanne thought that the inexorable moment had come, but she was soon left alone, without anyone seeming to be aware of her presence.

Little by little, saturated by terror, she fell into a trance, in which she continued uncomprehendingly to see the flames, the vile meal and the shadows of the forest, streaked with coppery gleams.

She did not hear a man approaching, and when the Forest Chief stood in front of her she hardly shivered. The enormous face loomed over her momentarily, and then a hairy hand seized her by the arm and lifted her up. Consciousness returned, but misty and indefinite; thinking that her time had come, she put up no resistance.

He did not take her toward the horde; he dragged her through the ancestral stones until they had arrived in an enclosure formed by four blocks of granite. As had been done with the captives, he threw her brusquely to the ground. An immense terror dissipated the mists. Suzanne knew that she was about to die and screamed loudly.

She was transpierced by a sudden pain, immediately followed by a release, and then by strange, inconceivable sensations, which accelerated, and her terror was confused by an intoxication...

Darkness. Branches, through which scraps of constellations filtered, enveloped Suzanne. Death had not come. For her ignorant imagination, something had happened in which terror, repugnance, astonishment and the strangest exaltation had been amalgamated. She distinctly remembered the hideous brute, breathing in his bestial odor, feeling herself gripped by pitiless hands—and while she had expected only pain and death, that unexpected event had occurred.

The Dutch girl, brought up by scrupulous and narrow-minded Calvinists, had had no inkling of the surprising act that perpetuates the human race. Its verbal revelation had filled her with stupor and had appeared to her to be both disgusting and grotesque—as, all things considered, it is for beings who, having emerged from primitive vileness, have created poetry, the arts, purity and propriety.

Lassitude ended up dragging Suzanne into sleep.

The phantasmagoric scene recommenced on a daily basis. The monstrous savage, groaning and uttering unknown words, suddenly appeared and threw Suzanne down. Every time, the poor girl experienced an incomprehensible exaltation in association with the brutal act. She did not seek to understand; she lived in a kind of bewilderment from which, by virtue of the repetition of the same things—the origin of all animal and human security—fear was now banished. At times when consciousness rose up forcefully, she experienced a profound disgust, and a homicidal nostalgia. Then, dreams rose from the depths of ages which, had we not been informed of their proximity, would have appeared as distant as ages lost for millennia. She bore within her an eternity that incessantly became the present moment…

A Dutch city surged forth on low-lying land: agricultural land stolen from the Ocean, which the Ocean, with a single bound, might fill again with its fecund waves. A placid discipline regulated time and human beings. Behind the little pools of windows one could see, through the *spioens*,[21] humans moving about monotonously; periodically, the patter of feet and the brazen voice of a child punctuated the slow adventure. In those days, everything was delightful. Like omnipotent gods, Jan and Anna van den Bosch watched over the wealthy child for whom miracles never ceased to be accomplished. Everything seemed immortal. Jan and Anna had always existed and would always endure. The child became a *jufvrouw* full of dreams, so content with life that her dreams did not even require much hope.

As to the essential event of adult life no one had ever given her any precision. Love was only a word, very familiar and bizarrely distant. The *jufvrouw* saw it surge forth from

---

[21] Literally "spy-holes."

colorless histories, devoid of taste, devoid of odor, only presented as an adventure as calm as warm bedrooms or well-scrubbed sidewalks.

Thus, her vile misfortune evoked nothing that connected with Suzanne's memories, ideas or dreams, and if she felt shame, it was because it was associated with regions whose very function rendered them vile. Any connection between her adventure and the mysterious, beautiful or touching thing that love became in sanitized periodicals or books would have seemed fabulous to the larval mind of the Dutchwoman. She was not far from believing it to be a kind of witchcraft, evocative of incoherent fairy-tales in which hideous creatures strangely combined good and evil.

She thought unrelentingly about running away, but the enterprise seemed superhuman. How could she get out of that fantastic and terrifying world? Even if she contrived to elude the Boar Men's vigilance, how could she get through the pitiless jungle? She wanted to, though. When she thought about returning to the human world, her entire being throbbed like a heart.

Simple cunning guided her. Since her movements remained free, she began taking short walks, which grew a little longer every time. She was allowed to do it. She sometimes thought she was really alone, shielded from all gazes, and, involuntarily, walked faster. Eyes shining within a bush, a face, limbs, or part of a torso would then appear, and she knew that she was being watched.

However, as she always returned to the dwelling, the surveillance relaxed, to the extent that she thought she was safe. There was more than one occasion when she had gone into the forest and nothing had betrayed the presence of a Boar Man. Then she resolved to test her luck to the limit.

She had been walking for an indeterminate time when she perceived muffled footfalls—human footfalls, which she had learned not to confuse with animal footfalls.

She pretended not to have heard anything, continued to wander for a few more minutes, and then returned to the abominable enclosure. Half way, the Forest Chief emerged, growled—as was his habit—and threw her on the ground.

She did not give up. Every day, she recommenced her excursions, moved more by instinct than by lucid will. She became strangely strong and resilient, as if the forest air had transmitted its millennial energy to her. She developed a subtle sense of smell: animal sense that allowed her to perceive invisible presences. She knew thereby that the moment had not come, and sometimes despaired that it would ever come—but youth was within her, which forbade resignation.

One afternoon, she arrived beside a river similar, in the rapidity of its flow, to the river on whose bank van den Bosch's men had camped. She had marked her path on hard stones. To reach the water it was necessary to descend through the rocks. Suzanne walked for a long time, her eyes and ears alert. Suddenly, a hope full of dread rose within her heart; in a sort of creek she had just perceived a primitive raft—which must have been there for a long time, since water-plants had grown through its interstices.

Suzanne realized that a chance had been offered to her within the inextricable tangle of events. All around her the forest was open, arrested by a ground of Archean rock that scarcely nourished a few paltry lichens, with the occasional fern whose roots descended into a fissure. The individual or individuals who were watching her had to be several hundred meters away, among the trees and bushes.

She had no thought for anything but the present. The perils to come were not manifest in her imagination, and she set about descending through the rocks. When she got close to the creek she raised her head, but saw nothing. Then she pulled out the raft, whose mooring had rotted away long ago.

The raft carried the woman on to the homicidal waves. In the torrential flow, menaced by the sharp rocks of the bank, clinging desperately to the damp wood that threatened to tip her into the abyss, Suzanne was only afraid of the man or men who were pursuing her.

A silhouette appeared among the rocks; a bestial face remained momentarily motionless, turned toward the fugitive. Then, bellowing like a buffalo, the man started to run down. He appeared and disappeared in the interstices. He was no more than 10 or 15 feet from the bank when he lost his footing. Then he fell, his arms extended, rolled on the hard rock and remained still, dead or unconscious...

For a long time, the fear of men remained greater than the fear of the waters. In the rapids and whirlpools Suzanne felt continually menaced by elementary life, the life of objects and energies that menaces the structure of perishable animals.

Finally, however, her raft was thrown rudely against a little promontory, and she disembarked. She was worn out by fatigue, her clothes as wet as if she had emerged from a bath. Her mind was in such disarray and she was so miserable that she no longer had the courage to fight. She climbed painfully on to a flat rock, exposed to the yellow Sun that precedes the red Sun, and remained as inert as a reptile. She was undoubtedly asleep, because she was unaware of the approach of night.

When she sat up again, her clothes were dry, but the red Sun was level with the river. Dazedly, she watched it disappear into a cleft in the rocks, and felt the immense solitude that descended upon her with the darkness. She was nothing. To destroy her, it only required a tiger, a bear, or even a panther—a wolf would suffice. She was not astonished; her faculty of astonishment was extinct. She searched instinctively for shelter. Night had arrived with its stars; the excessively pure sky drank the warmth, and the wind freshened.

Discouraged, Suzanne lay down between two blocks of stone, stammered a prayer, and sank into unconsciousness.

She awoke beneath scintillating constellations, amid the water, the branches and furtive beasts, knowing full well that living creatures were searching for living creatures in order to devour them. Fragile, without weapons and without instinct, she was a feeble prey—but she was no longer aware of any

ardent fear, fear full of images of civilized life; primitive resignation was already within her, and a brutishness that quickly
sent her to sleep again.

When she woke up yet again, the early morning Sun had
dried her clothes and warmed her flesh again. She was hungry,
but she did not know what to do to procure the humblest nourishment, either from the river or the immense forest, which
fed millions of creatures.

One can live for several days without eating, however—
she had even heard mention of a man who had fasted for 40
days. She dared not set off on the raft again, sure of having
risked her life 100 times the day before, but she followed the
course of the torrential river, in the hope that it might be the
one on whose bank van den Bosch had camped.

She walked all day without finding any nourishment,
dragged herself along the following day too, and part of a
third. Despair never ceased to increase within her soul. Then
weakness obscured her thoughts, and when she fell down in
the middle of the third day she stayed there for a long time,
half asleep and half unconscious.

When she came too, dusk was approaching. Almost in-
differently, she saw two men leaning over her. The first was
Matzal, the half-breed trail-beater, who had come to warn of
the approach of the bandits and the proximity of the Boar
Men. The other was one of the giant's servants.

Both of them had been sent to search for Suzanne. They
considered her with a mixture of amazement, joy and dread.
"You're safe, *jufvrouw*," said Matzal.

There was a gentleness in that swarthy face and those
hawk's eyes. The other had a face as inexpressive as a buffalo's.

It was joy that invaded Suzanne, but a muted joy, ponderous and fearful. "We'll be pursued!" she stammered.

"By the Boar Men, *jufvrouw*?"

"Yes," she said.

"They haven't killed you!" Matzal murmured, shaking his head. "They kill everyone—men and women! No captive has ever returned. We have horses...they can't catch us. Are you hungry, *jufvrouw*?"

She was not as hungry as she had been before falling unconscious, but when she had swallowed a few mouthfuls she was overwhelmed by voracity.

"You must eat moderately and slowly to start with," said the half-breed, who had only given her a thin slice of bread.

She obeyed. Matzal's companion went to fetch two horses, hidden in a thicket—thin beasts, but solid. The larger had to carry the young woman, who was a poor horsewoman, and the half-breed.

She learned that the giant, Lodewyk and Hendrik had searched for her in vain, and then Matzal had set out alone, with a companion of his own sort, into the depths of the jungle, where others would have gone astray.

All joy had disappeared; Suzanne was anguished by an obscure shame. It seemed that the whole world would divine her odious adventure, and the exaltation to which her flesh had submitted appeared to her to be an unforgivable action whose guilt she would bear forever. That idea floated within a chaotic and dolorous consciousness, an instinctive world into which rational thought only projected indecisive gleams, immediately extinguished.

A day went by, then another. The first night, they stopped in an abandoned cabin. The following night, Suzanne slept next to a fire lit by her companions. She had recovered her strength and felt safe; strangers to horsemanship, the Boar Men must be a long way behind, if they were in pursuit.

The sadness persisted, like the winter mists over the polders. She felt unworthy to return to the community of white men, fearing the sight of the person who represented, for her, the most profound human tenderness, on whom were concentrated all the persistent living entities that were her memories.

Sometimes, trying to define her state of mind, she thought: *What have I done? Why should I be guilty... and of what?*

A flux of blood rose to her neck and cheeks; she had ended up discovering where her responsibility lay: it was when, in spite of herself, in spite of the horror and in spite of the disgust, she experienced a return of the mysterious exaltation.

More days went by. On the fifth morning, Matzal said: "We'll get there before midday."

There was the immense desire to see Lodewyk again, and the shame of appearing before him...

The proximity of plantations was perceptible by the odor alone: an aromatic odor of dense perfumes, which preceded the sight of the plants. Then, her heart overwhelmed by hostile emotions, Suzanne saw a dwelling through the trees, flowers and bushes that was as spacious as a château.

It was not Lodewyk who appeared but the debonair giant. He took the adolescent girl to his vast bosom and hugged her with a timid tenderness. "I searched for you in vain, niece. Only Matzal could remain invisible in the forest, among the rocks and marshes." He dared not say that he had thought her dead, and asked in an almost fearful tone: "They haven't done you any harm?"

She lowered her head, feebly, stammering: "No...no..."

He was more skillful reading the tortuous minds of Malays than the minds of young women. "Lodewyk and Hendrik are searching for you too, my child, but they should return today..."

She was not astonished to see that he had not divined anything, so far beyond human affairs did her adventure seem, solely connected with the monstrous being with whom she had accomplished it—and she was slightly less fearful of Lodewyk's return.

Then there was the waiting: the strange projection of a creature into the future, which renders the present unbearable and attempts to erase it…

She was exhausted by impatience when van den Bosch told her: "They're coming!"

Then there was the great tremulousness of returns—and when Lodewyk appeared, she belonged entirely to the present of sobbing, joy and tenderness. That soul-storm covered her confusion when, to the same question that the planter had posed, she replied: "No…they didn't mistreat me."

Pell-mell, she recounted that which she was able to tell— the devoured prisoners, her patience, her attempts to escape, the raft, the encounter with Matzal—and because neither Lodewyk nor Hendrik went beyond words, she hoped that the abominable secret would never be revealed.

Suzanne lived a new life, which would have been charming. A sweetness fell from the high summits on to the van den Bosch lands; the evenings and mornings were warm, with sudden fresh breezes that caressed the flesh like promises of happiness.

Suzanne would have loved those strange constellations which, rotating gracefully around the Southern Cross, were suggestive of the austral legend, the forever-veiled history of a world whose annals were as lost in time as the ancient skeletons in the avid Earth.

She vaguely sensed the strength of vegetation and its vehemence; in a halo of aromas, she understood the poverty of the cultivated ground on which her race lived, and lapsed into a vast dream that would have been beautiful if it had not been so sad—but a terrible melancholy penetrated all the way to the marrow of her bones.

She felt like a foreigner among her own people, burdened by a shameful secret that others could not even imagine. Something awoke in the immense sunsets that made her, in her own eyes, a fantastic monster. She anticipated the arrival, in the cruel forest, of the man with the vile head, a frightful desire passing through her innocent and voluptuous body. Desperate and on fire, she refused and desired; a jet of flame penetrated her, of which she was so ashamed that she burst into tears. Thus, the horrible mystery lived on within her, mingled with the beating of her heart and the most intimate retreats of her thought.

She tried to take refuge in the nearness of others, especially of Lodewyk, the focal point of beautiful memories, but she felt indescribably estranged, exiled from the white race, and even from Malays or yellow men.

A double nostalgia caused her anguish by day and tortured her by night. With terrible sighs, she appealed to her homeland, its innocence and purity, its slow dreams, its calm canals and hours of song. Frissons dazzled the mornings, the birth of each recommencing day: legends of ancient Batavia drawn from the depths of centuries, boundless promises, evening stars that project youth into the skies…

Then, with tremors in her heart and her limbs, came the frightful nostalgia of the forest, the inconceivable mixture of horror and pleasure…the cruel night, the odor of amorous flowers, speaking the demonic language that got witches burned.

She got up, and she prayed, lifting her supplicant hands toward unknown stars.

One night, when she suffered thus, the dogs barked—only for a few minutes—and Suzanne, standing at the window, saw a shadow loom up among the coffee-bushes, in the silvery moonlight. She knew already. A mortal terror weighed upon her shoulders, and when she tried to cry out, she had no voice.

The monster surged forth into the light; in a few strides, he reached the building. Then Suzanne saw him grip the window-sill. She was made of stone, palpitating stone, a block of paralyzed flesh. He had only to grab her, to drag her into space…

Two dogs arrived, growling, which fell silent when the Boar Man had passed his hand over their skulls, as if they had recognized a fabulous master.

Suzanne did not move, gripped by a fatality comparable to the fatality of birth and death. The gardens and plantations succeeded one another without her having opened her eyes; she inhaled the brutal effluvia of the wild beast, the effluvia of a tiger or a panther, which became more odious as she emerged from her stupor.

The forest was there, the implacable land of trees and beasts, where human law ended, where everything was born and disappeared in accordance with encounters of strength, cunning and hazard.

Suddenly, she was deposited on the ground; she sensed, despairingly, what was about to happen...

The brute resumed his march through the forest, dragging his captive behind him—but this time, the journey was quite short.

Around a large red fire, beside a pool, a dozen Boar Men were asleep or on watch. As on the evening of the first abduction, the chief arranged foliage for Suzanne and left her an animal-skin...and for a long time Suzanne remained plunged in a mortal scorn for her own person that overwhelmed all peril and all disgust. She became irreparably estranged from her own humanity, a stranger to the frightful humanity that had seized her again, and stranger still to herself, her childhood, her youth, to all of her memories, and even to Lodewyk: every tremor of the forest, every palpitation of her heart condemned her; life became so impossible that Suzanne felt buried in the darkness, as a cadaver is buried in the Earth.

She got to her feet. She looked at the fire and the wild men. They all seemed to be asleep, and perhaps they really were asleep, but their subtle senses remained alert to the surroundings. The slightest unusual noise would have woken them.

The pool was close by, so close that Suzanne slid to its edge and contemplated the dormant water, where the cold life of fish, reptiles and batrachians was swarming frightfully.

Heads had been raised; eyes had followed the young woman's movements, but on seeing her immobile, the men went back to sleep, unable to imagine that a creature might escape into oblivion.

For one moment more, Suzanne allowed the shadows of the vanished world to pass by. Regrets were floating in the black sky; Lodewyk drifted past in a deadly fog. And, leaning forward, she disappeared among the algae, so gently and so softly that no ear perceived the annunciatory splash of her death.

IN THE WORLD OF THE VARIANTS

From the moment of his birth, Abel seemed to belong to a different race from his brothers; subsequently, a strange atmosphere seemed to isolate him from children and adults alike. No one ever discovered the reason for that anomaly. It was unrelated to his physical make-up—or, at least, did not seem to be. He had the fair hair and white face of men who set off from the North in their deckless boats to conquer lands, steal riches and rape women. In his province, the descendants of such men abounded.

He inspired a sort of disquiet, and the sentiment of very distant things, lost in Space and Time.

His speech also seemed unusual, even though, until the age of 12, he had not said anything extraordinary. Sometimes, some unspecifiable mystery was sketched out, quickly lost in familiar words. His gestures generated unease; even when he did exactly the same thing as other children, it seemed that he did so in accordance with a different orientation, as if he were carrying out left-handed movements with his right hand.

At an early age, he astonished some people with his subtle nature; for them, he evoked existences hidden in the islands or the solitudes of the sea, dreams enveloped in mist, depths in which obscure plant life and abyssal beasts were at war.

He belonged to a mediocre and placid family, untormented by any devastating dream. A few acres of soil surrounded a humble house, into which light penetrated through numerous little windows pierced in the four façades. The orchard yielded the fruits of the region; vegetables abounded in the kitchen-garden; two cows and four goats lived on exceedingly green grass. Because the family had a near-horror of meat, it led an easy life whose joys were not cruel.

The father, Hugues Faverol, a surveyor, assured the family's present and consolidated its future; the mother, gentle and incoherent, would have managed the household badly, but a maidservant and an old gardener regulated the affairs of the house, the stable and the land.

The turbulence and mischievousness of Abel's brothers was supportable; because he was the eldest and the strongest he had no difficulty defending himself. Although there were obstacles between him and those whom he loved from the outset, he scarcely perceived the singular dissimilarity between his universe and the universe of other men before his 12th year.

He saw, heard and felt all that they saw, felt and heard, but around and within every appearance an unknown appearance emerged. Thus, he perceived two distinct worlds, although they occupied the same space: two terrestrial worlds that coexisted, with all their creatures.

Abel eventually realized that he was linked to both worlds. That discovery, which became more precise by the day, he was fearful of revealing, even to his mother, and it was indirectly, by means of questions that alarmed his kinfolk, that he assured himself of his utter originality. Finally sure that the double world existed for him alone, he sensed that the revelation of his reality was pointless, and might be dangerous.

For several years, however, the world that penetrated every part of the world of human beings remained indistinct. One might have thought that Abel perceived it by means of rudimentary senses, as a sea-urchin might perhaps perceive the ocean and the rock to which it clings. At length, the world diversified. He began to establish there the order that a child establishes among the incessant metamorphoses of his environment, and it did not take long for him to realize that in the other universe, he was younger than he was in the human world.

No human terminology could express the existences and phenomena that he discerned; apprehended by senses whose development became increasingly rapid, they revealed nothing of that which hearing, sight, touch, taste or smell reveal to us, nothing that we could perceive or imagine.

The living things were the last to appear to him. It took him several months to assimilate their total appearance; unlike our animals and vegetables they had no fixed structures: a series of forms, incessantly changing, unfolded in a near-constant order, repeating themselves and thus forming cyclic individuals. As Abel subsequently learned, they live much longer than the living beings of our realm. As soon as he had grasped their mode of existence he recognized them, at first in their essence, then in their individuality, as easily as we recognize a song or a symphony.

Their diversity was as great as, and perhaps greater than, the diversity of our fauna and flora. The inferior species had slow and monotonous cycles. As one ascended through the hierarchy, the variations became more rapid and more complex; in the highest degrees, several cycles unfolded in concert, confused and distinct at the same time.

Abel perceived all this, with increasing clarity, in the manner of children—which, by virtue of not being embarrassed by method, is swifter and more penetrating. He soon found out that the Variants, as he named them, developed differently from animals or plants. Their extent did not increase; they were no smaller at birth than subsequently, but were vaguer, with incoherent cycles; gradually, their movements gained in coherence; they attained their full harmony after evolutions that were more numerous the more highly placed they were within the hierarchy.

It was on a June evening that Abel realized that he was himself both a human and a Variant—an evening when the clouds prolonged their metamorphosis. Weary of grazing the warm air, the swallows were chasing one another with hectic cries, drunk on a pleasure that filled the young man with compassion and tenderness. They seemed to him as ephemeral as those fragile countries hollowed out in crepuscular vapors—and, seized by an anguish, he had taken the hand of his mother, whom he loved more than any other creature.

They were alone. They seemed to be seeing the same appearances of the Universe, but, sensing instinctively that he was going further than she into the mystery of things, his mother said, with a touch of fear: "What are you thinking about?"

That was a moment when the world of the Variants was superimposed more narrowly upon the world of human beings, and Abel had his Revelation.

Until then, his human life had been so predominant that Variant Life had seemed entirely exterior. That evening he knew that he participated in the two Lives. Bowled over, he ceased to perceive his mother's presence. Frightened by the sight of a face as motionless as a mineral and staring eyes whose pupils were expanding in the dim light, she squeezed his hand in anguish.

"Abel...my little one! What's the matter?"

He looked at her without seeing her; then, like a man coming out of a trance, he murmured, without thinking about what he was saying: "I was living in the other world."

She did not understand; she thought that he was thinking about death and the eternal soul. "You mustn't think about that, my darling. You need to live with us!"

So distant as she was from Abel's reality, she would have been vainly and sadly burdened by a confidence. Embracing her with a gentleness mingled with considerable anguish, he acquiesced in an ambiguous manner. "I don't have to think about it," he said.

The human evening returned, with its stars, its infinity lost in other infinities. Abel was still awake, his heart in tumult, when the other members of his family had gone to sleep.

In spite of his revelation, Abel only had a confused consciousness of his own cycles, similar to that which we have of our bodies, whose innumerable functions are only known to us, very imperfectly, by virtue of the experience of thousands of ancestors. Just as we know that we are human, however, he knew that he was a Variant.

There was nothing to indicate to him the species—if one can speak in terms of species in this instance—to which he belonged. Was he one of those whose intelligence could not communicate with others, or could only communicate in the elementary fashion in which it is transmitted between our higher animals? Or had he received the gift of communicating his ideas to other Variants—a gift that did not seem, as it is on Earth, to be the prerogative of a single species?

While he sought to discover this, his terrestrial life passed through the essential crisis; for several seasons it dominated his Variant life to such an extent that the latter, without ever ceasing to be perceptible, sank into a kind of torpor. Still a child among the Variants, he became an adult among humans, submissive to the sparkling folly of puberty.

Woman, becoming the redoubtable principle of his two existences, saturated him with visions that were tragic, by virtue of their sharpness, centralized around the savage receptacle of generation, the image of which is, for so many young humans, an Eden that they despair of ever attaining.

Because he was timid to the point of dementia, he lived in a storm of desires exasperated by the fictions that our ancestors have accumulated around the Act, already fabulous in the darkness of primal instinct. He was the insect ready to die for the sake of fecundation, the wild beast maddened by the hectic pursuit through the desert, the savage prowling around the female with a club or spear, the barbarian warrior raping the wives and daughters of the vanquished, the poet assembling the reflections of Earth and sky, the morning light, the beauties of vegetation and the innumerable elementary sensations sublimated by centuries of dreams.

From brutal desire, already magnified by an extraordinary primitive legend, and from instinct brought down to and concentrated in sex, emerged the mystical grace in which the adolescent, prostrating himself before a sacred creature, fears the Act as a sacrilege...

The woman of instinct surged forth initially, with her brutal face, her thick jaws and a man as coarse as that of thoroughbred mares. Merely in seeing her walk, revealing her strong ankles, parting her legs, he knew the vertigo of forests, and glimpsed the cave ready to seize him...[22]

He thought of her frenetically during the nights of August; he extended his arms, he begged, moaned, wept. He encountered her every day, and everywhere. How near she was!—and so distant, at the other end of life, ungraspable and inaccessible. Overwhelmed by his timidity, in spite of many contacts, in spite of his loneliness, he had never made the gesture...

One day, sitting next to her, the others having departed one by one, his audacity went so far as to let him remain there, trembling and shivering, until dusk fell...

She did not put on the light. They said nothing. Intolerable fever tortured them. Finally, despairing of seeing him take action, she moved closer to him with the slowness of the minute-hand of a clock. She took possession of that young intoxicated body and gave him a mute dream, boundless joy, glory and triumph. She saturated him with a wild happiness, for which he retained an eternal gratitude, which did not impede the other dream of emergence.

There was almost as much difference between the two adventures as between a female gorilla and the whitest and most delicate human female...

When he recovered the woman with the coarse hair, the trees, the grass and the Earth exuding a phosphorescent scent, he immersed himself in the caress as in a river of flesh—but when he arrived next to the other, whom he never possessed, he knew the miracle of every form, every sound, every odor, of the cloud floating over the hill and of that other cloud, made of stars without number, which throws a milky veil over the estival night.

---

[22] Sexual symbolism is inevitably difficult to translate, because French *double entendres* and English ones frequently lack correspondence, so English readers will have to take it on trust that such passages as this one seem somewhat less inelegant in French.

Thus passed six seasons, during which, an adult on Earth, he remained a child in the twin world.

Then the woman with the coarse hair left him to pursue other adventures; replete, he scarcely missed her. The other, taken away by her family never to return, was lost in one of those lands that the Assassins of Humankind have stolen from red-skinned people.

In the era that followed, the world of the Variants began to dominate the human world within him, and he finally recognized his species—one of those that was able to communicate thought.

After six more seasons, he finally approached adulthood there, and began to be moved by the legend of their generation. It differed strangely from our animal legend. The sexes had no definite existence. A Variant could be male relative to some of his own kind, female to others. At the limits, however, rare beings existed who were purely male, and others purely female.

Abel had not yet experienced the union that presentiment announced by way of the disturbance caused by certain Presences, especially those belonging to the purely feminine category. While he completed his radiant increase he linked himself with Variants toward which he was attracted by a predilection they showed for him. Incapable of perceiving his double nature, they were surprised by his appearance; linked to his human body, his variant body was confined to a limited sphere in which it moved very rapidly. He dared not offer any explanation, and the Variants did not ask him for one. Gradually, he came to understand them almost as well as he understood human beings.

They escape the worst animal necessities—including the necessity of nourishing themselves at the expense of other lives—and possess no means of destroying one another; disease and fatal accidents were unknown in their world. None of the terrestrial cataclysms disrupt the rhythms by which they live; death only occurs by virtue of an exhaustion whose cause is unknown to them; it is a slow and gentle decline into unconsciousness.

Their existence involves some suffering, but tolerable ones. Their lives are not without chagrin or adventures, nor without sexual love, but the mysterious universal distribution has spared them ferocious tragedy, the immolation of the weak by the strong, frightful tortures and monstrous deaths.

Their nutrition is primarily energetic; their physiology is economical and maintains itself at the expense of inanimate substances, although their activity requires a perpetual collaboration with the environment. They obtain their nutrition by the absorption and incessant transformation of radiations of every sort.

It seems that their sense of beauty is more complex, more intense and more constant than those of human beings, and involved in all their actions. The kinds of rudimentary art that involve a taste for nutriments, vegetal perfumes, the forms of certain plants, flowers or animals, are replaced in them by an indefinite number of esthetic sensations, much more intense than those known to humans. To "assimilate" phenomena they have a legion of senses, which form harmonic series that have a "grasp" of the environment that is both powerful and subtle.

Love attains an incomparable splendor there; all the powers and sensibilities of creatures participate in it. It escapes the repugnant servitudes of terrestrial love, the odious mixture of vital functions and grotesque movements. Physical contact is no more necessary than it is for us to have physical contact with a melody, a painting, a statue, a flower or a landscape, and yet no contact can awake sharper or more subtle sensations. It is, in sum, an exchange of rhythms and imponderable fluids. It can last longer, without any fatigue, only ceases by virtue of the extinction of a superabundance of energy, and is not long delayed in resumption. It requires the absolute acquiescence of the two beings. Possession by violence is impracticable among the Variants; desire cannot develop unless it excites desire; the idea of egoistic enjoyment is scarcely conceivable.

Apart from a few obscure instincts to which nothing responded, Abel remained ignorant of Variant love for some time. He only began to understand when he encountered the individual whom he named, in terrestrial language, Liliale.

Entirely feminine, she was more sympathetic than any of her peers to Abel's latent strangeness. In spite of her considerable youth, she had a superior perception of her universe; among the Variants, experience depends much more on the perfection of persona cycles than the duration of circumstances. An individual like Liliale absorbed the variations of ambient life with an extreme intensity, rapidity and surety.

Although surprised by the limitation of Abel's movements, she did not see it as an infirmity, sensing a composite nature strangely different from and strangely comparable to Variant existence. Also perceiving that only he revealed himself partially, not for reasons of duplicity but out of some mysterious dread, she refrained from interrogating him; it was he who finally understood that a confession was inevitable.

It was one morning in terms of the mortal Earth, but in the world of the Variants, where time is not measured in terms of the motion of a central star, there are no mornings, evenings or seasons, only variations due to the interactions of worlds. Abel was simultaneously aware of the earthly morning, which was a morning in spring, and the complex phase of his other life. His double nature was subject to an excitement full of charm.

"What's the matter?" his friend had asked. "You seem to be somewhere else."

"It's just that there's a harmony within me more vibrant than my two lives," he replied.

"Your two lives?" she queried, less surprised than he might have expected.

"It's time you knew, Liliale. I'm different from all the other beings in this world we all inhabit…and those of another world, to which I find myself bound. Or rather, I am bound to both at the same time."

"That's a fearful mystery," said Liliale, "and so dolorous! I sense that it's true…everything about you speaks of existences beyond my own, a world incomparable with ours…and I love you more because of it, in spite of the fear—which will never cease—of losing you!"

"Ah!" he said. "In spite of their melancholy, those words are sweeter than all the joys of the other world…where, however, I have known marvelous joys…"

A profound disturbance began to overtake them, which was already changing the nature of their tenderness and could not be hidden—for although the Variants have their secret life, which none may penetrate without consent, it is impossible for them to hide their love from beloved individuals as soon as the latter love in their turn. Reciprocal love is a mutual penetration of two consciousnesses, although there is a period of growth during which each may guard the secret, always with increasing difficulty. Then the communication becomes perfect, and when the lovers are in one another's presence, nothing that happens in the mind of one can be concealed from the other.

That moment had arrived for Liliale and Abel; almost abruptly, they found that they were a single being. All speech became unnecessary. Liliale understood Abel as directly as he understood himself. Terrestrial love, for Abel, was no longer anything more than an exceedingly poor sentiment, for which he felt pity…

That lasted until the time when Liliale began to bear the being that she had conceived with Abel. Like the creative act itself, maternity did not have the repulsive aspects that it assumes in humans; the child comprised subtle rhythms added to Liliale's rhythms, and rendered the mother more harmonious and more beautiful. Then Abel experienced strange moments in which the world of the Variants was almost completely effaced by the world of human beings, and other moments in which humans were no more than the shadow of a dream. Then he was extraordinarily happy in the two existences.

The child was born, whose cycles were vague and disordered for some time. It was a young chaos; slowly it became a harmony, which resembled Liliale. Abel loved it profoundly, and was loved by it. It had a sense of the human world that its mother lacked, but it did not live doubly, as Abel did. Men, animals and plants were for the child a world fantastic and real, intangible and impenetrable, the life and movements of which it could perceive without understanding their meaning. As it did not possess any organ comparable to eyes or ears, its perception was extremely different from that of its father—as sharp and as subtle but without embracing relatively motionless forms. On the contrary, humans and animals were, from its viewpoint, series of very numerous vortices, with less mobile nodes and centers that corresponded to specialized organs like the heart, the liver, the stomach and the brain.

That was a happy time, among humans as among the Variants—a time of plenty, in which Abel lived his double life fully.

However, his terrestrial body was approaching old age while he was still young in his other life. A time of dolor succeeded the time of felicity; Abel's mother died and his father shortly afterwards, and with his dispersed brothers there was only negligible communication.

Terrestrial years passed, and the day came when Abel consented to quit the human world. His death was almost voluntary—a renunciation devoid of suffering—and he then belonged uniquely to Variant life, without ceasing to perceive the milieu in which he had lived, but no longer possessing the same senses. His memories being fragmentary, the creatures who had been his kin melted into scarcely-individualized collectives...

And he had time before him: the centuries that the Variants live, while his descendants increased and multiplied indefinitely...

Afterword

"Nymphaeum" established an important prototype within Rosny's *oeuvre*, providing a template to which he frequently returned, even though it is an inherently confused work that changes direction several times. The initial encounter between the explorers and the tiger was a confrontation that he was to echo incessantly as a supplier of melodrama, as was the chase after an abducted bride-to-be. Both these devices seem, however, to be mere accessories, awkwardly recruited to impart a measure of narrative drive to what is, in essence, a Utopian romance of how human life might have been, had evolution only worked a little differently. The heart of the story is the Rousseauesque innocence and happiness of the light-skinned Water-People—an exercise in pure Romance that is sufficient in itself to belie Rosny's hastily-acquired reputation as a Naturalist.

Given the manner in which the story changes direction several times, it is hardly surprising that Rosny found "Nymphaeum" a difficult piece to continue or conclude; it was obviously planned as a novel, but the story had to be finished off with brutal rapidity in order that it might be sold as a novella. As an adventure story, therefore, it remains direly unsatisfactory, but lovers of speculative fiction are bound to be glad that it did creep into print in some form, for the sake of the vision of the Water-People and their strange way of life.

The fact that the story, as published, embeds its poetic component within a narrative frame that is not far removed from crude pulp fiction, might reflect the fact that the opening was tacked on at a late stage in composition, not long before the ending, but the greater likelihood is that the piece really was composed in sequence, albeit with at least one substantial break, and that the preface burdened Rosny with a necessity that proved burdensome, of having to bring his narrator back

257

home to tell his story. The character would doubtless have been happier—and the author too—had he not been forced to do that, no matter how inevitable it might have seemed in terms of the literary conventions of the day. Indeed, the story might have worked better, in poetic terms, had it not been forced to continue representing itself as a "real" adventure at all, being allowed an ultimate retreat into the realm of dream. Perhaps, after all, it would have been better had the narrator not recovered from his encounter with the tiger, but merely hallucinated the whole Romantic adventure on the point of death.

There is, undeniably, a similar quasi-hallucinatory quality about "The Depths of Kyamo," "The Wonderful Cave Country" and "The Voyage," in which the commitment to an anecdotal format holds the first two stories back from the kind of general conclusion to which the third eventually breaks through. Alglave is only able to hint at his conviction that the life of the advanced great apes of Kyamo is preferable to that of civilized men, and that the scrupulous predation of the giant vampire bats is morally superior to our own use of other animal species, and even Villars, in the third story, is compelled to reflect on the symbiotic relationship of his giant elephants and primitive humans from a vast distance, perhaps spoiling its proto-ecological message with the rather fatuous offhand remark about what elephants might have accomplished had they had two trunks instead of one. In spite of that flaw, however, "The Voyage" deserves recognition as a significant ecological parable, which avoids the mystical excesses of the contemporary works of W.H. Hudson.

It cannot be a coincidence that the seemingly-anodyne title of "Le Voyage" reproduces that of one of the key exercises in Decadent symbolism featured in Charles Baudelaire's *Les Fleurs du Mal*—a book more frequently quoted by Rosny's characters than any other. The journey that it features is not only symbolic, but wryly symbolic, in a fashion of which Baudelaire might have approved, as he would surely have approved of the calculated paradoxicality and perversity of the commentary contained in the opening paragraphs. Rosny did not often let the "poetic" side of his conflicted personality show through in the era in which this story was published, but if "The Voyage" was actually written then, it testifies to the fact that the repression of that element of his literary personality was not contrived without rebellion.

"The Great Enigma" takes up that poetic thread, albeit in a straightforwardly nostalgic vein, but it is not surprising that Rosny was tempted to develop the basic theme of the story into a much more elaborate adventure story, of a sort that he was able to tackle much more confidently after 1920 than he had in the 1880s. "The Treasure in the Snow" is, in fact, one of the most coherent and level-paced of all his adventure stories, its relative lack of ambition in terms of the population of its lost land being compensated by a much greater willingness on the part of its author and its hero to involve himself intimately with its personnel. Indeed, "The Treasure in the Snow" can be regarded as a straightforward wish-fulfillment fantasy, whose sexual component is reasonably forthright and quite unashamed. It is that element of its plot which is extrapolated—in two different but not incompatible directions—in "The Boar Men" and "In the World of the Variants."

Rosny must have been painfully aware, in penning "Nymphaeum," of the blatant dishonesty of having the heroine carried off by a brutal abductor while forbidding any actual spoliation. He must have felt that, however necessary it might be in terms of reader-appeasement, it was a hypocritical fudge, and it is not surprising, given his willingness to write uncompromising *contes cruels* when the occasion warranted it (see, for instance, "The Witch" in vol. 6), that he was willing to look at the other side of the coin. Indeed, the more surprising thing is that when he decided to use the same formula again, in the relatively straightforward transfiguration of "The Boar Men" that became "Adventure in the Wild" (see vol. 5), he embraced a different kind of hypocrisy so readily. By the time he wrote "The Boar Men," he had already expressed the view, in "The Navigators of Space" (see vol. 1), that all human sex,

259

brutal or not, was a poor and ugly thing by comparison with more elevated forms of imaginable love, so it is not surprising that he went on from "The Treasure in the Snow" and "The Boar Men" to pen a very different kind of sexual fantasy in "In the World of the Variants," which moved beyond the scope of conventional lost land stories to feature one of the multitudinous coexistent realms that Alglave confesses to have always believed to be far closer at hand, although invisible, than any remote polar Eden.

The stories in this volume illustrate Rosny's lack—through no fault of his own—of an accurate time-scale for the discussion of evolutionary variations, and certain idiosyncrasies in his understanding of evolutionary theory, but those features of his work stand out even more clearly in his prehistoric fantasies, and are more conveniently discussed in that context (see vol. 4). They are, however, the stories that make the most conspicuous display of his occasionally-crude racism. When he was reading popularizations of anthropology in the 1880s, he could hardly help encountering race theories of the crudest sort, because anthropological theory was saturated with them at that time, and Rosny belonged to a generation—and, for that matter, to a colonial culture—that took it for granted that white people were superior to people of other races. It is, however, worth noting the evidence that these stories provide that Rosny did not suffer from the horror of miscegenation that afflicted so many 19th century race theories, and that he compensated for his racist assumptions with a frank xenophilia that made hypothetical new races—as well as the recovered prehistoric race of "The Treasure in the Snow"—more attracted to him than his own. Again, this is a topic that will be developed more fully in the commentary to volume four of this series.

The lost land subgenre is so obviously unviable in the context of modern geographical knowledge that stories of that sort cannot help but seem dated, and irredeemably quaint. Indeed, it is arguable that the subgenre was obsolete even before it was pioneered by ambitious Utopian writers, let alone adapted into quasi-Romantic adventure fiction by such late 19th century writers as H. Rider Haggard. It may be the case, therefore, that the primary appeal of all Rosny's ventures in this vein to modern readers is nostalgic, but they are deliberately and quintessentially nostalgic in their substance as well as their appearance, and their superficial nostalgia might actually be held to add to their inherent nostalgia for evolutionary circumstances that never were, but might have been—and which might perhaps have represented better paths of development than the one that humankind actually took.

That possibility is intrinsically Romantic, and has a particular enshrinement in French Romanticism by virtue of the contribution made to its inspiration by Jean-Jacques Rousseau. It is not at all Naturalistic—but the kind of "poetic passion" for science that Rosny had is itself intrinsically and irreducibly Romantic, and in developing that thread of his work in the winding way that he did, he was only following its logic in a slightly more forthright and ambitious fashion than other, less audacious, explorers of strange lands.

SF & FANTASY

Guy d'Armen. *Doc Ardan: The City of Gold and Lepers*
G.-J. Arnaud. *The Ice Company*
Aloysius Bertrand. *Gaspard de la Nuit*
Félix Bodin. *The Novel of the Future*
Didier de Chousy. *Ignis*
C. I. Defontenay. *Star (Psi Cassiopeia)*
Charles Derennes. *The People of the Pole*
Harry Dickson. *The Heir of Dracula*
 Sâr Dubnotal *vs. Jack the Ripper*
Alexandre Dumas. *The Return of Lord Ruthven*
J.-C. Dunyach. *The Night Orchid. The Thieves of Silence*
Paul Féval. *Anne of the Isles. Knightshade. Revenants. Vampire City. The Vampire Countess. The Wandering Jew's Daughter*
Paul Féval, *fils. Felifax, the Tiger-Man*
Arnould Galopin. *Doctor Omega*
V. Hugo, Foucher & Meurice. *The Hunchback of Notre-Dame*
O. Joncquel & Theo Varlet. *The Martian Epic*
Jean de La Hire. *Enter the Nyctalope. The Nyctalope on Mars. The Nyctalope vs. Lucifer*
G. Le Faure & H. de Graffigny. *The Extraordinary Adventures of a Russian Scientist Across the Solar System* (2 vols.)
Gustave Le Rouge. *The Vampires of Mars*
Jules Lermina. *Mysteryville. Panic in Paris. To-Ho and the Gold Destroyers. Mysteryville*
Jean-Marc & Randy Lofficier. *Edgar Allan Poe on Mars. The Katrina Protocol. Pacifica. Robonocchio.* (anthologists) *Tales of the Shadowmen* (6 vols.) (non-fiction) *Shadowmen* (2 vols.)
Xavier Mauméjean. *The League of Heroes*
Marie Nizet. *Captain Vampire*
C. Nodier, Beraud & Toussaint-Merle. *Frankenstein*
Henri de Parville. *An Inhabitant of the Planet Mars*
Polidori, C. Nodier, E. Scribe. *Lord Ruthven the Vampire*
P.-A. Ponson du Terrail. *The Vampire and the Devil's Son*

Maurice Renard. *Doctor Lerne. A Man Among the Microbes.*
The Blue Peril
Albert Robida. *The Clock of the Centuries. The Adventures of*
Saturnin Farandoul
J.-H. Rosny Aîné. *The Navigators of Space. The World of the*
Variants
Brian Stableford. *The Shadow of Frankenstein. Frankenstein*
and the Vampire Countess. The New Faust at the Tragicomi-
que. Sherlock Holmes & The Vampires of Eternity. The Stones
of Camelot. The Wayward Muse. (anthologist) *The Germans*
on Venus. News from the Moon
Kurt Steiner. *Ortog*
Villiers de l'Isle-Adam. *The Scaffold. The Vampire Soul*
Philippe Ward. *Artahe*

MYSTERIES & THRILLERS

M. Allain & P. Souvestre. *The Daughter of Fantômas*
Anicet-Bourgeois, Lucien Dabril. *Rocambole*
A. Bisson & G. Livet. *Nick Carter vs. Fantômas*
V. Darlay & H. de Gorsse. *Lupin vs. Holmes: The Stage Play*
Paul Féval. *The Black Coats: The Companions of the Trea-*
sure. Gentlemen of the Night. Heart of Steel. The Invisible
Weapon. John Devil. The Parisian Jungle. 'Salem Street
Emile Gaboriau. *Monsieur Lecoq*
Steve Leadley. *Sherlock Holmes: The Circle of Blood*
Maurice Leblanc. *Arsène Lupin: The Hollow Needle. The*
Blonde Phantom. Countess Cagliostro
Gaston Leroux. *Chéri-Bibi. The Phantom of the Opera. Roule-*
tabille & the Mystery of the Yellow Room
G. Marot & L. Pericaud. *Nick Carter vs. Jack the Ripper*
William Patrick Maynard. *The Terror of Fu Manchu*
Frank J. Morlock. *Sherlock Holmes: The Grand Horizontals*
P. de Wattyne & Y. Walter. *Sherlock Holmes vs. Fantômas*
David White. *Fantômas in America*